CW00879741

Weave of Love

Choices and Consequences: Book 3

By Rachel J Bonner

What if the choice you have to make has devastating consequences for others?

How can anyone know the right thing to do?

Bruno,

Congratulations!

Rachel J Bonner

Published by Isbin Books, Lancashire

Cover artwork and design by
Oliver Pengilley © 2019 by Rachel J Bonner

Editing by Sarah Smeaton

ISBN: 978-1-912890-07-1 (ebook – epub)

ISBN: 978-1-912890-08-8 (ebook – mobi)

ISBN: 978-1-912890-09-5 (paperback)

Dedication

To Kathy.

I can't remember when you weren't part of my life.

Thank you.

Description

What if the choice you have to make has devastating consequences for others?

How can anyone know the right thing to do?

Leonie chose to sacrifice everything to save other people. Now those around her have to face the consequences – and those consequences are not what they expected.

Prospero must deal with his own guilt. He was the one who gave Leonie the tools she needed – her life was in his hands. To make the most of what she did, he will have to face up to all the family issues he has avoided for so long. Whatever he chooses to do, someone he loves will be hurt. For Leonie's sake, is he now strong enough to make the choice he couldn't make before?

The crisis predicted by Lord Gabriel has come and gone. But his task isn't over. Leonie's very existence may be out in the open but Gabriel discovers that the past is never what it seems – and nor is the present. How can he use what he now knows to bring together those who have been enemies for as long as anyone can remember? If he fails in this, everything he's had to do so far will be in vain.

Table of Contents

Story So Far

Weave of Love is the third book in the Choices and Consequences series. If you haven't read Strand of Faith, or Thread of Hope I strongly recommend that you do read those first as you will get a lot more out of Weave of Love that way. They are available at all the major online ebook retailers and can be ordered at all good bookshops.

But, if you are really eager to get on with Weave of Love, or you have read the first two and would like a quick reminder of what's happened up to now, here is the story so far.

Strand of Faith

The story is set in a post-apocalyptic feudal society ruled by a few powerful families.

It begins with a young Lord, Prospero, coming across a feral child, a meeting which changes his life. Subsequent events lead to him becoming a monk.

Years later, using his extraordinary mental powers, he senses a stranger hiding in the monastery at House St Peter and becomes obsessed with finding them. While dealing with a student having a nightmare (a consequence of developing mental powers) he discovers his stranger is Leonie, an orphan girl, masquerading as a male student. Abbot Lord Gabriel adopts Leonie as his ward, aware through his own mental powers that she unknowingly holds the key to the world's future. He believes he must push Prospero and Leonie together for a chance of world peace – and this will potentially lead to their deaths. He makes Prospero and his close friend, Andrew, responsible for Leonie, using Andrew to influence Prospero's actions. Tormented by his choices and troubled by a lack of progress in the relationship, Gabriel also turns to his sister, Eleanor for help.

Prospero is terrified of falling in love with Leonie. Leaving the monastery means facing the issues which previously drove him to a breakdown. Andrew – who has long hidden feelings for Prospero – initially considers Leonie a trouble maker, but Eleanor leads Andrew to see Leonie as a victim not a villain and the two become friends.

Previous experiences mean Leonie is afraid her feelings for Prospero will lead to his death. When Prospero confesses his love to her, she is unable to reciprocate verbally, but her actions indicate she feels the same way. Prospero decides to leave the monastery, face up to his issues and impulsively proposes to Leonie.

Leonie thinks that marriage to her will put him in danger. She cannot take the risk and runs away, determined to find a new start elsewhere.

Available at https://www.books2read.com/strandoffaith

Thread of Hope

Prospero discovers that Leonie is missing. Eleanor encourages Gabriel to carry out a wide search for her, and once they find Leonie, ensures that Prospero is the one to bring her back.

Prospero finds Leonie and convinces her to marry him. She shares her past with him and later he realises that he knows who she is – a detail he inadvertently shares with Gabriel. Knowing that this puts both Leonie and Prospero in danger, Gabriel blocks Prospero's memory so that he can't share the information with Leonie.

Prospero leaves the monastic order and reverts to his past nickname, Perry. He faces up to some of his past issues, but postpones facing the expectations of his family to concentrate on being with Leonie. Leonie is terrified of the consequences of their relationship but finds marriage brings her a sense of completeness, happiness and confidence that she wasn't expecting. Perry and Leonie rescue a group of feral children and Perry takes them to the orphanage at Taylor House. He tells Lord James, who runs Taylor House, all about his recent marriage and his wife.

Gabriel now knows that Leonie is the child of an infamous and scandalous relationship between heirs to the two largest warring Great Houses, and as such, those from both Houses either want her dead or at least under their control. He starts negotiations about her future with one of those Houses but is very much aware that his actions may yet lead to Leonie's death.

Whilst attending a conference in a neighbouring Great House, Perry and Leonie are involved in an explosion. Perry shows Leonie how to access almost unlimited reserves of mental power which enable her to save many of the victims. They are both aware that using power in this way will almost certainly prove fatal to Leonie.

Perry manages to bring the almost lifeless Leonie back to House St Peter, where every effort is made to treat her. Despite this, her life hangs in the balance.

Available at https://www.books2read.com/threadofhope

If you would like to know more about the Great Houses and people of this world, you can find more information and a 'cast list' on my website at http://www.racheljbonner.co.uk/people.html

Prologue

This part of the ride was pleasant enough. He was on their own land, the afternoon sun was warm despite the time of year, and, although the route was narrow and twisted, his horse was surefooted and he could relax, riding with a loose rein. His thoughts, as always when he rode this way, were of his brother. They had been together since the womb, sharing everything, rarely apart for more than a few hours. Their sudden and total separation still tore at him like an open wound, unable to heal. How many times had he ridden this route now, since the first time he'd come alone, to grieve, the loss fresh in his soul?

His destination on that day, all those years ago, had been the rock formation on the very boundary of their lands. It had been a special place to the pair of them, him and his brother, a secret place, somewhere they'd come to escape, to adventure, to explore. Somewhere they'd toyed with challenge, excitement and danger. It had been the natural place for him to try to make sense of his loss.

Years ago, she'd been there too. Grieving like he was, and hoping in a way that he couldn't, caught in uncertainty. They had met there again over the next months. Not often, for it wasn't easy for either of them to get away unnoticed and the consequences of being followed were unthinkable. And then, once, she hadn't been there. It had become much harder for her, in her condition and she was near her time so he hadn't been altogether surprised.

Still he'd gone back again as they'd agreed, knowing that this could happen. He'd seen a figure moving near the rocks and his heart had leapt with anticipation. He'd thought it was her, cloaked and hooded, until the figure had heard his arrival and turned towards him, pushing back her hood. Then he'd seen the loss and sadness in her eyes and known the girl he had expected to meet was dead. He'd slid from his horse and sunk to the ground, burying his head in his hands at this fresh loss.

The girl waited until he was ready to look up. She was sitting with her back to a rock, hunched over, as though she was sheltering something in her arms. It looked like a bundle of clothes, rags even, and then it made a small sound.

"The child?" he asked hoarsely, barely able to breathe with the additional grief she'd brought him.

She nodded.

"Show me!" he commanded.

Why, he didn't know. What interest could he have in this bastard? The girl flipped back the blanket by the baby's face and he took one look and fell head over heels in love. Not like the love he'd had for his brother, nor for the girl who was this child's mother, or any of the women who had formed part of his life. This was an overwhelming love, a consuming desire to protect the child, to be there for her in whatever she needed. Instinctively he reached out and took her, cradling her to his body, crooning to her. Somehow, she soothed the pain in his soul. He could see her mother in her, and such a look of his brother. When he found the words, he said as much to the girl.

"Of course," she said. "She looks like her parents."

"Why?" he asked. "Why have you brought her to me?"

She shrugged, turning away slightly. "I thought you had a right to see her."

"And now what? You just take her back and I never see her again?" His pain and sorrow made his voice bitter.

"Not back. I can't go back. What you do is up to you." Her voice was dead, devoid of feeling.

"Not back? Why? What happened?"

"I heard things. I'm neither heir nor spare so no one pays me any attention. They – one of my uncles, I think and someone else, I don't know who – were going to get rid of her and the baby, that's what I heard them say. I told her and she made me promise to keep her child safe. She wasn't well by then, already. She died soon after the baby was born. I was ready. I took the child and came here."

"I'll take care of you," he promised. What made him say that? What could he possibly do?

"It's okay," she said. "We made plans. I had some help. We'll be fine."

"Where will you go? I can't take you onto our lands, you wouldn't be any safer there. But one of the Sanctuary Houses? Or House St Peter? I could help you get there."

She shook her head and gestured at the baby. "She is the heir. These lands are hers, her place, in her blood. She should be raised on them. I won't take her somewhere else."

"If they want to kill her, you're not safe. Let me take you somewhere else."

"No." She was adamant. She indicated back down the trail on her side of the rocks. "There's a hut down there, a couple of miles or less. It's hidden, difficult to reach, and it's warm and dry. We'll be safe there."

"It's hardly what you're used to. It won't be easy, not with a small child too," he protested.

"We don't live as richly as you," she said disparagingly. "And I've been helping raise my siblings for years now."

He could see she wouldn't give in, so he stood up, the child still in his arms. "Very well, then," he said. "But at least let me escort you there now."

Once she was mounted on his horse, reluctantly he passed the baby back to her. "Does she have a name?" he asked.

"Not yet," the girl said.

He sighed. "Her mother wanted to call her Leonie."

The girl nodded. "I know. But I thought you should have a say."

He was touched, and rested his head against the horse's neck to hide the tears that sprang to his eyes. Eventually, he looked up. "Call her Leonie," he said and then silently led the horse down the track.

He needed directions to find the hut, which reassured him, and he was relieved to find it dry and reasonably well equipped. There was a cradle for the baby, already housing a small soft toy, worn with age. The girl saw his eyes drift to it. "That was hers," she said. "I thought Leonie should have something from her mother. He's called Taylor."

Eventually, he left them there.

He'd been back many times since then. To start with he'd constantly tried to get her to move somewhere safer, but she'd been insistent and so he'd given up. She did have other help, besides him. He'd met her conspirator, early on and, of course, they'd recognised each other despite the ancient enmity between their families.

The first time, they'd watched each other warily, all but circling and baring their teeth at each other like a pair of wolves. The girl had snarled at them to behave and passed the baby between them. They had managed at least to accept their common ground in love of the child. Gradually, they had learnt to work together. Silently to start with, at opposite sides of whatever area they were in, simply doing whatever the girl had ordered. Then more closely together, communicating as the job needed, sharing tools, helping each other. Eventually, he had come to understand that what they had in common was far greater than their historic differences. Now he thought of the man as his friend. In a way, the girl's other helper had come to fill some of the hollow left by the loss of his brother.

Today was the child's fourth birthday and, as he crossed the rocks and descended into the alien territory, his thoughts turned from his brother to her. He couldn't help but smile as he thought of her. She had grown into a happy, active child, healthy if a little too thin. Full of mischief which was to be expected given her parents, and smart as anything. Bilingual, too. She spoke the common language with him, but with her aunt she spoke the ancient patois of her lands. In his saddlebag was his birthday gift for her, a new edition of her favourite book. He'd read it to her so many times, but this time he hoped she would read it to him.

She met him as he rode through the woods that surrounded the hut, dropping off a low tree branch to stand beside the track, Taylor clutched in one hand. She was never without Taylor.

"You should be more careful, Leonie," he said. "Anyone could be coming along here."

"But they weren't," she said. "Just you."

"I could have been a stranger. It's not safe." He couldn't keep the smile off his face, just at the sight of her. He knew it was taking the seriousness out of his warnings. "You need to make sure you're not spotted by those who could hurt you."

"I could see it was you, from ages away," she told him. "I

can always tell who it is."

He lifted her up to ride the rest of the way perched in front on him on his saddle, Taylor balanced in front of her.

"It's my birthday," she said to him proudly. "My first real birthday. The one that doesn't happen every year."

The other two were waiting for them at the hut and greeted him with pleasure. It was a small celebration but a happy one. The book from him, a new outfit made by her aunt, with the scraps made into something for Taylor, a jigsaw from his friend. And a birthday tea with chocolate cake, a special treat in in this household. He stayed until the child was asleep in bed, exhausted with pleasure, Taylor, still resplendent in his new clothes, tucked in beside her.

"You're an amazing mother to her," he said to the girl as he returned to the main room.

"It'll be your birthday soon," his friend told the girl. "Twenty one. We should do something to celebrate."

She smiled slightly. "Maybe," she said. "But it's a couple of months yet. There's time to think."

They did manage to arrange a surprise party for her in the end, working together. How the girl didn't suspect anything he would never know. When he arrived, Leonie was jumping up and down in front of the door with unsuppressed excitement. His friend was trying – and failing – to keep her quiet.

"You're here, you're here," Leonie exclaimed, leaping into his arms.

"You got everything?" his friend asked.

He nodded at his bags. "All here," he said. "Let's go."

The three of them charged through the door, shouting "Surprise" — Leonie clearly the loudest. The girl jumped in shock, but her face lit up with a broad smile as soon as she realised what was happening. The afternoon passed in a haze of noise, fun and food until Leonie at least was exhausted, curled around Taylor and nearly asleep.

The girl reached to kiss his cheek before he left. "Thank you," she said. "I loved my party."

Afterwards, that always brought him some comfort.

Chapter 1

Thursday Midday – Early June

Perry

How often will I have to do this? How often can *I even do this before it breaks me?*

Perry groaned and buried his head into the pillow, trying desperately to recapture those fuzzy moments on the edge of waking. Those warm, happy moments of forgetfulness before the memories of the last few days hit him. Before his mind was swamped with thoughts of Leonie sacrificing everything to save others, of her almost lifeless body as he brought her home, of earlier this morning when they'd had to stop supporting her.

I won't think about it. I won't. Just the happy times, I'll think of the good times.

"Sit up," said Lord Gabriel. "I know you're awake. You have to face this, not run away from it."

Gabriel's voice reached somewhere below Perry's conscious mind and obedience came without thinking. He sat up. "Andrew was here," he said slowly.

"I took over from him. I have a confession to make to you. Under the circumstances, I think it needs to be before tomorrow," Gabriel replied with a slight smile.

Perry stared at him, frowning and puzzled. "Okay then," he said, relieved at the distraction from his own issues.

"Not yet. You need to eat first," said Gabriel, nodding towards where food was set out on a nearby surface. "Many years of experience have taught me never to confess to someone with low blood sugar."

Despite the circumstances, that brought a slight laugh to Perry, and he moved to comply. As he ate, he kept glancing at Leonie's body on the other side of the bed.

"She's not been alone. Never alone," Gabriel told him. "And my confession is for her, too, even if she won't hear it."

"I can't keep secrets from her," Perry confessed.

"I know. And this isn't secret, not now. Although I'd rather my behaviour didn't become public knowledge. At least, no more than it already is."

Tendrils of intrigue wound into Perry's mind, challenging the numbness he was desperate to hold on to, detachment his only protection against the ocean of pain awaiting him.

Gabriel took a deep breath and started. "For the last seven or eight months, I've been having visions and dreams again."

Now fear rose through Perry's chest, hot and vicious. "Did you know that what happened at House Eastern was going to happen?"

"Not exactly. Not until that morning. All I knew was that something was going to happen and that it would be soon. And I knew that it would have consequences that would change the world – for the better if I took the right actions, for the worse if not. And those actions included pushing you and Leonie together." He hesitated and then continued. "I knew that Leonie would die and I expected that you would too."

"I wanted to. Without Leonie…without Leonie, I can barely breathe. I can't stand what I feel. When I think of a world without Leonie in it, then I want to die."

"I can understand that. Doing what I knew I had to do became harder and harder as I came to know her better."

"Why didn't you tell me? You should have told me. I might… We could… I should…" Perry couldn't take it in. Gabriel had known what was coming? Had set them up? Had caused the pain Perry was now feeling?

"I didn't make it happen," Gabriel said, very softly. "I'm not defending myself. I am responsible for what I did and its consequences. I am so sorry for the hurt and pain it has caused. But I had to do what I was called to do, and act for the greater good."

Somewhere deep inside himself, Perry started to think about what Gabriel had known and faced for the last few months. "You've suffered this," he said, his speech slow as each thought bubbled to the surface. "You've lived with the responsibility for her death and mine for months. That's why you didn't tell me. It's better not to know." He looked up at Gabriel. "How?" he asked. "I can't face it. How in the name of… How on… How do you deal with the pain? How do I deal with the pain? The loss? The fear?"

Gabriel shook his head. "I can't answer that, other than with prayer and with time. I will be here, whatever you need. So will Andrew and any number of others."

"Who else knows then?" Perry asked.

"About the visions and my actions? Only Benjamin and Eleanor, though others may suspect."

"Not Andrew?"

"Not Andrew. He has done what he has been told to do, whilst arguing to defend and protect you at every opportunity. He realised I was pushing you together; he doesn't know why. He's been a good friend to you. To you both."

"And Leonie?"

"Knew nothing. Less even than you."

Perry buried his head in his hands, fighting to regain the detachment that provided the only way he could find to function, the only way he could manage to survive the next minute, the next hour. Eventually, he lifted his head and looked straight at Lord Gabriel. "How does what happened benefit the world? What happens next? And why did Leonie have to pay the price?" he asked.

"I don't know the answers to any of those. My vision tells me that this route leads to a more peaceful, united and prosperous world. I still don't know how we get there, just that the key moment is past. If I'd done nothing, it would have led to wars and famines, trouble on the scale of the Devastation times. As for Leonie, perhaps the answer is because she could? Can you think of anyone else who could have done what she managed? I know I couldn't have done it."

"Would you have told me had she not..." He gestured again at the bed, unable to complete his sentence.

"Yes, I would. Just not yet. Under the circumstances I felt you should know before tomorrow."

"I would have chosen to have these past weeks and months. Even knowing what was to happen I'd have chosen to have them rather than not to. So would she. However it started, what's between me and Leonie is real."

Gabriel nodded. "I know. I found that a comfort." He paused. "Can you forgive me?"

Perry stared at him blankly, his mind unable to process what he was being asked. "It helps to understand why," he said in the end. "I know I need to. I want to. I do forgive you, I just... I just... I'm afraid I'll struggle. On the bad days."

"Then we will work at it together, and we will pray."

They continued to sit together, both watching the bed. The rest of the day floated past Perry; he simply sat or ate or slept as others directed, his whole focus on what would happen the following morning.

***

Friday Morning

"Just me," Perry said. "Just me and her here. No one else." He glanced down at the bed beside which they were all standing.

"No," said Benjamin firmly. "That's not going to happen. Gabriel and Eleanor will wait on the far side of the room. Andrew and I will be right here."

Perry narrowed his eyes, looking at Benjamin, taking a breath for his retort, not caring about the consequences. Then Andrew touched his arm and spoke, just to him. *"It's not just about what you want, Perry. We all understand you want to be alone with her. It's about what could happen and what's best all round. No one will interfere with what you're going to do. I'll see to that."*

Perry swivelled round, turning his stare on Andrew, sighed then nodded, his shoulders slumping. "Okay, then."

He sat on the edge of the bed and then reached to stroke Leonie's cheek. "Leonie," he said softly but insistently. "Leonie, it's time to wake up."

Leonie

Where am I? I'm dead. At least…I should be.

My mind was full of fog, nothing seemed to be working. I

couldn't sense any other presence. There was no light, no dark; just greyness. The last thing I remembered was the sound of Perry singing. The pain of never seeing Perry again coiled round my heart, a physical ache as I drew breath.

I'm breathing?

A voice intruded on my thoughts, calling my name. Perry's voice.

Perry is here?

I strained to open my eyes. It was hard work; my eyelids were stuck together, my eyeballs scratchy and dry. The light was too bright, my sight was blurred, a jumble of colour with no meaningful shape. As my vision cleared I saw Perry sitting beside me, looking down at me. His face was so drawn, so worried and concerned that I tried to reach for him, tried to speak his name, but my body was as unresponsive as my mind, my voice not even a whisper. He placed his fingers on my lips.

"Don't try to talk or move yet. You've been hurt, but everything's going to be okay. Sip this."

He held a straw to my mouth. The juice was neither too sharp nor too sweet and it soothed my dry throat. This time I managed his name. "Perry."

Again he silenced me. "I'm going to help you sit up a bit, okay? You might feel a little dizzy."

He slid one arm round and underneath me, and that gave me the chance to wrap both arms round his neck, bury my head in his shoulder, and drink in the scent and feel of him. "I couldn't find you, I couldn't find you," I kept repeating.

He adjusted his position so we were sitting wrapped together, his arms around me. "You did find me. Do you remember? You rescued me."

He didn't understand. "No, after that," I told him. "After the power left. I couldn't find you, and then I heard your voice and now I'm here."

He held me like he'd never let me go, and that was more than fine by me. After a while, someone coughed and I became aware there were others in the room. Perry drew back a little. I knew my eyes were wet; I hadn't expected his to be, too. He busied himself making sure I was sitting comfortably against the pillows. I didn't want to let go of him so I kept one hand twisted into the fabric of his top and as soon as he had a hand free I tucked my other hand into his.

He didn't look round at the others but spoke to me. "Now you're awake, Benjamin and Andrew need to examine you, alright?"

I nodded but I kept tight hold of him. Lord Gabriel spotted that – he noticed everything – and he stood up and spoke quietly but very firmly, "Prospero is going to wait outside with me."

Perry looked as reluctant as I felt, but there was no way I would disobey Lord Gabriel and neither would he, so I untangled my fingers from his top.

"It won't be long, and I won't be far away," Perry said trying to reassure me and then I was left with Andrew and Benjamin.

Andrew came over to me. I grabbed his arm as he sat down beside me. "Is Perry alright? He looked so... so..." I couldn't think of the right word.

"He'll be fine," Andrew said. "He's just been worried about you."

I tried to reach Perry to reassure him and found I couldn't. My mind was still foggy, not working. An icy swell of panic rose through my middle, clouding my thoughts further. "I can't reach him, I can't find him," I said, my voice rising with my fear.

"Don't try," said Andrew hurriedly. "You won't be able to and it won't be good for you. He's okay."

"He needs me," I pleaded, tugging on his arm. "I need him."

Lady Eleanor appeared beside Andrew and, despite my pleadings, Andrew moved away and she took his place. She put her arm round me. "You can't use your Gifts right now," she told me gently. "Gabriel's looking after Perry. He'll be fine. He'll be back as soon as Benjamin and Andrew have done what they need to."

Not use my Gifts? How can I not have my Gifts?

After the time of Devastation, as our world healed and the population regrew, people discovered they could do things with their minds – things like telepathy, telekinesis, and fire starting. Now around one person in four could do something, and some people – like me, and Perry and many of those around us – could do a lot.

How can I be me without them?

But with Andrew and Benjamin pestering me, I couldn't think. They tried to be gentle, but they were thorough and it wasn't particularly pleasant. I supposed medical matters rarely were. I wanted to scream at one point but I choked it back because I was afraid Perry would hear and worry. Eventually it was over. Benjamin left the room first, closely followed by Lady Eleanor.

"Andrew," I hissed, and he turned back towards me. "Take this drip out."

He shook his head. "I know you don't like it, but medically, we have to leave it," he whispered. "And it's bandaged like that to stop you pulling it out. But Perry'll take it out in a moment if you ask. Everything he'll need is on the table."

And then Perry was there. Andrew winked at me over his shoulder, nodded towards the table and disappeared. Finally I was alone with Perry. I held my arm out to him. "Please?" I begged.

He understood instantly and set about removing the drip. "If I do this," he said, "you have to agree to eat and drink anything and everything you're told to, understand?"

I nodded but he'd almost finished before he spoke so it didn't really matter. When he stood up to put things away, I swung my legs round and sat on the side of the bed trying to hide how weak and dizzy I felt.

He turned back. "And what do you think you are doing?"

I was pretty sure I wasn't going to get away with it but I tried anyway. "I want a shower."

He sat back next to me, sliding one arm round my shoulders. "No way. You aren't strong enough. That can wait until tomorrow and I'll help you."

If I wasn't strong enough to shower alone, I certainly wasn't strong enough for his help, with its inevitable consequences. I tried for my next option. "Then I want to sit there, with you." I pointed at the large armchair we had in the bedroom, where we'd often sat curled up together. I could see he was weighing up how stubborn I was likely to be, but he gave in. I guessed he wanted that, too.

"Okay," he said. "But I'm going to get a blanket so you don't get cold, and you're to drink that juice."

He indicated a glass standing on the table. That seemed a

good deal to me so I drank it, and we snuggled into the chair together, me partly sitting on his lap, with my head tucked into his shoulder. I made him take his top off, so I could feel and smell his skin, and for the first time I saw the bruises spread across his ribs. I traced them gently with my fingers. "I didn't know you were hurt?"

I should have known; how could I have missed that?

"They're nothing, they're nearly better; I didn't know myself till we were back here."

I trailed my fingers along to the monitor disc on his chest and down his arm to the patient bracelet. "If they're nothing, why these?"

He took my hand in his, placing it on his chest between us, then tucked the blanket round us before answering. "I thought you were going to die on me and I couldn't handle it. And I was drained by what we did. They spiked my drink to make me sleep. That's why."

I looked towards the now empty glass of juice and he followed my glance. He answered my unasked question. "Probably not. But honestly, you're not going to stay awake very long whether they did or didn't. For the next little while you aren't going to want to do anything but eat and sleep."

Actually, I could feel my eyelids growing heavy already. I didn't mind; I was where I wanted to be, and that was enough. I'd worry about everything else later. I rested my head on Perry's shoulder and let my eyes close.

Chapter 2

Perry

Perry could feel Leonie's breathing becoming more even and her body relaxing against him as sleep overcame her. He was overwhelmed by how possessive and protective he felt and how unwilling he was to let go of her. Fancy her trying to get out of bed, demanding a shower. That was so like Leonie, wanting to do more than she was able, sooner than she could. Mind you, he'd have indulged her in practically anything. He suspected he'd have given in on the shower, had she pushed any harder. Letting his joy at her survival sweep through his body, he rested his cheek on her head and closed his eyes.

It was a couple of hours before Perry awoke, conscious first of the warm weight of Leonie as she still slept on him, the feel of her breath on his chest, the heat of her hand resting on his skin. With his eyes still closed, he could even sense her heart beat, steadily, strongly, in time with his own. Eventually, he opened his eyes, to see Andrew sitting across the room from them, watching closely.

"Your turn on the rota again, is it?" he said drowsily. "I'm glad it's you."

Andrew walked round the bed to stand over them, looking down. "I think the rota's pretty much over now. You look stuck."

"Oh, I am. Are you planning to rescue me?"

"Do you want to be rescued?"

"Not really, no. I'm quite happy here."

"Stay there then. It seems to be doing you good, you look a lot better than you did earlier."

"How can I help but feel better?" Perry couldn't stop

smiling.

Andrew sat down on the edge of the bed, facing them. "I owe you an apology."

"I can't think how, but right now I'd forgive anyone anything, so if you do it's a good time."

Andrew paused, looking anywhere but at Perry, his fingers playing with the covers on the bed. Then he raised his head, met Perry's eyes and said in a rush. "You were set up, you and Leonie. Gabriel pushed you together, trying to force something to develop."

"I know. Gabriel confessed yesterday. But however artificial the situation, what Leonie and I feel for each other is genuine. Is that what's worrying you, that you helped in pushing us into this? Because that doesn't need an apology, rather I owe you my thanks."

"No, that's not exactly it. I did help, but I was following orders. No, it's that I argued against it, I said it wouldn't work, it wasn't fair, that they'd be playing on your shortcomings. And I guess I was jealous. And then, these last few days, I've seen what you risked, how much you've hurt and that's shown me just how much you love her, and I'm sorry I tried to prevent it."

Perry smiled at him. "There's nothing to forgive. I know you were just looking out for me. Gabriel told me you'd been a good friend to both of us." He looked down at Leonie. "I do love her. I didn't know it was possible to feel like this about anyone."

"There isn't anyone I love so much that I would hurt for them the way you've hurt," Andrew answered.

Perry adjusted his position slightly and winced. "Andrew," he said sheepishly. "I think you're going to have to rescue me after all. I need the bathroom."

Andrew grinned and started to lift Leonie off him, revealing Perry's topless state. Perry was more concerned about Leonie. "Don't let her get cold," he instructed.

"Stop fussing, I won't, she's quite safe," Andrew responded as he carried her across to the bed and gently laid her down, tucking the covers round her.

Perry watched them for a moment, seeing a range of emotions cross Andrew's face. "You love her, too," he said in wonder, experiencing a moment of revelation.

"Of course," said Andrew, tranquilly. "Just not like you do. And anyway, she loves you." He grinned at Perry. "When you're done in the bathroom, I'll see if we can discharge you. Then you can go down to the kitchens and get something to eat, and see if you can stop Pedro baking all these cookies!"

It had become a source of much amusement, despite the circumstances, that the head chef, Brother Pedro, had dealt with his own fears and emotions by baking large and continual quantities of chocolate chip cookies, Leonie's favourite. Perry laughed, the tension broken, and went to obey. He didn't want to leave Leonie but Andrew shooed him out of the room. "You need to eat, and you need a break from being here," he said. "Leonie will be fine; she won't be alone for a moment."

When he thought about it rationally, Perry knew Andrew was right, but he still planned to be as quick as he could manage. The kitchens were pretty quiet, in that lull after lunch had been cleared but before any preparations had started for the evening meal. Pedro came rushing to meet him. "How is she? How's Leonie? Is she…?"

"She's woken up. She's asleep again now, but she woke up. And she remembers a lot of what happened. So far, it's looking good."

Pedro stopped in his tracks and sighed deeply, closing his eyes. "Thank you, Lord."

Then he opened his eyes and looked straight at Perry. "Come on, you need to eat. Sit." He pushed Perry onto a chair by a small table and hurried off, before quickly coming back with a bowl of thick soup and fresh bread. "Eat, eat," he instructed. "You need to keep your strength up too."

Pedro sat down opposite Perry and started plying him with questions about Leonie's recovery. He didn't seem to expect any response, which was as well given that Perry was eating and no one knew the answers anyway.

"I think of her as a daughter, you know," Pedro confessed. "Poor little nestling."

Perry looked up sharply. "You knew she was a nestling?" he asked. "Since when?"

"I knew we had a nestling around sometime in the autumn but I couldn't tell who or where. I knew it was her that first time you brought her into the kitchen. If you've been one, you don't miss the signs. And I assume she was taking food to feed another nest."

"She was. We rescued them, they're safe now. I didn't know you'd been one until she told me. Not many make it to adulthood."

"It was a long time ago. And someone rescued me." Pedro shook his head slightly as if to disperse the memories. "Now," he said, "we need to think about what Leonie should be eating. I've got some plans."

Leonie

I slithered to the edge of the bed and stood up. I wobbled

for a moment and then arms slid around my waist from behind as Perry caught me.

"I need the bathroom," I told him.

He didn't object, but kept his arm round my waist and supported me on the short walk to the bathroom door, Andrew hovering behind. Only then Perry started to come in with me.

"No way," I said. "I can do this on my own."

He shook his head. "It's not like a hospital," he protested. "There's no grab rail or call buttons. What if you fall?"

"I'm going to be fine," I insisted. "And besides, I want clean clothes." I gestured towards the nearby chest of drawers.

Without thinking, Perry let go of me, opened the drawer and found me some pyjamas. That gave me the moment I needed to slip through the bathroom door. I just didn't quite close it in time. He grabbed for the handle, held the door open and glared at me through the gap, before relenting and passing me the pyjamas.

"Don't lock it," he instructed. "And call if you need any help. Promise?"

"I promise," I said and shut the door.

Of course my definition of needing help might not have been the same as his. I tried not to look in the mirror, but I couldn't help it when I was washing my hands. My face looked like a skull, all sharp angles and bones with sunken eyes. My skin was washed out, no longer its usual golden honey colour, and my hair was just a matted mess. I managed to wash my face and attempted to brush my hair although it made little difference. I sat on the chair to put the clean clothes on. What I really wanted, still, was a shower, but I had to admit I didn't feel strong enough for that right now. Instead, I reached in, turned the shower on, then sat back down to see what would happen next.

The door burst open and Perry shot through, skidding to a halt when he realised the shower was empty and I was just sitting there. The look on his face was well worth it. "Back to bed for you," he said, picking me up and carrying me there.

Andrew was right behind him and he at least appreciated the joke. I could see him trying hard not to laugh out loud. "Don't be mad at her," he said, defending me. It's a good sign, shows she's feeling better."

Perry turned towards him, still holding me. "I'm not cross with her. I was just worried."

That made me feel instantly guilty. "Perry, I'm sorry."

"It's okay, beautiful. I just don't want you to do too much, too soon."

Andrew butted in, "He's going to be seriously overprotective for a while even for him. He won't be able to help it. You might as well get used to it for now. He'll get over it eventually."

"I'm going to be seriously overprotective forever," Perry growled at him. He turned back to me. "And you don't get a choice in the matter so yes, you'd better get used to it."

But he was smiling now as he said it so that was alright. I got back into bed and Andrew ambled off to our kitchen to find me something to eat. He came back with a tray holding some of Pedro's soup and bread and a cookie. It didn't look like much to me but it was all I could manage. I dozed through most of the rest of the afternoon, not really wanting to do anything but sleep and hold onto Perry. He must have felt the same because every time I woke, even for just a few minutes, he was right beside me, his hand in mine. I was a little bit more awake when Lord Gabriel came in later to find Perry and take him to the evening meal.

"Your presence at the meal, looking happy and relaxed will do far more than I can to convince the rest of my House that Leonie is recovering," he said.

Perry got off the bed reluctantly, but really he didn't have any choice. "I'll be back soon," he said. "Andrew will stay with you."

Lord Gabriel had a bandage on his hand, but he seemed to be ignoring it and I didn't get an opportunity to ask about it. He looked pale and drained himself, and thinking about it, so did most of the people I'd seen around since I'd woken up.

"Why is everyone so pale and worn out looking?" I asked Andrew as soon as we were alone.

"You've had the easy bit, being unconscious or asleep," he said, teasing me. "The rest of us have been worrying about you. Everyone will start to feel better now you're awake."

"Why aren't I dead?" Andrew was the only person I felt I could ask.

He smiled slightly, no doubt at the bluntness of my question. "Perry saved you," he said. "He – I suppose the best way to put it is, he shared his life with you. And then he brought you back here where we all could help. It takes a lot of energy, that's one reason people are looking so drained."

I understood what he meant; I'd done it myself a couple of times. I'd shared a part of myself, my energy, my desire to live, with someone else so that they'd had a chance to live. Katya – the Trader Headwoman I'd been apprenticed to – had taught me how but she'd had very strict rules on when to use it. We'd only ever used it for a minute or two, to get a mother or a baby, or both, through a traumatic birth. I'd never heard of it being used for anything else, nor of it going on longer than a few minutes. No wonder those around me were looking tired. And no wonder Perry was feeling overprotective – I'd barely been able to let those babies out of my sight for about a week after helping them.

"You helped me too?" I asked him, because he looked just as pale as everyone else.

"Yes," he said. A fleeting shadow passed across his face, so quickly I might even have imagined it. "Though most of it was Lady Eleanor and Melanie."

"Melanie's here?" I asked. "I'd like to meet her."

"What do you know about Melanie?" Andrew asked cautiously.

"She's Lady Eleanor's daughter," I told him. "Perry's friend, ex-lover. Your friend, too."

"Perry told you all about her then?"

I nodded. "Ages ago. But I knew before that, anyway."

Andrew smiled. "I'm sure you'll get to meet her soon enough. She wants to meet you, too."

"Was it worth it? What I did? All the trouble I've caused here?"

"Yes, it was," he answered quickly and certainly. "What do you remember about it?"

"Mostly just needing to rescue people, to get them out of the damaged building," I said, trying to remember. "But I had so much power, so much knowledge. I could do anything, know everything. And now I can't do or remember any of it." I paused, then looked straight at him. "And I thought I would die."

"You saved a lot of lives. Many of those you rescued would

have been killed by the building collapsing further, or died while they waited to be rescued. And they'll make a better recovery because they were treated sooner. It was well worth it."

For a while we sat quietly while I thought about what I'd done and what I could remember. Andrew had always been someone who knew when I needed just to be silent. Then Perry's absence started to tickle at my mind. I pushed it down; Perry wouldn't be much longer. It fought back, tormenting me like an itch I couldn't scratch. What was taking him so long? Where was he? I couldn't stand his absence; I needed him there with me. If he wasn't there… Panic was flooding up, ice cold fear rising from my stomach, through my chest. I knew Andrew was right there but still I needed Perry. I looked at Andrew again. "I want Perry," I said, unable to keep it in.

He tried to be reassuring. "He's not far, he'll be back soon, don't worry."

It didn't help. The panic rose further, my chest and throat tightening. I couldn't sit still. I needed to run, to escape, to find Perry.

And then the door opened and Perry was there, and I was launching myself across the bed and into his arms almost before he could cross the room. Once I touched him I was safe again, but still I wrapped my arms around him and buried my face in his shoulder. He spoke to me, his voice soothing, but I didn't really pay any attention to what he was saying. He picked me up and sat down on the bed, keeping his arms round me and holding me on his lap. I knew he was speaking to Andrew, but again I chose not to pay any attention, I just wanted to stay where I was. I heard another voice and Benjamin was there, saying my name, softly but insistently, so I turned my head to look at him. He had squatted down so his eyes were at my level and he smiled at me.

"I think," Benjamin said, his voice still quiet, "I think that despite being asleep or unconscious you've been shut up in here too long. If we were in the hospital, I'd send you out to sit on the terrace or in the garden for a while. But as Eleanor has unaccountably failed to provide you with a balcony here" – that made me smile – "I think we'll have Prospero carry you down to sit in the courtyard. How about that?"

I nodded eagerly, liking the sound of getting outside. "I can walk down," I assured him.

"Maybe you can," he said, "but let's not do too much too soon. And whilst you're there we'll get this room tidied up for you." He stood up. "Andrew, you go too in case they need anything. It's a pleasant evening; you'll not get cold, but take a blanket and some cushions anyway."

I just let everything happen around me. They let me walk as far as the main corridor but by then I was quite happy to let Perry carry me the rest of the way. Soon we were comfortably settled on the bench outside, me on Perry's lap with my head on his shoulder and Andrew at the other end of the bench, my feet tucked up against him. We talked a little, about nothing in particular, and then, with Perry's arms around me, and the warmth of the evening sun on my skin I let my eyes close.

Andrew

Andrew relaxed into the corner of the bench, resting one arm along the back of the seat and watched as Leonie drifted off to sleep. Her feet were warm against his thigh and he tweaked the blanket to ensure they stayed that way. He smiled to himself; right now Perry was broadcasting unrestrained feelings of happiness and contentment. At least that meant he was well on the way to recovering. Andrew didn't have the heart to point out the extent to which he was sharing his feelings. Anyway, there was no one else around so it didn't matter.

Leonie had asked him why she hadn't died, and despite giving her an answer, he really didn't know. He – like Benjamin and several others – had been researching the consequences of using master stones in the way she had done. Master stones were technological constructs, made to look like jewels, that someone as Gifted as Leonie could use to enhance their energy and abilities. There was a cost – most users had died immediately once they'd stopped using the stones. Of those who had survived, few had ever regained consciousness and those who had woken, had had no memory even of who they were with no ability to relearn. And the few who'd woken up with their memories intact as Leonie had done had either seemed to slip into a suicidal depression at the loss of their Gifts or died as a consequence of problems with their abilities re-establishing themselves. But there had been too few of those to make any real judgement on what might happen, along with some rumours – totally unsubstantiated – of someone who had made a full recovery. The only things they were certain of were that the first one hundred days were crucial and that each day Leonie survived improved her chances of recovery, with or without any return of her Gifts. He hadn't shared any of this with her; he thought it better that she didn't know. Perry would work it out when he stopped to think about it, but again, Andrew had no wish to put a dampener on his happiness, at least not right now.

He hadn't been able to explain to either Perry or Benjamin what had unsettled Leonie so much; they'd both asked, of course they had. But she hadn't been upset by their conversation, rather she'd seemed reassured. Perhaps it was just being separated from Perry. He hoped it wouldn't make Perry even more overprotective and possessive; that wouldn't help anyone.

Benjamin wandered across the courtyard towards them. Andrew lifted Leonie's feet further onto his lap and shuffled along a little, giving Benjamin room to perch on the arm of the bench. Benjamin nodded at the sleeping Leonie. "She's going to be doing a lot of that for the next little while."

Perry smiled at him. "I know. It doesn't matter. Awake or asleep, at least she's alive. And she remembers."

Benjamin's slight smile dropped as Perry turned back towards Leonie. "Perry," he said slowly.

Perry brushed a stray lock of hair from Leonie's face before he answered softly, without looking up, "It's okay, Ben. I know what the odds are as well as you do. I know what's most likely to happen." He turned back towards Benjamin, his voice quiet but strong. "But whether we have hours left or years, I am going to hope and pray with every fibre of my being that Leonie will be the one to beat the odds."

Benjamin agreed, "Amen to that." He stood up. "The room is ready whenever you are, but take your time."

Benjamin left, but Perry and Andrew continued to sit together a little longer in companionable and supportive silence.

Chapter 3

Friday Night

Perry

Perry lay still, barely daring to breath, let alone sleep. Leonie was curled on her side, her back towards him and he kept one hand resting on her in his need to reassure himself that she was there, alive and breathing. He didn't care that there was another doctor watching the monitors who would be with them in a minute should there be any problem, or that Benjamin was less than five minutes away. That made no difference. He still felt responsible for her care and he intended to be the first person she turned to, and the person who dealt with anything she needed.

He was jerked out of sleep – how had he dozed? – as Leonie sat up, eyes unfocused, grabbing frantically at the bedding and muttering words that made no sense. He pulled her into his arms, trying to soothe her. "It's okay, you're safe. I've got you, everything's alright."

It didn't help; she was stiff and resistant, shaking her head at him, more incoherent words tumbling out. By the time Sister Hannah – the doctor on duty – entered the room less than a minute later he had deciphered just the words 'necklace' and 'bracelet'. He gestured to Hannah to wait whilst he continued to try to work out what was troubling Leonie. "It's about your necklace and bracelet?" he asked.

Quieter, she nodded against his chest. "Want them. Can't find them," she told him, with a deep sigh as her body – finally – relaxed into him. Perry had no idea where they were either. She wasn't wearing them but this was the first time he'd thought about them and he didn't know where they'd been put. He glanced at her right forearm and her neck. There were dressings on both but there were a number of dressings on what he'd been told were minor injuries all over her body.

"Don't worry," he said, holding her closer. "I don't know where they are but I'll find them." He looked at Hannah to see if she knew.

She shook her head. "I don't know either," she said. "Perhaps a jewellery box?"

"Leonie doesn't have a jewellery box," he said. "That's all the jewellery she had." Well, apart from her rings, and he could feel those on her hand, tucked into his and nestled between them.

Before Hannah could respond, Benjamin walked in. Hannah brought him up to date, but instead of answering her query about the location of the jewellery, Benjamin sat on the bed close to Leonie and gently took her right hand in his. She turned her head to look at him with huge, dark, solemn eyes.

"You're missing your necklace and bracelet?" he asked her, and she nodded. "When you use master stones like you did," he said, "and Gabriel says both were set with master stones, then—"

Leonie interrupted him with a whisper, "I saw them. They spun."

"Did they? When you're stronger, I'd like to talk about what you remember." He paused for a moment. "When you use the master stones, they disintegrate, destroyed by the power, and they destroy their settings too. I'm afraid your necklace and bracelet no longer exist."

Tears started to roll down Leonie's cheeks and she turned to look at Perry as if for confirmation.

"I didn't know," he murmured. "I'm sorry." He wiped her face with his hand, brushing her tears away with his fingers, aching for a way to console her.

Benjamin spoke to her again, "To you, they were signs that you belonged, weren't they? And now they are gone, you're afraid of not belonging?"

She nodded. Perry looked at Benjamin in astonishment. How did he know so much about what Leonie feared when Perry himself had barely worked it out? As he carried on speaking, Benjamin stretched Leonie's right arm out and began to remove the dressing there. "When they disintegrate, they mark you with the symbol of their setting. Not a burn or a brand exactly, more sort of a tattoo." He lifted the dressing to reveal the eight-spoked-wheel design that represented the Traders etched on her inner forearm.

Leonie stared at it for a moment. "Trader sign," she whispered with a sigh and then her fingers moved to the dressing at her throat.

"Yes," agreed Benjamin as he reached to remove that dressing also. "You're marked forever as belonging to them. And here..." He paused a moment to ask Hannah to pass him a hand mirror so Leonie could see. "Here, the crossed keys of St Peter."

With the fingers of her right hand touching her throat, and those of her left hand around her right arm, Leonie rested her head on Perry's chest, her arms between them and his arms around her.

"You match Gabriel," Benjamin told her and she turned her head back to stare at him, wide eyed. "The stone in his Abbot's ring turned out to be a pair to the one in your necklace, designed to work together. He was holding it in his hand as it burnt out when yours did, so he's got the crossed keys on his left palm."

"I hurt him?" Leonie whispered, shock sounding in her voice.

"No, no," Benjamin reassured her. "He chose to use it to

find out what was happening. It was very useful."

Leonie accepted that, closing her eyes as she leaned against Perry. Benjamin turned towards Perry with a grin. "Gabriel did say he wanted to know how you knew the necklace had a master stone. I suggest you and Melanie get your stories straight."

Leonie opened her eyes and tilted her head to look up at Perry, raising her eyebrows in question.

"It's a long time ago," he told her. "I'll tell you later. Sleep now."

He held her close as she fell asleep, unwilling to let go of her, rocking her in his arms, his head bent over hers. As soon as he was sure Leonie was asleep, Benjamin left, but Hannah remained in the room a little longer. "You should take your top off," she said to Perry.

He looked up at her in shock and surprise. "I'm sorry, what do you mean?" he asked.

She grinned back, clearly amused at having shocked him. "Have you never heard of skin-to-skin nursing?" she asked.

"Well, yes," he admitted. "But only for premature or sick babies."

"It works just as well for children," she told him. "And there's evidence to suggest it works for some adults too. Did you not use it when you did your time at Taylor House?"

He shook his head. "No, I didn't have much involvement in longer term care of the children, mostly just when they were first rescued. Were you there long?"

Hannah nodded. "A couple of years, rather than the usual six months we all do. My specialism is the care of malnourished and traumatised children, so I fit in pretty well with what the kids they rescue need. I'm going back soon."

Perry was silent. It gave him little comfort to think that perhaps Hannah's specialism might be the most appropriate for Leonie's care now.

Hannah seemed to interpret his silence as indecision, or perhaps modesty. "Don't worry," she said, smiling. "I'll leave you to it. You can decide what you want to do. I won't be far away if you need me."

After she'd left the room, Perry laid Leonie down carefully and then removed his top. Skin-to-skin nursing or not, he certainly enjoyed skin-to-skin contact with Leonie. Lying down himself, he gathered her back into his arms and settled comfortably to sleep again.

Saturday Morning

Leonie

The pillow was smooth under my cheek, Perry's arm warm as it rested over me, his breath a slight breeze on my hair. I had to be awake, so I reached out with my mind to check my surroundings and...couldn't. My eyes shot open to see Perry lying beside me, his arms around me, watching me warily. He had to have known exactly what I'd tried to do.

"Don't worry about it. We don't know what will happen," he said gently. "If your Gifts come back, that's great, if not, that's fine too."

"But I'm not me without them," I whispered, voicing my real fear, but only for him. Only he would understand.

"Yes, you are," he told me, his voice certain. "You're far more than just a few odd abilities. You'd still be you if you'd lost part of your physical body and you're still you without your Gifts. And I still love you, no matter what." He smiled at me. "Do you remember what happened in the night?"

I did. I reached for my arm and my neck, tracing the markings there with my fingers. He laced his fingers into mine, tracing them too. "They suit you," he said. "And you'll always belong."

"Lord Gabriel has one," I said. "That must be why he had a bandage on his hand."

Perry nodded, but then we both jumped as Andrew came through the door, carrying a tray.

"You ever think about knocking?" I asked, sitting up and pulling the covers closer.

He grinned at us. "Just be grateful you're not in the hospital," he said. He lifted the tray slightly to draw our attention to it. "And anyway, which hand do you suggest I use?" He put the breakfast tray down on a table. "You hungry?" he asked.

I was, so abandoning the bed covers, I scrambled across to the table and started to eat. Perry wasn't far behind me although he stopped to put a top on. Andrew sat down and ate with us. After that, he removed the rest of the various dressings on me. I squinted over my shoulder as he removed one from my lower back. "How did I get hurt there?"

"I have no idea at all," he said. "They're mostly very minor burns, healing well. Was there debris flying around?"

I shrugged – I didn't remember – but Perry answered for me, "No, not really, not after the first explosion. Nothing that was alight. And anyway, her clothes would have offered some protection."

"Her clothes were riddled with burn holes, matching all these injuries," Andrew told us. "Although yours weren't," he said looking over at Perry. "Yours were torn, certainly, but not burnt. I'd have expected similar damage for both of you."

"Perhaps it was the power, arcing out of her at the end," Perry said. "Perhaps these are all exit wounds?"

"You know I'm still here?" I asked sharply. "You're doing it again, talking about me as if I'm not there."

"Sorry," said Andrew. "There, I'm all done. You can shower now if you want."

Perry wrapped his arms round me. "Sorry, too," he whispered in my ear. Then slightly louder, "I'll help you shower. Andrew, you can disappear. Now."

Andrew just grinned and left. At least we were allowed privacy to shower. Perry got in with me – he didn't give me a choice and I certainly didn't mind. I soaped him, running my hands over his body, checking on his scrapes and bruises. He was far too thin and gaunt for my liking. He stroked my body as he washed me, gentle and caring, helping me rinse away the traces of the last few days, and again he traced the marks on my arm and neck.

"How did you know it was a master stone?" I asked him, remembering the conversation from the night.

"Mel told me," he said. "She was proving to me that master stones existed and that she knew all about them. She got hold of the necklace and showed it to me. I touched it with my mind." He paused, clearly remembering. "It felt dormant, not ready to be used, at least not by me. When Gabriel gave it to you I assumed it was a copy – Mel showed me a copy, too – until we were sitting by the fire on Christmas afternoon and then I felt it." He paused again. "It was still dormant but it was ready. It was where it had been designed for and it was ready to be used."

"You didn't tell me," I said.

"I didn't know you very well then," he said. "If Gabriel had made a mistake I couldn't reveal how I knew; if he'd given it to you deliberately for some reason and chosen not to tell you, I wasn't going to be the one to mess up his plans."

"And now it's gone," I said sadly.

He put his arms round me and held me close, the water running over us both, hiding the tears that slid down my cheeks.

"I'm sure you could have the copy, if you wanted," he said.

I wasn't sure about that, not sure that I wanted it, not sure that I wanted the constant reminder. "Maybe," I told him.

He left it at that, turning the shower off and reaching for a towel to wrap round me.

I did feel better for washing, but I was exhausted again so I climbed onto the bed, curled up and went straight back to sleep.

***

"Leonie, Leonie."

Someone was calling my name. And the world seemed to be moving backwards and forwards. I opened my eyes to see Perry looking down at me, one hand on my shoulder as he shook me awake.

"You have to eat as well as sleep," he said with a grin, passing me a tray of food as I sat up.

Obediently – for now – I ate what was there then pushed the empty tray away and lay down again. Perry had said all I'd really want to do was eat and sleep, and so far he was right.

The next time I woke, it was to the sound of Perry's voice, from a distance, the other side of the room. "She's still asleep," he hissed. "She needs to sleep. I'm not letting you disturb her."

"We're going to need to examine her again." Another voice, probably Benjamin.

I scrunched my eyes tighter. If he was planning that, I was going to stay asleep.

"Half an hour." That was Andrew. "Let her sleep another half hour, and see if she wakes naturally by then."

I didn't hear Perry's answer but there was a 'snick' as the door closed and then the sound of footsteps as he returned to sit by the bed. I risked opening my eyes a little. Perry was grinning at me. "I thought you were awake," he said. "We've got a little bit of leeway, but then Gabriel wants to discuss what we're going to do next. And Benjamin and Andrew want to examine you."

I was sure they'd want to do what they'd done before – the bit that made me want to scream. It wasn't going to be any better this time. I shuddered slightly, trying to keep my reaction from Perry.

"Officially, you're still a patient," he told me, reaching over to finger my wristband. "They're going to want to check on you every day at least."

I scrambled my way up to sitting. "But not for half an hour, right?"

He nodded and held his arms out. "Come here for a few minutes and then I'll help you get dressed."

Usually he was more interested in me getting undressed, but I wasn't going to miss a chance to be close so I launched myself onto his lap. By the time Andrew knocked on the bedroom door at the end of the half hour I was dressed and sitting cross legged on the end of the bed, watching Perry tidy stuff away.

Benjamin and Andrew turned Perry out of the bedroom again while they examined me. He muttered under his breath as he left. I stayed on the end of the bed trying not to snarl at them. Yet.

"That monitor you're wearing tells us most of what we need to know," Benjamin said as he sat down on a chair. "But we do need to look at your mind. Nothing can report on that for us."

"No," I said. That was exactly what I was afraid of.

He just looked at me.

The Them flashed across the room, black, cloaked and hooded, long arms reaching for me.

I. Am. Awake.

"No," I said again, louder now, as the Them disappeared.

"I'll be here," Andrew said. "You'll be quite safe. You can hold my hand if it helps."

One of the Them shot between us, arms outstretched.

I. Am. Awake.

No one was holding me. The door was close by. Perry was just the other side. I leapt off the bed, yanked the door open and ran. Away from the Them, away from Andrew, away from Benjamin. I headed for Perry and cannoned straight into whoever he was talking to.

Chapter 4

Melanie

Andrew and Benjamin had gone to examine Leonie and Perry had come over to talk to Melanie while they did so. Not that he was paying any attention to her. He was staring at the bedroom door, shifting his weight from foot to foot, twisting his fingers in the fabric of his top.

Melanie took the opportunity to look around the room, taking in the changes since she'd last been here, barely a couple of days ago. Then, it had been filled with people worrying over Leonie and piles of medical supplies and equipment. Now it had returned to a large, open living space, lit by a wall of windows. There was a kitchen at one end, and doors down one side which she knew opened onto a couple of bedrooms and a bathroom. The space was still full of people, though, all those that had gathered to discuss how to care for Leonie. Melanie's mother, Eleanor, was there, Gabriel, Chloe, Edward, and a couple of others Melanie didn't know.

Then the red-headed *waif* they'd all been fretting over hurtled through the bedroom door, spun round Perry and bounced straight into Melanie, putting them between her and Benjamin and Andrew who were following.

"Don't let them! Please! Stop them!" she pleaded breathlessly.

Perry pulled her into his arms, but he kept his body angled to protect her from the other two.

Perry and Andrew on opposing sides?

That was so unusual as to be almost unprecedented. And what had they been doing to scare Leonie so? Benjamin was clearly upsetting Leonie, and Melanie wasn't having that. Leonie was *hers* to protect. Why did men have to be so confrontational? Really, they weren't that different from the small boys she'd left at home. She stepped between them.

"What are you doing to your patients these days, Benjamin? She's clearly scared stiff," she drawled.

Leonie spoke up from the safety of Perry's arms, her voice still showing signs of panic, "They want to be in my head and I'm not even there! I don't want them there. How do I know what they are doing? Or if what I'm doing is me or them?"

Did 'them' mean Benjamin or the *Them*? Melanie suppressed a shudder. She'd seen the *Them* in Leonie's memories.

Andrew answered Leonie, "We have to look in your mind, or we won't know how you're healing, or what to do next."

"Perry can," Leonie volunteered. "I don't mind Perry looking."

"No!" burst from three throats at once – Benjamin, Andrew and Gabriel.

Leonie looked up at Perry, dark eyes wide in surprise.

"I can't," he said, his voice regretful. "It all drained me, too. Tomorrow maybe, or the next day, but today, I just can't."

Leonie reached up to stroke his cheek and attempted to comfort him. Over the past week, Melanie had seen how Perry felt about Leonie; now she could see that love reciprocated. She shook her head gently.

Can't they tell she's terrified? Time for me to take charge.

"Benjamin, Andrew, you sit down over there. Leonie, sit here. Perry, sit next to her and keep your arms around her so she knows she's safe."

Somewhat to her amazement they all did as they'd been told. She sat down herself, opposite Leonie, took her hand and spoke gently, "Perry's your safe place, isn't he?" She didn't wait for an answer. "I'm not going to let anyone hurt you or do anything to you without your agreement, okay? Do you trust me?"

Leonie nodded slowly, and Melanie smiled at her. "Good. Now, Benjamin does need to see how you're healing so we can look after you properly. But suppose I watch him for you while he looks in your head? And Perry will keep his arms round you, and I'll hold your hand. Do you think you could manage that? I think you can."

Leonie gave another reluctant nod, gripped Melanie's hand tighter, and hid her face in Perry's shoulder. Melanie could feel the tension in her body, but she gestured to Benjamin to begin. She mirrored his link to Leonie's mind herself, seeing what he was seeing as he visualised the damage. Benjamin saw it as a network of memories and abilities, but with every node now disengaged from every other. Wordlessly he pointed out where the nodes appeared to be reconnecting and then, apparently satisfied, withdrew his link. It had taken just a few seconds. It wasn't Melanie's area of medical expertise but even she could tell that Leonie was making better progress than anyone had dared to hope. She squeezed Leonie's hand reassuringly. "All done," she said. "You can relax now. You're doing really well."

Benjamin murmured his agreement and then described her progress in medical terms for Andrew and Perry. Leonie lifted her head from Perry's shoulder to question Melanie. "What do you see in my head?" she asked.

Melanie answered quickly, to reassure her. "We see your memories, loose and unconnected with each other, trying to join up in a pattern and the same with the various components of your Gifts. We've seen a lot of your memories while we've been supporting you."

Leonie snapped her head round to Perry, eyes wide open in horror. "Others have seen what I showed you? Everyone knows about everything? All about me? They all know?"

He nodded, and there was concern in his dark eyes. "Everyone who has looked after you, yes."

Leonie twisted round, burying her head into his neck again, her shoulders shaking with sobs, and tears running down her face. Perry stroked her hair, whispering to her, but he clearly didn't know what to do. Feeling guilty over the problem she'd caused, Melanie squatted down beside them and reached out, placing her hands either side of Leonie's head and turning her gently so that they were eye to eye.

"Leonie," she said, her voice little more than a whisper. "Those of us who've been supporting you have been in your memories. And yes, we saw some horrible things, but they were done to you, not by you. No one here is going to reject you because of something that happened in the past. We've been fighting to keep you alive because we love you and we want to keep you because you belong to us. We want to keep it that way."

Leonie turned her head to Perry for confirmation. Melanie understood that, even if she'd provided the words, only Perry had the ability to provide full reassurance.

"Truly?" Leonie whispered.

"Truly," he replied, wiping her cheeks with his thumbs, his words echoed by others in the room. "Some people here have only just found out, others – Andrew, Benjamin, Gabriel, Pedro – have known for weeks, months even. It didn't change how they felt, did it?"

She shook her head. "Nobody minds?"

"They mind only that you suffered. That's all," he told her.

Once more she buried her head in his shoulder, and this time Benjamin spoke, "She's not strong enough to deal with this right now."

"She's stronger than you think," Melanie snapped back, still exasperated at Benjamin. "Just give her a minute or two."

Perry mouthed "thank you" at Melanie over Leonie's shoulder, and then worked at persuading Leonie to lift her head and turn back to face the room. He was successful; she settled down beside him and apologised to Gabriel for disrupting everything.

He smiled at her. "You have nothing to apologise for. Right now you are the most important person in this room – this is about what is best for you."

Still twisted into Perry, Leonie slid one hand into Melanie's for reassurance. Melanie sensed a flash of jealousy from Perry, but kept hold of Leonie's hand anyway. Perry could learn to deal with it.

Leonie

"All I can suggest," Benjamin said, "is to eat well and sleep well, and we'll arrange some physical therapy sessions, and Gift therapy sessions and see what they do. But I really don't know what will happen long term."

That was hardly surprising. I'd been listening to him, Lord Gabriel and some of the others talking and it was quite clear that I was a medical puzzle to them. And it was obvious that they were trying to avoid talking about the fact that I should have died. I tightened my grip on Melanie's hand. At least she'd been honest with me and she'd protected me from Benjamin. Taking a deep breath, I interrupted the discussion.

"Lesley might know," I volunteered.

"Lesley?" echoed both Perry and Benjamin. There was an undertone of something in Perry's voice too. Perhaps it was a mistake to mention her. She and I had both known Perry would try to sacrifice himself to protect me and we'd collaborated to protect him. We'd obviously succeeded but I had no idea how Perry had reacted at the time. Not well, would be my guess. He'd probably been absolutely furious with Lesley.

"She told me how to release the power," I said slowly then turned to look at Perry. "And she helped me protect you, at the end," I confessed.

Perry's face was a picture as he shook his head slowly. He glanced at Lord Gabriel who was smiling, almost smug.

"You were right," Perry said to him and then turned to me. "So the pair of you set me up. Remind me never to let you conspire together again."

"Lesley is otherwise engaged anyway," Lord Gabriel said. "I was sent a message that says her son was born last night. She's planning to call him Peter."

"Is she okay?" I asked.

"Both mother and baby are doing fine," Lord Gabriel said. "There's to be a service of thanksgiving for the baby sometime in the next week or so. I'd like Prospero to attend on our behalf."

I thought Perry was about to say no, so I nudged him. "You should go," I said.

He shook his head. "No, I'd rather stay here with you."

I glared at him but before I could say anything, Lord

Gabriel spoke. "I wasn't giving you a choice," he said, his voice quiet and mild.

Perry spluttered quietly, but even he had more sense than to argue with Lord Gabriel.

"Moving to other matters," Lord Gabriel continued, looking straight at Perry, "I've been speaking to your mother. I know you were planning to visit, later in the summer, but I think that would be a good place for Leonie to convalesce. Chloe will arrange for you to travel there as soon as Leonie is strong enough for the journey."

I turned to Perry. "Can we?" I asked. "I'd really like to do that. As soon as we can."

Perry may have had some reservations – he hadn't visited his family in years – but he smiled at me. "Of course we can. As soon as they let us."

"Ten days or so, then," Benjamin said to me. "Depending on how you're progressing. For now, you're going to spend time each morning with Lucy working on physical exercises, and Andrew on the Gift related ones. And while you do that, Prospero and I will research every possible potential problem and make sure he's equipped to deal with it."

That all made sense. Lucy was a physiotherapist and Andrew's specialty was the development of Gifts. And dealing with things going wrong when using Gifts was Perry's specialism. If we were going to be with his parents, he'd be the one best equipped to deal with any problems.

Tired again, I curled against Perry and let the rest of the conversation wash over me as they all sorted out the details. Idly I watched Melanie, letting my mind freewheel. In person, neither Lesley nor Melanie looked quite how I had expected. Up to meeting them, I'd only seen them in Perry's mind where the image wasn't just visual; it incorporated feelings, sensations and memories – all the things he associated with that person. People he saw every day looked pretty much the same in his mind and in real life but the longer it was since he'd seen them the more they changed.

Had Melanie felt familiar to me because she'd been in my head supporting me, or because I'd seen her in Perry's thoughts? It was strange how two of Perry's previous lovers had been instrumental in saving my life. Had they done it for him, because they still loved him?

Melanie

With the meeting over, Melanie's mother headed across the room towards her, but it was Perry she was aiming for. He unwound from Leonie and stood up to talk to her. Melanie stayed seated, looking at Leonie who studied her back, head tilted to one side, clearly curious.

Does she even know who I am? What does she know about me? About me and Perry?

"I'm Melanie," she said, watching Leonie's reaction closely.

A slow smile spread across Leonie's face, lighting it up. "Hello, Melanie," she said. "I didn't recognise you when I bumped into you, not until you touched my mind. Unless he sees them every day, the people in Perry's head don't look like themselves but like how they made him feel."

Perry turned back at the sound of Leonie's voice.

"I need to talk to Andrew," she told him.

"Of course. Go on. He's over there." Perry indicated

Andrew with a nod.

Leonie started to move, but Melanie put out a hand to stop her for a moment. "How I made him feel?"

Leonie turned back towards her, still smiling. "You made him feel trusted and safe," she said and then slipped across the room to Andrew.

Melanie looked at Perry, bewildered.

He grinned back at her as he sat down again. "Disconcerting, isn't she?"

"I feel like she's very gently pointed out to me something I should have known but was too slow to see," Melanie confessed.

"Happens to me all the time," he told her.

"Trusted and safe? Is that right? I thought I led you into all sorts of trouble."

He nodded. "You did. But that's still how you made me feel, at a time when I needed it."

She carried on, "What does trusted and safe look like anyway?"

He shrugged. "I don't know. To me people look like they always do. It's Leonie who sees them looking different in my memories. Knowing what matters to her, I should think trusted and safe looks very beautiful indeed, so she should have recognised you."

Melanie found herself blushing at the compliment. "Does she know about us? I wasn't sure."

Perry was more serious now, the smile gone from his face. "Oh yes, I've told her everything I could remember. Andrew and a few others have added bits that I didn't remember. Some of that time is rather…blurred. Some of it I don't remember at all."

"And she's not bothered by it?"

He took a moment or two to respond. "She's not bothered to the extent that she's not the slightest bit jealous, not of you or any of the others. And you're not the first she's met, either, there are several still around the House and hospital, and of course she met Lesley. She just doesn't see any point in worrying about things that happened before she knew me. What bothers her more, if that's the right word, is the effect people in my past have had on me. Most of the women I slept with she considers utterly unimportant; a few she has opinions on. She's convinced you were there for me when I needed someone – trusted and safe, remember – so I don't think you could do any wrong in her eyes."

They both looked across at Leonie, now standing talking with Andrew.

"Who else does she have opinions on then?" Melanie asked.

"That you know of? Lesley and Marie."

"Are they bad?"

"No, not exactly. She may see people how they made me feel, but she's doing it with hindsight, so she also sees the outcome. And she thinks about their side of things. And I did care about Lesley, so a lot of what I felt was very good."

"Did she know Lesley was going to be at the conference?"

"Oh yes, Leonie was expecting to meet Lesley, just not quite how it happened." He paused, remembering and sighed. "My world is turning into before and after and I don't even know what to call the thing that divides them!"

Melanie responded gently, "Whatever it was, I'd call it an accident."

He looked at her, grateful. "You're probably right. Anyway, they were on good terms from the start and Leonie was very protective of Lesley's baby. And then Lesley looked after Leonie. What she did then made what you did later possible."

Leonie shot back across the room into the space she'd vacated earlier and curled close into Perry again.

"Alright, beautiful?" he asked softly as he wrapped his arms back around her.

Leonie nodded. "I didn't know Andrew knew about me. I needed to know how long he's known," she said.

"And now you do know?" Perry asked.

Leonie nodded again. "And he looked after you—I wanted to thank him."

That rendered Perry speechless for a moment, and a variety of expressions – relief, guilt, love – crossed his face. What did he have to feel relieved or guilty about? He couldn't possibly be jealous of Andrew, though perhaps Andrew could be jealous of Leonie. Perhaps even now Perry might not realise how Andrew felt about him.

"You looked after him, too," Leonie said to her, twisting round in Perry's arms to talk to her. "And me. You did so much for me, and I don't know how to say thank you enough."

Melanie smiled at her earnest face. "You're welcome. I was glad to help and I've enjoyed coming back here and visiting old friends. But I haven't been looking after Perry, just you."

"But you looked after him before," Leonie stated. "After Lesley. When you loved him."

This time it was Melanie who was rendered speechless.

"Whatever we did, we were just friends, Leonie," Perry said, but Leonie gave him a look that suggested she thought he was being either slow or stupid.

"Yeah," she said, disbelievingly. "Perry, I'm really hungry."

Chapter 5

Leonie

"Leonie, if you're hungry we'll go to the Buttery and ask Pedro to serve afternoon tea," Lord Gabriel said. "Lucy, go on ahead and warn him."

"It'll be too demanding, emotionally." That was Lady Eleanor.

"She's not strong enough." Benjamin.

"People will crowd her when they see her, fuss over her, swamp her." Lady Eleanor again.

Me, I didn't care. If this was what Lord Gabriel had suggested, I wasn't going to say no. I just desperately needed the safety and security of being next to Perry. Only moments ago I'd felt an equally desperate need to be with Andrew.

"I'm a doctor," Andrew had said softly, stroking my cheek. "And I've worked at Taylor House. Do you really think I don't know how to recognise a nestling? And that I don't know what that means? It doesn't make any difference."

I'd flung my arms round him and kissed his cheek. He'd hugged me back.

"Thank you," I'd whispered. "And thank you for looking after Perry. I couldn't manage without him."

I was brought back to the present by Lord Gabriel silencing all the fuss with a wave of his hand. "You are all invited to join us. With such medical supervision I am sure Leonie will be fine, and with me she will not be disturbed by others. Prospero, you bring Leonie. Melanie, perhaps you would care to accompany me? The rest of you can make your own arrangements."

With that, he offered Melanie his arm and we followed them to the Buttery. I liked the Buttery. A small room off the main dining hall, it was both cosy and welcoming. On weekend mornings we served Pedro's hangover recipe from the hatch between it and the kitchen. I'd seen what Pedro put in his remedy, which was more than enough to put me off drinking for ever. I wondered how often Perry and Melanie had needed it – frequently from the stories I'd heard.

I felt safe and protected, tucked between Perry and Lord Gabriel, with Melanie and Lady Eleanor both close by. Everyone from the meeting seemed to have joined us.

Pedro was busy making sure they all had plenty to eat. He nudged me with an elbow. "Cookies here," he said offering a plate piled high with my favourites. "And cake there, fruit over there."

As I reached for a cookie my sleeve dropped back, showing the Trader marking on my arm. Without thinking, I glanced towards Lord Gabriel's hand. He spotted me, smiled, and laid his hand palm uppermost on the table so I could see it. The mark looked like a perfect match for the one on my neck.

"I knew my ring and your necklace were twin stones, designed to work as a pair," he said. "But it turns out they were triplets, and the one in your bracelet was designed as the third in the group."

I looked up at him, full of curiosity, and Lady Eleanor spoke, "You should tell her how you came by them. I think Leonie deserves to know."

"Very well," he said, moving a little to settle himself in his chair.

Everyone turned to listen as he started, "When I was a teenager, my father thought it important that I should learn about other cultures, other ways of life. So he sent me to join a caravan of Traders for a time."

I caught his glance towards Lady Eleanor, with a slight smile that suggested shared memories. Of course, she'd been fostered to a Trader caravan too. I turned my attention back to Lord Gabriel.

"The caravan I joined were specialists in jewellery," he continued. "They were very welcoming and they had a fairly new Headwoman who was like a mother to me."

I must have made a noise as I realised who he meant because he turned towards me. "Yes, Leonie, it was Katya."

I'd known Katya well when I travelled with that caravan. I still missed her and thought of her nearly every day. Apart from my aunt, she'd been the closest I had to a parent.

Lord Gabriel carried on, "The merchant then was Eshley. Merchant Ethan's a little younger than me, but I knew him then too. My time with them was a happy time and then I returned to my father and carried on with my life. In time, I was called to join this Order and eventually I became Abbot."

I figured he was probably missing out quite a lot of story there but I supposed it wasn't relevant at the moment.

"Katya and Eshley came to the service at which I was inducted as Abbot and they brought me gifts. They brought my Abbot's ring which I've worn ever since, until this past week." I glanced at his hand where he still appeared to be wearing the ring. "Katya had the Sight, you know," he said, acknowledging my look, "the ability to see something of the future. So they also brought a duplicate ring knowing that one day the master stone would burn out. This one only has a power stone, not a master stone. And with the ring, they brought a necklace which they told me was for my daughter."

He looked directly at me. "That really puzzled me," he continued. "I knew I didn't have a daughter and I didn't expect ever to have one. For a while I wondered if it meant Melanie but I became sure it didn't. I put the necklace away and waited. Then you came along and almost immediately I wanted to give it to you. When you wore it the first time I knew I was right. The stone felt like it was now where it belonged. A few days later I received a letter Katya had left for me. She asked me to care for you as she had cared for me. She'd been like a mother to me – so I took that to mean I should consider you my daughter, as I do."

"The stone felt right, with Leonie wearing it," Perry said.

"Yes," agreed Lord Gabriel. "I saw you recognise it on Christmas Day." He put his hand up to stop both Perry and Melanie speaking. "Don't tell me. I know the pair of you were up to some mischief by which you discovered the necklace and the stone originally and I've decided I don't want to know more."

They both subsided, looking guilty and relieved at the same time. I wanted to know more, but I'd get the full story from Perry eventually. Lord Gabriel turned back to me. "There's a copy of the necklace, too. I'd like you to have it."

"I don't need it," I told him, fingering the mark on my neck.

"I know. But I'd like you to have it anyway. I'm sure Edward will find it for you some time." He looked at Edward who nodded.

Perry frowned, a crease between his eyebrows. "This doesn't add up," he said. "Master stones are linked to an individual, to their brain pattern, as distinct as a finger print. You must have had that necklace for nearly twenty years. How could it possibly be geared to Leonie's mind?"

Lord Gabriel looked around as if he was assessing something. "I wondered that, too," he said. "For those who don't know, master stones and power stones are constructs, technology designed and built by Traders."

I hadn't known that and I'd lived with them; from the intakes of breath I suspected most of the others at the table hadn't known either. He went on, "I can think of several ways in which this could have been done. But I think the most likely is that the stone in the necklace wasn't actually locked to Leonie's mind."

Now everyone looked at him, bewildered. He grinned at that, took my wrist and touched the Trader sign emblazoned on it. "I think the stone in the necklace was linked to the bracelet," he said. "So it could be accessed by whoever could access the bracelet stone. And the bracelet stone could easily have been adjusted to work for Leonie, after she came to join the Traders."

That made a lot of sense to me, and from the way Perry was nodding, it clearly satisfied him too. I decided to take the opportunity to ask something else that had been on my mind for a while. I took Perry's hand and rested it on the table, our fingers entwined. "Our rings are Trader rings?"

"Yes," Lord Gabriel said. "Your caravan sent them for you. Their current Headwoman, Katila has the Sight too, you know. They'll be coming by in the autumn sometime, and bringing the rest of your portion." He reached into his pocket and held something out to me. "She sent this too, as part of that."

I recognised it, of course. It was a Deathstone, a form of jewel in an intricate setting. It was prepared for a Trader child around the time of their birth and held by a parent, usually their father. At some point – maybe on marriage or a significant birthday – it might be given to the child to keep, in recognition that they are responsible for their own life. Or a father might keep it until his own death in recognition of the bond between parent and child. When a Trader died, the Deathstone was burnt on their funeral pyre. It would melt, usually partly contained by its setting, and when it cooled, it would be kept as a memento of the deceased. Katya had told me it was a hangover from the time just after the Devastation – if the Deathstone melted it meant the fire was hot enough to kill the remnants of any disease.

"I've kept it with me this past week in case the opportunity arose," he said.

He'd had it close in case I died. I took it from him, looked at it and then handed it back. "Will you keep it for me?" I asked. "I don't have a need for this right now, either."

He took it with a smile and dropped it back in his pocket. I was certain he understood what I meant by handing it back – that I was both accepting him as my father and telling him that I had every intention of surviving. Then I realised what else he'd said. "My portion?" I asked.

"You're a Trader too," Lord Gabriel pointed out, indicating the mark on my arm. "You have a portion due from the caravan you left, a share in it."

Any Trader who left a caravan, say through marriage or to be a Settler, would take their share with them. I just hadn't thought it applied to me, an *Osti*, an Outsider. It didn't seem very important right now; I was more pleased at the idea that I would see Ethan and Katila and the rest of the caravan in a few months. I yawned.

"Enough," said Perry, with a grin. "I think you need to go back to bed before you fall asleep." He pulled me to my feet and shepherded me back to our rooms.

Chapter 6

Leonie

The Them surrounded me, cloaks billowing in a non-existent wind.

I tried to gather the power but it wasn't there. I reached for a weapon but none came to hand. "Not fair," I told the Them. "I have no Gifts."

They shrugged, not caring.

Hang on. They responded to me?

I didn't have time to think about it as they oozed closer. I did the only thing I could. I ran. There was a cave, small, deep, dark. I dived in. They couldn't get me here. One of the Them reached towards me.

Perry was holding me and I was safe. I slept again, secure in his arms, waking much later to the sound of rain drumming on the roof and walls.

Sunday

I couldn't sit still but I was too tired to keep moving. I didn't want to sleep in case the nightmare came again. My head felt wrong, empty and itchy.

"What's the matter?" Perry asked me.

"Nothing," I snapped. "I'm fine."

"You didn't sleep very well. Why don't you go and lie down?" he tried.

"I don't want to sleep." I knew I sounded whiny, petulant. I turned away from Perry so I couldn't see the hurt and worry on his face.

"How about you just sit down then? Rest a little?" His voice was very calm. I was sure he was trying not to sound worried.

I climbed onto the sofa and rolled into a tight ball in the corner, rocking backwards and forwards. Perry sat down at the other end, not touching me, just there, nearby. He started reading out loud. The sound of his voice was soothing in itself and I crept closer. Holding onto him, I'd be safe, of course I would. Then I listened to the words and they were comforting too and I could rest.

When I woke again my head was on Perry's lap, his hand twisted into my hair. He smiled at me. "Hello, beautiful. Feeling a little better?" His voice sounded relaxed and content, and his arms were wrapped around me as I took my time waking up properly.

"I expect you're hungry," he said. "Come on."

I followed him into the kitchen and sat at the table watching as he put bread, cheese and meat out and heated soup. He kept smiling at me, and I revelled in us being together, just us with no one else around. The peace I got from that sleep and time together lasted well into the afternoon. Then it started to rain again and the restlessness came back.

I wandered around our living space, moving from window to window, staring at the view without seeing it. I picked up a book and put it down. Pushed a chair from here to there, just a fraction away. Went back to the windows.

Perry came up behind me, taking my shoulders to turn me to face him. He enveloped me in his arms, pinning me to his body, whispering in my ear, breath warm on my neck. Desperately, I wanted him. I yanked my arms free, took his head in both hands and pulled it down so that our mouths met. Eagerly, almost roughly, I claimed him as mine. He hesitated for a moment and then responded in kind, hands sliding down my back to cup my bottom and lift me up. I wrapped my legs round his waist, one hand in his hair, the other frantically searching for the touch of his skin beneath his shirt. He moved and somehow we were in the bedroom, lying on the bed, still tangled together. He was already topless.

"Get these clothes off," I hissed, yanking at any fabric I could reach. For a moment I was swamped by guilt. I was just using him, using sex to calm the restlessness, using his body to take away the power of the nightmares. And I didn't care. Then we were skin to skin, bodies joined as one and a wave of peace drove the guilt and restlessness away. This was about love, about sharing ourselves with each other, about giving each other what we needed. It wasn't using, it was giving – and receiving.

Perry

Perry lay in bed, Leonie's head tucked against his shoulder, her arm draped across his chest and the covers thrown loosely across the pair of them. The day was definitely improving. He'd woken in the early hours to the sound of torrential rain and the realisation that Leonie was not beside him in bed. He'd been out of bed like a shot, frantically looking for her, reaching for the glow in his mind that meant Leonie. It hadn't taken long; she was curled up in a dark corner of the living area behind an armchair. Without thinking he'd just pulled the chair away to get to her. She'd launched herself at him in attack like a wild animal disturbed in its lair, and that's when he'd understood that she was having a nightmare. He'd wrapped his arms around her as she attacked him, and that had woken her, leaving her shivering and shaking against him.

Honestly, he'd panicked at the time. Now he realised that Leonie was still being monitored and had the disturbance gone on for more than a moment or two, someone would have come. And the nightmare was probably a good sign. They were usually experienced by the Gifted as their talents developed so it could mean that she was starting to heal.

She'd been restless all day, though, as had he and he hadn't known what to do about it, especially when she'd curled up in a ball and started rocking back and forth. He'd started reading the day's Bible passages out loud, just to calm himself. And then Leonie had uncurled from her ball and settled close to him to listen. She'd fallen asleep again sprawled across his lap like a cat, waking too late to go to the main hall for lunch, so he'd fixed them something to eat there. He'd enjoyed it just being the two of them, quietly together.

When she'd kissed him in the afternoon, hard and passionately he'd felt her desire but then, remembering her health, he had pulled back.

"Leonie, you've been injured, you aren't strong enough," he'd protested.

She'd answered by kissing him again, with an almost desperate edge to her desire, and he'd wanted her too, so badly. Making love had exhausted her, certainly, but he was also certain that in some way she had needed it as much as he had. She was asleep again now, more deeply and peacefully, her body more relaxed, than at any time since the accident.

He rested his cheek on her head, and the first thought that came to him was that Leonie belonged to him again. It shocked him deeply.

I'm not that possessive. I'm not. Surely I'm not?

He'd certainly viewed all that power as possessing her, as taking her away from him. And since they'd returned neither of them had had any control over their lives, with other people making all the decisions for them. Yesterday, he knew he'd been unwilling to let go of Leonie, jealous of anyone else she'd turned to; today he was pleased to have her to himself. But he didn't want to own her, to control what she did. He wanted her to be her own independent person, the one God had designed her to be. It was just that he was terrified of letting her out of his sight, afraid that any goodbye might be the last time he saw her. And that was still a very real risk.

He shuddered slightly at the thought and dipped his head to kiss the top of hers. Even in her sleep a smile crossed her face at his touch and a happy sigh escaped her lips. Since she'd first woken, after the accident, their personal connection had felt misaligned, out of kilter, not quite right. Now, he felt back on track.

We belong together again, not her to me, but us to each other.

Had Leonie's restlessness today been because she'd felt the same lack of belonging together? Whatever the problem, making love appeared to have had a healing impact on them both.

Thinking of healing, for the first time he felt both ready and strong enough to look at the damage to Leonie's mind, even curious. Up to now he'd shied away from it, barely able even to take in what Benjamin had told him and glad to have the excuse that his own mind was not recovered enough. Leonie'd been willing enough for him to look yesterday even if the thought of Benjamin doing so had terrified her. If he was the one to look, he could spare her that fear again. After all – and he grinned to himself with remembered pleasure – she had had no problem with him touching her mind whilst they made love.

Gently, he touched the surface of her mind again with his and then sank deeper, letting his own mind find a way to visualise the damage. Her mind was a fire, one where the coals had been scattered, but they were still whole, still glowing, not burnt to ash. To his amazement, and joy, he also saw signs that some of the coals were joining up again, slowly rolling together, although there were so many he couldn't begin to estimate how long it would take for them all to join, if ever. Carefully he retreated from her mind pleased also that he hadn't disturbed her; she was still draped around him and sleeping deeply.

***

Later he sat beside the bed watching her sleep. The many hours he'd spent doing that in the past few days took on a dream like quality, as if he'd only just woken up himself.

Leonie stirred, opened her eyes and said simply, "Perry."

He smiled at her. "Do you know, my name is almost always the first thing you say when you wake?"

She nodded and smiled back. "It seems like a good way to start." She sat up, the sheets tangled around her still naked body, and looked at him.

He thought of the last time he'd seen her like that, the morning of the accident, less than a week ago. He read on her face the same thoughts that had been there then.

"No, no, no. Stop looking at me like that or I'll end up back in bed with you, and then Andrew will turn up and find us and he'll be shocked."

Leonie giggled. "I don't think he'd be shocked."

"Maybe not, but it still wouldn't be a good idea."

Nonetheless, unable to resist, he pulled her into his arms

for a kiss. He was still smiling when they both came up for air. "Seems to me that you're feeling better. Is that right?" he asked.

She nodded. "Definitely better."

"In that case, how would you like to go to the evening service?"

Her eyes lit up. "Can we?"

"I don't see why not. There's plenty of time; you get ready, and I'll go and keep an eye out for Andrew."

Giggling again at the thought of shocking Andrew, Leonie headed off to do just that.

Andrew

Andrew practically stormed into the room as soon as Perry opened the door. "Honestly, Perry," he said. "What were you thinking of? She isn't well enough, not strong enough."

Perry was defensive. "She's stronger than you think. Anyway, what are you on about?"

"You know perfectly well what I'm on about. You and her…"

"It didn't do her any harm, quite the opposite."

"Seriously? You're claiming that having sex with someone who almost died a few days ago is *good* for her?"

"Yes, I am. And anyway, how could you possibly know? Am I not entitled to a private life?" Perry snapped.

"Your life hasn't been private since Lesley," Andrew said dryly.

"I had thought that maybe Leonie and I were entitled to

some privacy," Perry retorted.

"Normally, perhaps. But in this case, had you forgotten that Leonie is still wearing a monitor? The trace is unmistakable."

Perry paled as Andrew watched him. Then he took a deep breath, visibly trying to calm himself. "So tell me, how many people have seen that trace?"

"Not many," Andrew assured him. "But you do know that her strongest memories are being with you, and anyone who supported her this past week has seen those, quite explicitly?"

Perry sighed heavily. "I guess I did. Benjamin told me early on, but I'd forgotten. Don't tell Leonie. I'd rather she didn't know if possible. And the sooner that monitor disc comes off, the better."

"I won't tell," Andrew confirmed. "And, look, I'm sorry. It's none of my business really. I was just worried about Leonie."

"I know," Perry said. "I'm sorry too. I shouldn't have snapped at you. But it really was good for her. You'll see in a moment."

They'd barely finished their conversation as Leonie came into the room. Smiling happily at both of them, she did indeed look much better than she had all day. "Hello, Andrew," she greeted him cheerfully. "Has Perry told you we're going to the evening service?"

He smiled back at her. "I think this is the first time I've seen you awake today." Then he turned towards Perry. "No, he hadn't told me that." The two men locked eyes as Andrew continued, "Do you think that is wise?"

"Oh, yes," Perry replied decisively, clearly certain he'd won as Andrew dropped his gaze and turned towards Leonie. Andrew did his best to hide the delight he felt. The compliant Perry of the last few days had been worrying him considerably; he'd never expected to be so pleased at the return of the somewhat arrogant 'I know best' one.

Andrew hovered round Leonie as they headed to the service, almost jostling Perry as they both tried to protect her.

"I'll stay here with you," he said once they reached the Abbey.

"Don't be daft," Leonie told him. "You're supposed to be over there." She inclined her head towards the monks and nuns in their part of the building. "I'll be fine."

She nudged Perry with her elbow. "You can stop being quite so overprotective too. I can handle the service."

The doubtful look on Perry's face amused Andrew, although he kept that to himself as he went over to where he was supposed to sit. As soon as the service was over he headed straight back to Leonie, intending to help guard her from well-meaning but inquisitive acquaintances. She'd been right though. She didn't need it; looking tired but peaceful, she circulated and answered questions for a few minutes. He wasn't the only one trying to protect her either. Both Melanie and Eleanor were close by.

Melanie nudged him. "Who's that dark-haired man there?" she whispered.

Andrew looked in the direction she'd indicated. "That's Aidan," he whispered back. "Don't you remember him?"

"No," she said, "but he's watching Leonie very closely."

Andrew shrugged. "He used to be a monk, now he's visiting, covering for a lecturer on sabbatical. He and Perry used to sing together. I should think he's just concerned for a friend."

"Maybe," Melanie agreed. Then she grinned. "Have you

noticed that Gabriel and Benjamin keep looking over at Leonie too? As bad as we are."

Andrew grinned back. "We've all got an excuse, haven't we?" he said. "It'll wear off."

It wasn't long before Perry had clearly had all he could tolerate of sharing Leonie and, declaring her to be in need of rest, he swept her off and back to their rooms. Andrew accompanied them, just to make sure they had everything they needed for the night and that the monitor was working properly, or so he told himself.

Chapter 7

Monday Morning

Perry

"Are you sure you'll be alright?" Perry asked Leonie as they headed towards the hospital for the first of her sessions with Andrew and Lucy. Perry knew he was fussing excessively over her; knowing didn't stop him. "I could do these exercises with you, at home. Or Andrew and Lucy could come to you? You don't have to go into the hospital."

"I'll be fine," she said quietly, tucking her hand more firmly into his. "I don't mind the hospital so much now. And it's nice to get out of our rooms."

He shook his head doubtfully. "I don't want you doing too much, over tiring yourself."

She smiled at him. "I think they both know what they are doing, don't you?"

He had to concede that, in fairness, but he tried again once they reached the room Andrew and Lucy were using. "I could stay with you, if you wanted?"

This time it was Andrew who grinned at him. "Get out," he said firmly. He took Perry by the shoulder, turned him round then pushed him out of the door, shutting it sharply behind him.

Perry reached for the handle to reopen the door, then thought better of it, and trudged towards Benjamin's office, feelings of possessiveness sweeping through him.

"This is what I've found so far," Benjamin said, pushing an open book across his desk towards Perry.

Perry picked up the book and glanced at it, then put it

down, shaking his head. "I'm sorry," he said. "I can't concentrate. It was so hard, leaving Leonie with Andrew. Am I really that possessive?"

Benjamin looked almost amused, a smile playing at the corner of his mouth. "You're worried about feeling over possessive?" he asked. "Think about this and tell me what you're missing. Henry and George have asked for and been sent on a month's posting to Taylor House. Melanie won't go home to her husband and kids. Gabriel and Eleanor are spending at least half their time mind linked so they can watch out for each other. Andrew is spending every moment he can and probably quite a few he shouldn't with you and Leonie, and I'm struggling not to keep a constant eye on her charts and monitor output. What do we all have in common?"

Realisation flooded through Perry. "It's bonding isn't it? It's the bonding effect doing it."

"Yes, it is. We thought it would be less intense because we all care for Leonie anyway. Turns out it's the opposite. It's worst for you because you're the closest to her and what you did was the most concentrated. Easiest for Henry and George and they've also been able to get furthest away. Hard for Melanie and Eleanor as they did more of the support. It will ease; it's already starting to, but it will take time."

Perry sighed with relief. Bonding was the name given to the link formed between those who needed support in the way Leonie had and those who gave that support. It was one of the reasons that such activity was strictly regulated. It was normally relatively minor, expressing itself as close concern for the well-being of the supported person and faded naturally within a couple of weeks.

Benjamin carried on, "When we realised it was an issue –

George spotted it first – we changed who was doing what and sent George and Henry away. Then we had Melanie do as much as she could, only that backfired too, because now she won't go home."

Perry nodded his acknowledgement. At least now he knew why he felt this way, and he could only hope that knowing would help him deal with it.

A Few Days Later

Perry could tell that Leonie found the sessions with Andrew and Lucy hard work, but they'd settled into something of a rhythm. She worked with them in the morning then usually, although not always, managed to stay awake for an early lunch. She would sleep for a few hours in the afternoon and then they spent the late afternoon and early evening together, just the two of them.

Today, when she woke, he had a picnic ready. "Let's go up to the lake," he said. "I know it's further than we've been recently, but I think you're strong enough to make it up there."

She grinned at him, nodding. The lake was one of their favourite places, secluded and private, just a mile or two away through the woods. They took the journey slowly, ambling along, hand in hand, but it still wasn't long before they reached the lake, and the decking that hung out over the water. Perry spread a blanket on the decking and then sprawled on it. Leonie lay down next to him, resting her head on his lap.

"Read to me," she said. "I love the sound of your voice. Here, in the sun, listening to you…everything's okay again."

Perry tried not to hear the wistfulness in her voice as he reached for a book. Reading to Leonie was one of Andrew's suggestions, as was today's choice of book – a children's book, one of Leonie's favourites. "Being read to is less tiring than reading for yourself," Andrew had said. "And there's something soothing about the cadence of children's books."

After a couple of chapters, Leonie rolled over onto her stomach, propping her chin on her hands, elbows on the ground. Perry put the book down. "How are you doing, beautiful?" he asked.

"'M okay," she said. "It's hard work with Lucy and Andrew. And the nightmares scare me. Every night. And they disturb you."

He reached over to stroke her cheek. "You don't have to worry about me," he said. "And I'll ask Benjamin about the nightmares, see if there's anything more we can do."

She nodded at that, then pulled herself along his body to lie next to him. She was warm against him, her very touch on his skin exciting him. Constantly wary of the monitor disc Leonie still wore, Perry had refrained from initiating love making and when Leonie made a move towards him, he had found a number of excuses. But here, here they were out of range of the monitor. A smile crept across Perry's face. Here they could do whatever they wanted and no one would know. He rolled over so they were facing each other and ran his hands down Leonie's back and up under her shirt.

***

Perry spoke to Benjamin the next day. "Leonie has nightmares every night," he said. Well, almost every night. There hadn't been one last night, after their time at the lake but he wasn't going to share that. "How can I take her away if I can't stop them?"

"I don't think it will be a problem," Benjamin told him.

"From the looks of the monitor there's only the tiniest hint of power there. So it's not surprising that you aren't preventing them. I think they're more related to the trauma of what happened and will ease as time passes."

Perry shook his head. "There's definitely power involved. I can feel it. I should be stopping that bit for her, at least."

Benjamin took a deep breath and paused a moment before he answered. "I'd hoped we'd be through this stage before it became an issue. You were far more drained by what you did than I think you realise. It's just that you don't have anything like the same power and strength that you did. Give it another week or so and you'll be fine."

"I'm fine now," Perry protested.

"No," said Benjamin gently. "No, you're not. Not yet. Take a proper look in the mirror sometime, or weigh yourself. You're recovering well but you're nothing like fit yet. You'll be fine by the time you and Leonie leave. As for Leonie's nightmares, we're still monitoring her. You don't need to worry about not waking or not stopping them. If she hasn't calmed down in a few minutes after one starts someone will be there. If she leaves your rooms sleepwalking someone will be there. It's only been a few days. I think we'll find it sorts itself out."

Leonie

The Them came for me again, circling our bed, hoods covering their faces.

I rolled onto the floor, leading them away from Perry, keeping him safe. "Go away," I snarled, but they just shrugged again.

They followed me, drifting behind me, reaching towards

me. I ran. I couldn't throw power at them and I had no weapons, but I could entice them away. There was an archway ahead of me. I knew I'd be safe on the other side but the Them had almost caught me. I lunged at the closest one. It faded to nothing and I turned and ran for the Arch with a last burst of energy.

I was inside the Abbey. Without thinking I ran across to the side chapel where I had hidden out so many times before and curled up on one of the seats. With his amazing talent for being where he was needed, Andrew appeared beside me. "Want to tell me all about it?" he asked.

The words burst out of me, "It's not fair. I have to put up with the nightmares but I can't do anything. And why doesn't being with Perry stop them anymore? Doesn't he love me any longer? Doesn't he want me?"

Andrew put his arm around my shoulders. "Oh, Leonie," he said sympathetically. "Which do you want me to answer first?" He didn't wait for me to tell him but answered the one that mattered most to me. "Perry loves you desperately. He always will. I've never seen anyone hurt so much as when he brought you back. He wants you and he needs you. Never doubt that."

"But why then? Why's he being so…so cautious, so…so protective?" I pleaded.

"You have to know he was so scared you would die. He's still terrified of losing you, of doing something that will make that more likely. And he feels guilty that he did this to you, by telling you how to use the master stones."

"That's daft."

Andrew grinned. "This is Perry we're talking about." That was a good point and it made me smile too.

Andrew went on, "As for the nightmares, at the moment

they aren't truly nightmares."

"They have the *Them*, and I sleepwalk. That seems pretty much nightmare to me."

"Yes, I suppose it does. But because there's very little power there, there's little for Perry to stop. And they're normally stopped by his touch stimulating hormones in your body which aren't working at full effect because you're still healing. And Perry's still recovering himself so he's not as effective at stopping them. As you both recover, and strangely as the power gets stronger, you'll find he'll stop them again. It won't take much longer."

That was reassuring. "But why won't he… I mean… They used to stop if we…" I didn't know how to say it, not to Andrew.

"You mean making love used to stop the nightmares, don't you?" Andrew asked. "And now Perry is sometimes reluctant? When it should be a good solution?"

I nodded. That was exactly what I meant but I hadn't wanted to say so knowing how Andrew felt about Perry.

Andrew sighed. "There isn't anything you can't tell me, you know. This problem I can solve for you." He tapped the monitor disc where it was stuck to my skin under my clothes. "He didn't want to worry you but he's concerned this will tell everyone what you're doing. Let's go to the kitchen and get some milk and cookies and I'll find a bit of alcohol to dissolve the glue and take it off for you."

That sounded like a good idea to me so we did just that. Perry found us there a few minutes later. He sat down next to me, straddling the bench I was sitting on. He put his arms around me, pulling me close. "Hey," he said quietly. "I was worried about you."

"I'm okay," I told him. "It was a nightmare, but I'm okay now."

He accepted that, for now anyway, and reached for my mug of milk to take a sip. Andrew stood up to get him his own mug, and I put my hand over my mug. "Don't drink that," I told Perry. "Andrew's put something in it to make me sleep."

Andrew turned and looked at me in surprise. "How could you know that?" he asked, astonished.

I grinned back. "I didn't, I guessed and you just confirmed it."

Perry laughed out loud at Andrew's startled face. That was good to hear; I realised I hadn't really heard him laugh over the last few days. "She's got you," he said. "She's caught me that way before." He looked down at me. "Are you going to drink it?"

I nodded and leaned against him. "Now you're here, I will." I drank it down, made myself comfortable against Perry and closed my eyes.

"You're not meant to drink it that fast," Andrew protested.

Perry laughed again.

Perry

"You're an idiot," Andrew said to Perry as soon as Leonie was asleep. He dropped the monitor disc on the table. "No one would have thought anything of what the trace might show, not now she's so much better. Or you could just have taken the disc off. And Leonie was fretting over what your behaviour meant."

"I'm not stopping her nightmares. That disc means someone else will see and help her when I fail to. Like you, tonight. Or Benjamin. He told me where you were. I was frantic when she was missing."

"If it worries you that much, stick the disc back on when you go to sleep and remove it when you wake up. But you're both recovered enough that you'll be stopping her nightmares before the week is out. Meanwhile, making love is likely to reduce their incidence anyway."

Perry looked at Andrew, astounded. "I can't believe that you, of all people, with all you know, are recommending that I use sex to reduce the likelihood of a nightmare. You know where that led before, what a mess, what damage I did."

Andrew shook his head, smiling slightly. "I didn't say sex, I said making love. There's a difference, or hadn't you noticed? You and Leonie, expressing your feelings for each other physically, inside marriage, is not going to lead to the problems you had before, so you might as well enjoy the benefits."

Now it was Perry's turn to shake his head. "I don't know," he said doubtfully. "It seems a lot to risk, removing the disc."

"I told you, if it worries you, stick it back on when you go to sleep. But the more normally you treat her, the more confidence she'll have in her own recovery."

That made sense to Perry and he said so before carrying Leonie back to their rooms. Andrew went with him, intending to open doors for him. "I didn't mean it to work quite that quickly," he said, referring to the sedative he'd given Leonie.

"No," Perry agreed, his equilibrium restored by his close contact with Leonie. "Benjamin warned me that she's overreacting to everything."

"Yeah. You'll have to watch out for that if you need to treat her. And she might develop allergic reactions to stuff, too."

"I'm not that comfortable with being the one to treat her anyway," Perry said, finally voicing another of his concerns. "Admittedly, I don't like anyone else doing it, but treating your own family, that's hardly good practice, is it?"

"It's not ideal," Andrew agreed. "But there's no one who'd do a better job. Even if you stayed here, it would be you treating her if anything happened, because it's your area."

"But here I'd have you and Benjamin to discuss it with. There, I'm on my own."

"You're just looking for a safety net. If we disagreed with you, you'd do what you thought was right anyway."

Andrew had a point, although Perry wasn't prepared to concede that. "And it's not just that either. The doctor there left a couple of weeks back. I'll be covering while we're there, just afternoons and the occasional evening, but I'll end up treating a whole bunch of family."

Andrew shrugged. "In small rural communities the doctor has to treat family because they're related to most of the community and there's no one else. You'll be fine. And you'll enjoy the work. It'll be good for you."

He would enjoy the work and actually he was happy to take it on; despite his specialism, day-to-day clinic work was his favourite part of practicing medicine. He had discussed it with Leonie before he'd finally agreed but she seemed happy for him to do this. He wasn't entirely sure she'd understood what he'd planned, but at that point he'd still been desperately trying to protect her from anything stressful so he hadn't pushed it. Benjamin and Gabriel had sorted out a deal and a suitable workload. He'd even have a couple of assistants, nurse practitioners, one of whom would be Lizzie, who was going to marry his brother Sam.

Once Leonie was tucked into bed, Andrew left although not without a final reassurance that Perry was more than capable of taking proper care of both Leonie and the rest of his parents' community. Back in bed himself, Perry's thoughts went round in circles as he tried to consider everything Andrew had said. But before sleep overcame him, he resolved to stop treating Leonie as breakable and instead make the most of every minute they had together.

Chapter 8

Late June

Leonie

Something was tickling my face. I brushed it away, but it came back and there was quiet laughter. I opened my eyes to find Perry, fully dressed, standing over me, but the room dark. I struggled to sit up. "What time is it? What's happening?"

"It's okay," he said. "It's still early. I didn't mean to worry you. I have to go or I'll miss the train, but I didn't want to leave without you knowing."

Of course. Perry was going to the thanksgiving service for Lesley's son. I put my arms round his neck and kissed him, but he made sure I'd snuggled down to sleep again before he left.

Next time I woke the sun was on my face, and I could hear someone moving about in the living area. I poked my head out of the bedroom door and discovered it was Andrew.

"Good morning," he said. "Hurry up and get dressed. I've got breakfast here for you."

I was pleased Andrew was there— I didn't want to be alone at all. But surely I ought to be fine on my own, ought to be facing up to doing that by now? I'd been perfectly used to being on my own in the past.

"Andrew," I asked over breakfast. "Why are you here? I mean I want you here but does it mean Benjamin thinks I need someone with me all the time? Am I not as recovered as I think I am?"

Andrew grinned. "Firstly," he said, "not one of us, not even Lord Gabriel, is prepared to face up to Perry if we left you alone for a minute and something happened in that minute."

That made me laugh.

"And secondly, after having the power and knowledge of all those people in your head, being alone is going to be much harder for you for a while. When you're ready to be on your own, you'll know. Until then, don't worry about it."

"I am much better," I told him, holding out my arm. "Look, not just skin and bones any longer. And I haven't had a nightmare since that time you found me."

"You're doing well," he agreed. "Now, do you think you're up to working on our surprise for Perry?"

I nodded. "I just about managed it yesterday. I want to be ready for when he gets back."

"It'll be hard work."

"I know," I said. "We'd better get practising."

***

Chloe caught up with me as Andrew and I left the dining hall at lunchtime. "I don't want to put pressure on you," she said, "but I could really do with going over a few things with you in the office."

Puzzled, I followed her along to the main office, Andrew trailing after me. It seemed less tidy than usual, with packages piled against the walls, and envelopes and letters spread over a large table. Chloe sighed and turned to me. "People have wanted to respond to what you did," she said. "There's been cards and letters, flowers, gifts, money. I've got it all organised. I just need to tell you, so that I know you are happy with what I plan and what I've done."

I nodded, unable to think of anything to say.

"Right," she said. "The flowers have all gone to decorate the hospital and the Abbey. Any food gifts have already been taken by Pedro, and the non-food gifts will go to Edward. They'll both arrange for them to be passed on to those who need them. Any money, and anything suitable for children, I plan to send on to Taylor House."

"I like that idea," I said, finding my voice.

"It was Lord Gabriel's suggestion," Chloe told me. "He thought you'd like it."

That left the cards and letters which Chloe had opened and sorted into two groups. One was cards and letters from people Chloe didn't think I knew, which I could look through one day when I felt strong enough.

"That's not going to be soon," I told Chloe.

"That doesn't matter," she said. "I'll deal with anything that needs a response."

The smaller group was from people that Chloe thought I would know. I managed to look through it, amazed at how many people seemed to care. One card struck me particularly; it was from Taylor House and signed by the children Perry had taken there, the ones I had found and we had rescued. That was touching enough but the card design featured a little cartoon zebra. It struck some chord in my foggy brain but I couldn't work out what. The zebra was the logo of Taylor House; maybe I'd seen it before. I kept that card with me in the hope that it would trigger something in my memory.

The other card I kept was one from Perry's family. Everyone had signed it and they'd included a photograph of the whole family. Andrew leaned over my shoulder, looking at it and pointing out who everyone was though it wasn't hard to work out.

"You've met them all?" I asked him, a little surprised. I thought of Andrew as always having been at House St Peter, even if I knew, really, that wasn't the case.

He nodded. "I used to stay sometimes, between quarters. You know, before. You'll love it there and they'll love you."

Well, maybe.

***

Andrew and I walked down to the station in the early evening sunshine. We stood on the platform waiting for Perry and I watched as the train appeared in the distance, slowed down and came to a stop. I was still amazed by how huge they were, up close.

Perry stepped down from a carriage further along, scanning the platform for us. His whole being looked weary, shoulders sagging. Although I knew Benjamin considered him pretty much recovered from all he'd done, I thought he was still far too thin, too easily tired. His eyes lit up when he saw us and that was all I needed. I ran down the platform to greet him, throwing myself into his arms.

"Hey, beautiful," he said, holding me close, even his voice sounding tired.

I kissed him and then, concentrating hard, I reached out and twisted my mind into his. The slow smile that spread across his face as he realised what I was doing was worth every drop of sweat, every tear of frustration that relearning this had cost me. He kissed me again, one hand in my hair, the other arm tight around my body, as if he couldn't hold me close enough.

Andrew came up beside us. "Did you like your surprise then?" he asked Perry.

Perry was smiling too much to answer.

"I can't do it for long or from very far yet," I told him. "But I'm getting better every time."

"That you can do it at all is nothing short of amazing," he said, finding his voice again. He kept his arm around me as we walked home, Andrew walking on my other side.

"How was it?" Andrew asked.

"Hard," Perry confessed. "Very hard. Seeing her there with a baby. I have forgiven her for what happened with my child, I know I have but it was still hard to see." I squeezed his waist in sympathy and he smiled tiredly at me. "Everyone was asking after you," he said. "They were all so pleased to hear how well you are recovering, and so grateful for what you did." He looked into the distance. "Lesley's dying," he said, his voice sort of remote. "Did you know?"

I nodded. "I did. But sometimes I don't remember what I know until you tell me again."

Both Andrew and Perry hurried to reassure me that was perfectly normal and would pass and not to worry about it, which actually I hadn't been. Then Andrew asked for more details about Lesley and Perry told him medical stuff that I didn't try to follow.

"That's perfectly treatable," Andrew said.

"Not at this stage. She delayed treatment because of the baby, and it's too late now. She has months, perhaps."

We walked in silence for a while after that, each lost in our own thoughts.

"Why do people have to die?" I muttered, kicking at a stone on the path.

Perry smiled tiredly at me. "Mortality rates are much higher now than they used to be, before the Devastation, whether you're talking about in child birth, or infants, or just in general."

"Why?" I kicked the stone again. "'S not fair."

Andrew shrugged. "Maybe the Devastation had a hidden impact on humanity's health in general. Maybe we've lost too much medical knowledge. Or perhaps it's just to do with differences in the way we live."

"Yeah," Perry agreed. "But that's not necessarily a bad thing. Higher mortality rates mean a slower expansion of population and less demand on our world's resources. And the stronger ones, those more suitable for our world are the ones who survive and pass on their ability to survive." He paused and took a deep breath. "That makes sense on a global scale. But when it comes to the individual, when it's my friend, my family, my wife" – his arm tightened around me – "my child, my sister, then I want that individual to live."

I understood that; there was a continual tension between what you might want or what might be best for an individual and what might be best for the world, for society as a whole.

Andrew spoke again. "Before the Devastation, medical knowledge meant that people went on living longer and longer. But they often had a much reduced quality of life, or were in considerable pain, or they had years of senility. And that meant everybody had less experience of their loved ones dying, so death became less and less familiar and more and more something to try and delay."

"How do you measure someone's quality of life?" Perry asked. "How much is too much pain to ask them to bear? Do you subject them to treatment for something when very likely they'll die of something else before the first thing kills them? How much

– time, energy, money – do you invest in keeping them alive? And who makes these decisions? In the end, everyone has to die sometime of something."

I shook my head, no idea how to respond.

"I don't know either," he continued. "I just try and live each day as a gift, each new one a bonus. Death will come one day and when it does, I'll be with God."

"But what about your patients?" I asked. "How do you decide what to do for them?"

Perry sighed and exchanged a glance with Andrew. "I try to give them choices and options. I try to tell them everything they need to make a decision, and where I think treatment will be pointless, or the side effects worse than the illness. And I tell them about my faith and how it helps me. And then, whatever they decide I do all I can to achieve that, whether I agree with it or not."

And I've held you after a patient's died. It tears you apart. Every time.

When we were alone, back in our rooms, Perry turned to me and his fingers touched the mark on my neck. "I didn't give you a choice," he said. "I didn't tell you that using the master stone would kill you."

"Yes, you did," I told him. "It was clear in your face. I read it there. And I still went ahead and did it, knowing what it would do to you. Perry, I'm so sorry."

I leaned against him and burst into tears. He put his arms around me and held me close, burying his face in my hair. "It's okay," he said, his voice muffled. "I chose to tell you. I knew you'd choose to use it."

He was crying too, and we clung to each other as we tried

to face together all the fear and loss and pain we'd each been trying to protect the other one from. We slept that night curled tightly together, both clearly needing the reassurance of the other's touch.

Chapter 9

Friday – Late June

Leonie

I stood looking blankly at the bag. It sat on our bed, and I imagined it staring back at me, laughing at me. Today, we would set off to visit Perry's family. This small bag was supposed to hold whatever we needed for the overnight journey. Our main luggage had gone yesterday; I hadn't been able to face packing that either so Edward had taken over. I suspected that he had probably sneaked a whole new wardrobe in there for me but I hadn't had the energy to argue about it.

I picked up my Bible, the little holding cross Perry had given me long before we'd been married, the photo of Perry's family and the two cards that I'd kept and put them in the bag. Perry appeared beside me. "A change of clothes, perhaps? And your washing things?" he suggested.

I found those and put them in, then looked back at Perry. "Anything else?" I asked.

He shook his head. "I'll finish off," he said. "You sit down for a moment and rest until it's time to leave."

I was more than happy to obey – for now, anyway.

"Are you worried about the journey?" he asked as he wandered round the room getting his own things. "Benjamin's a little concerned you might have bad memories about what happened after our last train journey."

I shook my head. "I don't think they're bad memories. Just...strange. It's more where we're going this time."

He came over to me, squatting down so we were on a level. "It'll be fine. I'll be there. And they'll love you."

Well, maybe.

***

This time we had our own private room in a carriage. I just stared around it in astonishment. On one side was a bed, already made up and turned down, small but sufficient for us both. On the other side, two comfortable seats with a table between, and in one corner a small but ingeniously equipped washroom. Perry watched me with an amused look on his face.

"You've travelled like this before, haven't you?" I asked him.

He nodded. "Quite a lot, yes. Just not for a long time."

I settled down in one of the chairs where I could watch as the train pulled out. I'd enjoyed that last time. After a moment, Perry put our bag down and sat in the other chair. We were well underway before he spoke again. "Benjamin wanted me to give you something to help you sleep tonight," he said.

His tone suggested to me that he disagreed. I didn't want to take anything; I didn't like taking medicine. "Do I have to take it?" I asked.

He shook his head. "No, this is entirely up to you. I'll be here if you need me, I don't think you'll have any particular problems sleeping, nor a nightmare."

"Then I don't want to take it," I said firmly. "Besides, last time we were on a train you made me a promise."

He'd told me that, despite all his previous experience, he'd never made love on a train. We almost had, then and there, except for the lack of a lock on the door to our compartment. This time, there was a lock. He smiled, a wicked grin, clearly picking up on what I meant. "I did, didn't I? Do you want me to keep that promise?" He moved to kneel by my feet, looking up at me.

I wove my hands into his hair as he slid his hands along my thighs to my waist, pulling us closer together. "Oh yes," I told him.

Gabriel

Lord Gabriel heaved a huge sigh of relief once Chloe had reported that Leonie and Perry were safely on the train. He sat back down at his desk, ignored all the papers piled on it, and thought back over the events of the last couple of weeks.

It had been tough, but at least Leonie was now recovering and headed somewhere safe, well out of the way. He didn't want her anywhere near some of the people who would be arriving at House St Peter in the next few days. In a way he was looking forward to face-to-face meetings, however difficult they might be. Since Leonie had arrived in his care, he had been led into taking actions that were entirely out of his comfort zone in order to fulfil what God required of him. Now that the crisis was over he felt on much firmer ground. He might not have the answers, but at least the next steps seemed both obvious and sensible, unlike many of his recent actions.

He glared at the telephone which sat impassively on his desk, refusing to glare back. He didn't like telephones and he'd had to use that one far too much recently. Come to think of it, he wasn't that keen on telepathy either, except with Ellie. Face to face was much better although, given a personal vow he'd made many years earlier, it wasn't an easy thing to arrange. And to make the arrangements he'd needed to make he'd had to use the telephone.

He had started with Lord Neville, High Lord of House Tennant. That had been almost two weeks ago now and he thought back over the conversation. At least Neville's first concern had been for the health and wellbeing of both Leonie and Perry.

"Of course they can come here," Neville had said. "They'll be safe on my lands and I should think the boy's mother will be overjoyed to have him back. And tell the boy I'll put no pressure on him. They can come and visit me when she's stronger and we'll find a way forward that suits us both."

"I'd like to put extra security round them for now," Gabriel had said. "I'm trying to keep it as quiet as possible while I sort things out, but her identity is going to come out and there'll be trouble."

"Yes," Neville had agreed dryly. "I saw a picture of her and put two and two together. You kept that pretty quiet. How long have you known?"

"A DNA test just before they married. It hadn't even crossed our minds before that."

"Well, it wouldn't have crossed mine. I thought the Lindum child and her aunt were long dead. But it does mean you've married one of my heirs to the missing heir to Lindum and she's got a strong claim to Chisholm."

"Do you mind?"

"Not at all. Chisholm and Lindum might have something to say about it. Who else knows?"

"Here, only Eleanor and Benjamin. Not Perry or Leonie. Both Lindum and Chisholm have been trying to get hold of me. I'll face up to them soon. When we know more about how Leonie is progressing."

"Rather you than me."

Neville and Gabriel had gone on to discuss security details, including bodyguards, and Neville had confirmed that he would liaise with Michael, Perry's father, to put extra guards around their farm. "Best if I keep that from Mary, I think," he'd said. The relationship between Neville and his sister was strained to say the least. "And they'll need to change trains on their way through and there's likely to be a wait. I'll arrange accommodation for them too."

Gabriel had then used Neville as a sounding board for his plans to start resolving the whole situation. The discussions had been careful and circumspect but Neville had agreed to help to the best of his ability. "If you can get the others to meet, I'll be there too," he'd said.

Today, Gabriel needed to fulfil his commitment to speak to Lindum and Chisholm. He couldn't put it off any longer. He'd start with Lord Leon, High Lord of House Lindum and therefore Leonie's great grandfather, a man well into his eighties. Eleanor had met with him some weeks ago and at least he was aware of Leonie's existence. Gabriel sighed, picked up the dreaded telephone and waited to be connected.

"Gabriel," Lord Leon said in greeting. "Finally we speak. You know you've put me in a very tricky situation. There are any number of rumours starting and I cannot honestly deny them, but nor can I safely acknowledge her."

"I may have a solution to that," Gabriel said. Through careful and circumspect conversation he outlined his plans.

"Very well," Lord Leon said, grudgingly. "If you can get *him* to come, then I'll be there."

Him referred to Lord William, High Lord of House Chisholm, Leonie's paternal grandfather, and the recipient of Gabriel's next call. To mitigate the risk of his descendants challenging for his House, he tended to keep them close and well cared for. One of their common characteristics was red hair of a particular shade, the same colour as Leonie's.

"Gabriel," he spluttered indignantly as soon as they were connected. "I saw a photo. She's one of mine. She has to be. You must have known that the moment you saw her. I'd have provided for her. Why didn't you tell me? What were your plans for her? What are you going to do now? How old is she? Is she…?"

His words petered off. Clearly he desperately wanted to know if Leonie was also the Lindum heir, but was unable to frame the question. Gabriel smiled slightly to himself. Lord William was playing straight into his hands. "Now, William," he said calmly, "you must know I can't discuss such matters over the telephone."

That didn't help William's mood but his need to know was so urgent that Gabriel persuaded him to join the planned meeting, despite telling him that Lord Leon would also be present. Gabriel was well satisfied with his efforts.

He did not expect that all his visitors would feel benevolent towards Leonie, quite the opposite. It was likely that one of them – he did not know which – had been responsible for implanting a tracker in the child at some point around the time of her aunt's death. Someone – and again he did not know who – had to be behind the fact that the dead child found with Augusta was not in fact Leonie. There was every reason to think that one or more of his upcoming visitors wanted Leonie dead, or, at the very least, under their full control. He was very relieved to think that she would be safely out of the way and not his direct responsibility during this meeting.

Chapter 10

Saturday

Perry

Perry sat by the window, watching the dawn and the familiar scenery unfold before his eyes. He'd woken early, remembering this journey from so many times in the past. He'd always woken early then too, and sat here, his eagerness to be home rising with every mile. He smiled to himself; that was exactly how he felt now. A little nervous, perhaps, given all that had happened since he'd last made this trip, but mostly just excited to be going home. And that farmyard they'd just passed – a little bigger than it used to be, but still easily recognisable – meant they were only about ten minutes from the Castle Tennant station but Leonie was still asleep. He shook her gently to wake her. "Time to wake up, Leonie. We're nearly there."

She sat up and mumbled at him, her words indistinguishable, but he persuaded her to dress and be ready. At least she was acting as if she was awake although he wasn't convinced she was entirely with it. As the train drew to a stop he picked up their overnight bag and guided her down onto the platform. Almost immediately the hairs on the back of his neck rose, his senses telling him that something was not quite right. Not dangerous, not wrong exactly, just not quite usual.

The place wasn't quite as he remembered – that bookstall had expanded, the bakery had a new frontage – but nothing that couldn't be explained by the passing of so many years since he'd last been there. It was just that, despite the early hour, there seemed to be slightly fewer passengers and slightly more staff than he would expect. He reached out with his mind but found nothing strange; he couldn't reach far and walk at the same time so he concentrated on heading them both over to the station hotel. One or other, perhaps both, of them were clearly recognised almost as soon as they were through the door. The manager came across the lobby to greet them quietly and show them to their room – the master suite – on the top floor. After showing them the room, and offering to arrange anything the two of them might want, the manager left.

Perry sat Leonie down on a chair for a moment and took the opportunity to look around carefully. Would Gabriel really have got Chloe to arrange something this luxurious? What was going on? They were in a central sitting area with comfortable chairs and sofas, assorted side tables, snacks and drinks set out on one of them. Those doors had to lead to bedrooms, or bathrooms and there were two full-length windows looking out onto the town. One of the tables held a note, a small card pinned down by a vase of flowers. Perry strode over to it, picked it up and read it.

'Relax, it's safe. I'm in charge and I'm watching you. Brin.'

Well, that told him quite a lot. Gabriel must have been liaising with Lord Neville and this suite would be the least that Lord Neville would consider appropriate. He reached out with his mind to see if he could spot Brin and smiled as he did so. His cousin Brin, also a potential heir to House Tennant, wasn't telepathic, but they'd worked out a way of communicating, many years ago. Sitting at the top of Brin's mind was a simple message echoing that on the card. Perry stepped to the window and waved towards where he knew Brin must be. The mental message changed.

"Good to see you, catch you later."

Perry had hoped that they would be able to travel quietly, unnoticed as they slid through this capital city on the way to his parents' farm. Obviously, that was not to be, but perhaps this was better, safer and more comfortable for Leonie even if he didn't like the way that others were attempting to run his life.

He turned back to where he'd left Leonie and found she had wandered off into the bedroom and climbed onto the bed. Thinking that it was still very early and a couple of hours more sleep would be good for her – and perhaps for him – he went to help her undress and get into bed. Instead, she wound her arms slowly round his neck and pulled him down. Suddenly eager to do something that showed he was the one in control of his life, he rolled over her and sat up in one movement, pulling her onto his lap. She wrapped her legs around his waist as he started to remove her clothes. Despite her sleepy state she responded actively, pulling at his top and reaching to undo his trousers.

Perry touched her mind with his, knowing without a doubt that she was as eager as he was. He slid his hand under the hem of her top, sliding it up her back, caressing her skin, soft and silky, the touch sending an electric thrill through his body. Did he feel a hint of something else in her mind? A fear of rejection? A sense of insecurity? He brushed her lips with his, trying to use both his body and his mind to convey safety, belonging, love. She wound her fingers into his hair, holding him close as she responded to him, the connection between them blossoming into passion, sensations driving away all conscious thought.

Afterwards, Leonie fell asleep in his arms. He stroked her hair, feeling so much more settled and relaxed than he had earlier. Just what Brin instructed, he thought drowsily before sleep claimed him too. When he woke, it was full morning and Leonie was leaning on his chest looking down at him, eyes now wide awake and full of mischief.

"Good morning, beautiful," he said, unable to stop himself smiling widely at the sight.

"Perry," she said. "I'm hungry!"

Laughing out loud at that, he tipped her off onto the bed

with a kiss and went to order breakfast for them both.

Leonie

I watched Perry as we ate breakfast; I couldn't believe how much l loved him, even if I still couldn't bring myself to say it. I was terrified that if I admitted how happy I felt with him, something would happen to take it all away and I wouldn't survive that.

"Want to see something?" Perry asked once we'd eaten. "We've plenty of time before the next train."

I nodded, so he opened one set of the floor-to-ceiling windows and guided me out onto a little balcony. We could see right across the town. "See that flag over there? Above those high walls? That's Castle Tennant, where Lord Neville lives."

"It's huge," I exclaimed. "He must be able to see for miles."

"It's not just his home," Perry said, slight amusement in his voice. "See the big archway? That leads into a market plaza and beyond that there's offices, workshops. His actual home is towards the back, looking over the river."

"Do you want to go see him?" I asked, twisting to look up at Perry. He shook his head. "No, not today. We'll have to visit sometime, but not yet."

He went on pointing out various important landmarks and places that had meant something to him. He had some story or anecdote that went with each one; I enjoyed that, it made me feel like I was part of his past as well as his present. He only stopped when there was a knock at the door.

Perry went to open it, and a man about his own age walked in, a broad smile on his face. Perry's face lit up in pleasure. "Brin," he said and they clasped forearms in a welcome greeting.

So this was Brin. I'd heard of him. He was Perry's cousin and that meant he was the first member of Perry's family I'd met. My stomach churned, nerves rising to close my throat. What if I messed this up? Made things difficult for Perry?

Don't be daft. Even you can't mess up saying hello.

I stepped out from my position sheltered behind Perry, and Brin bowed towards me. "At your service, my Lady Leonie," he said. "I thought I'd come and say hello and walk down to the station with you."

"Hello," I said, as Perry turned and picked up our overnight bag.

Brin just smiled at me as I studied him. My mind wasn't working properly, but I wasn't stupid. Brin was wearing a short sword at his side and I'd have wagered he had a number of other concealed weapons about him. As we walked to the station he kept his hands free and his eyes were constantly glancing about us. I'd done my share of lookout duty with the Traders – more than my share because I was good at it and my Gifts helped. Brin was a bodyguard for us and I suspected he had a crew around. I tried to work out where I'd place them but found I didn't know the people or territory well enough to spot them. Was this just a formality because of who Perry was, or was there something else? Whatever it was, Perry would be trying not to worry me with it, so I kept quiet.

Despite Brin and his crew, I was eager to look all around the station – I'd never been anywhere quite like it before. It was so much bigger than those I'd seen on our last trip. Perry was quite happy to let me and we kept stopping on our way to the train as I saw something new or Perry pointed something out. We did make it on time, though, and Brin waved us off. I wondered if we had a bodyguard on this train with us but again I couldn't spot anyone obvious.

It wasn't our safety that worried me but what was waiting at the other end of this journey. Suppose Perry's family didn't like me? Or I did something terribly wrong without realising and let Perry down? Or said the wrong thing? It was a big thing for Perry to be visiting his family again. Suppose I ruined it, or made things worse in some way? Perry must have realised how I was feeling because he put his arm round me. "It'll be fine," he said.

He wanted me to eat some lunch from the hamper the hotel had given us for the journey. I was hungry, but the nervousness made my throat close up at the thought of food. Perry took no notice of that. He just got out a knife and cut off small portions – a slice of fruit, a piece of a sandwich – and passed them to me one at a time. I tried to eat them just to please him. Then he leaned forward a little and started pointing out landmarks as we passed them. I knew it was intended to distract me but it did work because after a while I found I'd eaten quite a bit of the lunch.

As we got closer there were more and more things that Perry was pointing out. I looked at him rather than out the window. "You're excited about it," I said wonderingly.

"Yes, I suppose I am," he agreed. "I'm sorry, does it make things worse, make you more nervous?"

"No. In a strange way it sort of helps." That surprised me, but it was true. "If you are excited about it, it must be good, things will be alright."

"It will be alright. They're good people." He sounded very certain.

"But they tried to stop you doing what you wanted to, what you were called to."

"You can't hold that against them, Leonie. They were doing what they thought was right. I was the one who was out of order, who was disrupting things, not taking my responsibilities seriously." He sounded pretty serious about it now.

As the train reached our destination, he was up and collecting our things, clearly eager to be off. I followed a little more slowly. Perry's father was waiting on the platform. I'd have known him anywhere because he was so like Perry, just obviously older. The likeness was far more pronounced in person than it was in my photograph. They both hesitated a moment and then enveloped each other in a real hug.

"Welcome home, son," his father said as I stood to one side not quite sure what I was supposed to be doing. They broke apart and both turned towards me.

"You must be Leonie," this older version of Perry said to me. "Welcome to the family and to Deep River."

Then it was my turn to be wrapped in a bear hug. I felt so welcomed. Perhaps this wasn't going to be so bad after all. Perry's father turned back towards Perry. "Your ma's waiting at home," he said. "Wanted to make sure everything was ready." I hoped that didn't mean there were problems ahead.

We travelled the rest of the way by horse and cart. I pressed up close against Perry just for the reassurance of his touch. He was really quiet but his fingers were fidgeting with the edge of his top and his body got more and more tense the further we went. His father – "Please call me Pa," he'd said – took over pointing out local landmarks and telling stories of Perry's childhood. "Can you see that little clump of trees?" he asked me, pointing at them. "They're a lot closer to the farm than they look. All our boys used them as a place to hide out, avoid chores and school work, explore and climb. They've all come back bruised and grazed over the years. Even a few broken bones."

"Even Perry?" I asked.

"Even Perry," Pa confirmed. "Although not always his own bones."

"I did not break Sam's arm," Perry muttered.

Pa laughed. I looked between them, curious, eager to hear more about the child Perry.

"Sam was only about four or five," Pa said. "He climbed too high in one of the trees and got stuck. Perry, who was only about nine himself, went up to rescue him. Did a good job too, but on the way down, he slipped —"

"Sam wriggled," Perry interrupted.

"They both fell from several feet up. Sam landed mostly on Perry but with one arm underneath."

"*He* broke *my* collarbone," Perry insisted.

Pa grinned. "True. And, to be fair, you got him home and insisted that we saw to him before you'd let anyone touch you."

Now that sounded just like the Perry I knew. We continued to travel along the quiet little lanes between the fields.

"We live a bit out of town," Pa said, "but it only takes a few minutes to walk in when you want to."

Perry's tension made me feel far more scared than I had been, but Pa just went on chatting gently about this and that. We turned off the track and through an open gate into a large farmyard. A sprawling house formed one side of the yard and Pa pulled up by the door. "She'll be in the kitchen," he said.

Perry was off the cart in a moment and disappearing

through the door. Pa put his hand on my arm gently to stop me following. "Give them a minute or two," he said. "They were always so close and they hurt each other so much."

I looked at him in surprise. "Perry thinks he hurt her not the other way around," I said.

Pa shook his head. "He was caught in the middle of things he didn't know about and then it was too late to tell him. If our daughter had lived maybe it would have been different."

"Jenny," I said without thinking. "She's why Perry wanted to be a doctor."

Now it was Pa's turn to look surprised. "He told you that? I didn't know."

I nodded. "But I don't think I was supposed to tell you."

"Don't worry," he said "I won't tell. Come on, I think they've had long enough."

Someone came over to take the horse, and Pa directed me through the door and down a short corridor. It opened out into a large kitchen. Perry was there with his back to me and his arms around someone I couldn't see clearly. I was sure they'd both been crying but Perry was smiling when he turned round to me, took my hand and pulled me towards them.

"Ma," he said proudly. "I'd like you to meet my wife."

Ma opened her arms, and I simply stepped into them.

"Leonie," she said. "I'm so glad you're here."

This is what a mother feels like? Why would anyone ever walk away?

I was surrounded by unconditional love. When she let go I

leaned back against Perry just trying to take it in. The room started to go fuzzy and swirl around me. Ma said something I didn't catch, and then she looked at me. "You've gone very pale," she said. "Would you rather lie down and sleep for a while? Recover from the journey?"

I didn't know what to say; I looked up at Perry.

"That's a very good idea," he said. "I think you need to lie down before you fall down. Can you walk?"

I thought I could, leaning against him, but I had no idea where I was going and then the world wobbled and he picked me up and then sat me down on a bed. I grabbed his hand. "Don't leave me," I whispered.

He bent down beside me. "Don't worry, I won't leave you. I'm not going to go any further than the next room, okay? The furthest I'll be is right outside that door."

Ma was there too. "That's right," she said. "You sleep. Perry and I have got a lot of explaining and catching up to do."

I had to protect Perry. I tried to stand up in front of him and the words tumbled out, "Don't be cross with him, he just did what he had to do, what he thought was right."

"It's alright, child," Ma said gently. "He's not in any sort of trouble. We've just got years of catching up to do."

"I'm not a child." It came out automatically. Why did I say that? I felt so silly.

"Yes, you are," she replied smiling. "You're my child now. Just as Perry is, now and always, however big he is."

I leaned against Perry, but the next thing I knew I was tucked up in bed, holding tightly onto his hand. I couldn't let go. He was the only solid thing in a room that was moving round me.

Chapter 11

Perry

Perry sat beside Leonie waiting for her grip on his hand to slacken as she descended more deeply into sleep. With his free hand he stroked her hair. He was so proud of her; she'd been so scared and so brave. With all the emotions that had been swirling around she had to have felt utterly overwhelmed. He had, and he was very glad of these few minutes sitting quietly, to gather his own thoughts and regain his composure.

This morning he'd been annoyed that Lord Neville seemed to be interfering in his life but pleased to see Brin again. And then, on the train, just as Leonie had pointed out, he had been feeling more and more excited as they got closer.

When his mother hadn't been at the station he'd started to worry, getting more and more tense by the minute. When Pa had pulled up outside the door he'd been like a coiled spring and his father's words had been the release. With no thought at all for Leonie he had hurtled through to the kitchen, stopping dead when he'd seen his mother. She'd had her back to him and had turned round, starting to say something, thinking he was someone else. The words had died in her mouth and they had stared at each other in silence for a moment. Then they'd both taken a step forward and they'd been hugging each other. It was funny how someone so small – Ma really wasn't that much bigger than Leonie – could make you feel like you were totally enveloped in their arms.

"I'm so sorry, Ma," he'd said.

"Oh Perry, I am too. I've missed you so much."

"I've missed you too."

And then they'd both been laughing and hugging and

crying, although he'd tried to hide that from Leonie when she'd followed him into the kitchen. He'd felt so proud, so happy, to be able to introduce her as his wife.

He looked around the room. Since he'd last been here, his parents had converted a couple of rooms on the ground floor at one end of the house to make a fairly private guest suite. As far as he could remember, in his childhood these rooms had been a playroom, or a storeroom, or a little used study space. Now they'd been converted to a decent sized living space with a small kitchenette, a pleasant bedroom and a private bathroom. And while it was an integral part of the main house, it also had its own private entrance so he and Leonie would be able to come and go as they wished. Their trunk had arrived and been unpacked, there were flowers in a vase on the table, and everything possible had been done to make them feel comfortable. For a moment, he was overwhelmed again at the effort and love his parents and family had put in to welcome him home.

Leonie stirred slightly in her sleep and finally let go of his hand. Ma had known just what to say to reassure her and how to get her into bed more quickly and efficiently than Perry would ever have managed.

"Stay with her until she's asleep," she'd said. "It won't be long. I'll go and fetch tea and cakes for us in a few minutes."

He could hear her now putting a tray down on the table in the next room so he took a deep breath and went out to join her and his father, leaving the bedroom door slightly ajar in case Leonie needed him. Ma waited until he was sitting comfortably with a drink and a cake before she started on him.

"Now, whatever I said to Leonie, you do have some explaining to do. Lord Gabriel obviously didn't tell us the whole story. What we have here" – she gestured at the bedroom door –

"is a sick, scared child."

"She's not a child," Perry said automatically and then grinned at himself for picking up Leonie's refrain.

His mother gave him a look. "No? How old is she then? I assumed she'd be around Matt's age or Sam's but she doesn't even look as old as the twins."

He'd known this was coming and decided to face it head on. "Actually, she's a little younger than Jonny. She turned eighteen in February."

His mother's face was a picture but she had no problem finding her voice. "Prospero! Eighteen? How could you? What were you thinking? What on earth was Gabriel doing, allowing this?"

"Leonie wanted to marry me just as much as I wanted to marry her. Gabriel encouraged it and technically she's his ward. He hoped that, if necessary, you'd stand in for him while we're here."

"Thinking to get round me is he?"

Perry thought he probably was but it might be as well not to say so. "I can't think of anyone better, Ma. Please? Leonie needs more than just me."

It was Pa who answered. "Of course we will."

Ma nodded, but took up her interrogation again. "All the same, she's scared and she's sick. She looks like she shouldn't even be out of hospital, much less out of bed, and you've made her travel hundreds of miles across the world to get here – what is going on?"

Perry put his drink down on the table and leaned forward,

resting his elbows on his knees. "She is sick, very sick, but there's no benefit to keeping her in hospital. There aren't many who've been through what Leonie has and survived this far. Those who do survive are better out of hospital, surrounded by family, people who care for them, giving them a reason to live. There's so many things that can still go wrong – but a hospital won't help. In the end it's going to be down to Leonie herself fighting to survive. Ma, I love her so much, and she all but died on me, and she still could so easily…" His voice broke a little. "I didn't know it was possible to love someone this much."

His mother reached over to hug him in sympathy and understanding, but it was his father who spoke, thoughtfully, "We're your family, not hers. How can being here help her?"

"She's an orphan, no family. This is all she has."

"But there must be people who care about her, or that she cares about at House St Peter too?"

"Yes there are, any number, but…" Perry wasn't sure how to go on. "But there are also any number of curious doctors who want to know how she's doing, and so many adepts who are constant reminders of what she can no longer do. They love her but it's not the sort of environment that she needs right now."

"And if things go wrong, if she were to die, then you are here with us." That was Ma, cutting to the heart of things.

"Yeah," Perry agreed. "That's the thing everyone is thinking and trying not to say. At least not to me. It's not like I don't know what her chances are but everyone is being enthusiastically optimistic."

"So," Ma had to ask, "what are her chances?"

"Poor," Perry said, finally voicing what he had known for days. "Very poor. Perhaps one chance in five?" He leaned forward and hid his head in his hands for a moment.

"A twenty per cent chance of a full recovery?" Ma said. "That's not that bad is it?"

Perry shook his head as he lifted it. "That's not what I meant. There's no documented case of anyone making a full recovery. I meant that, of those who have actively used master stones, and survived and woken up again with their memories intact, four out of five have died within the next one hundred days."

His parents were stunned into silence for a few moments. Ma recovered first. "So, what can we do to help? No, hang on. You said a hospital wouldn't help and we've been talking about the sort of care a family can provide. If I were to guess that what she needs is lots of love, rest, good food and gentle exercise, how far off would I be?"

Perry grinned at her, feeling a sense of relief that she understood. "Pretty much spot on. The catch is, she can have no appetite one minute and be starving the next. She can be overtired yet unable to sit still. When she does sleep – and she needs about sixteen hours sleep a day – there's nightmares and sleepwalking to deal with. Oh, and she's scared stiff."

Ma waved a hand dismissively. "Most of that's quite manageable. What she needs is some sort of a routine. But why is she so scared? Does she know how sick she is, how likely it is that she could die?"

"No, no... I'm sure she doesn't. She hasn't been told—everyone thought it would be better for her if she didn't know. Anyway, I don't think that would scare her. It's because she's never been part of a normal family in a normal home, she doesn't know what it is like. Losing the Gifts and abilities that she's normally relied on has damaged her self-confidence. She thinks she's only got me and what terrifies her is that she'll let me down somehow or that something will happen to me…"

"Oh, the poor child," Ma exclaimed. "Well, she's got us now. Make sure she knows that."

Perry hesitated for a moment and then the words just came out, "There's something else I have to tell you. I did this to her. She didn't even know about master stones, let alone that she was wearing one – two as it turned out. She was using everything she had and it wasn't enough and she was distraught she couldn't do more, and I told her about them, knowing what she would do and what it would do to her. If she dies, it'll be my actions that killed her."

Ma reached across, taking his head between her hands, and shook him gently. "Don't be daft," she said. "From the little I know of Leonie already, she'd have done this anyway, wouldn't she?"

He nodded.

"Then you need to concentrate on her getting better, not take on responsibility for something that wasn't your fault. Understood?"

He nodded again.

"How long will she sleep anyway?" Ma asked letting go of his head and leaning back in her seat.

Perry shrugged. "I'm not sure. Perhaps a couple of hours. When she wakes we need to go and see Pastor Thomas, use his phone and get a message through to Lord Gabriel."

"If you go then, you might meet Jonny on your way back. He's out with Emlee, but he'll be heading back about then."

"I was going to ask where everyone was," said Perry,

relieved at the change of subject.

His father responded, "The twins are out in the home paddock working a couple of the horses. They'll have seen us arrive, but given us some space. They'll be in for their dinner later and meet Leonie then. Matt and Sam and the girls are up at their place. They were planning to come down for an hour or so after dinner but if you think that would be too much for Leonie I can send a messenger up."

Perry thought that meeting his siblings in stages was a good idea and was quite happy to go along with his parents' plans. Their conversation drifted on, turning to local news and events on the farm before his mother stood up. "I need to get back to the kitchen," she said. "Or there'll be nothing for dinner. You settle in and come find me when Leonie wakes up."

Perry's father waited for a moment after Ma had left, before getting up himself. "It's good to have you home, son," he said and then hesitated before continuing. "You might notice that I have some extra crew around the farm. I don't know the details but Neville's worried about keeping your lass safe so we agreed I'd have some guards disguised as farm workers. I thought you should know in case you spotted them following you or some such."

Perry nodded his thanks. "Does Ma know?" he asked.

His father smiled slightly. "Neville thought it better if she didn't, but I told her anyway. She wasn't best pleased at what she called 'his interference' but I think she'd put up with anything to have you back here again."

Chapter 12

Leonie

Perry was in the room as I woke up and looked around. For a moment or two I didn't know where I was so I just launched myself at him in panic, and he held me until I calmed down. It helped that he seemed happy and relaxed himself.

"Way back," he said, "right at the beginning, I told you that you'd cause chaos wherever you were. And I was right. You've turned my life upside down. But somehow, you've also sorted out so much that was wrong with it. It's so much better now. And it isn't anything to do with what you did at House Eastern. It's just by being you. I don't know what I've done to deserve you."

There didn't seem anything I could say to that. He'd made my life better, not the other way around. We just sat together, holding each other tightly.

When I was ready, he led me through to the kitchen to find his mother, and this time I was up to having a good look around me. It was a big room, divided into three distinct areas. One was the kitchen proper, large and well equipped, separated from the dining area by a breakfast bar. The dining area had a long wooden table with benches and chairs that would seat more than a dozen people easily around it. The third part was a seating area with comfortable squashy chairs, a sofa and a low table. It also had a dog basket with a dog curled up in it. I scooted round to the other side of Perry, putting him between me and the dog and keeping as far away from it as I could manage.

I didn't like dogs. I'd been chased and bitten by them as a child. Over time I'd grown to respect the Traders' dogs as working dogs – they were good guards, they knew their job and they left me alone – although I'd never come to like them. I'd known there would be dogs here, but I'd expected them to be working dogs too, outside, not in the house.

Perry looked over to see what was worrying me. "Is that Amber?" he asked his mother. "In the kitchen?" He sounded surprised.

"Yes," Ma said. She hesitated before going on. "Jewel died about ten days ago. Amber's grieving and she's sick herself. She's barely moved from that basket in days. She's not got long."

She looked at Perry, eyebrows raised, as if she was expecting something but he didn't seem to respond. Clearly there was something more to this that I wasn't picking up. Perry just shrugged and made sure he was always between me and the dog. I thought he was deliberately ignoring her. I didn't think it was the time or place to ask why.

Ma found us drinks and cakes then sat down with us to chat for a little while. Or more accurately, she and Perry chatted and I ate – I was starving again – but I put in the odd word when Ma asked me a question. Ma wasn't exactly a stranger to me; we'd written to each other a few times since Perry and I had got married. She'd described the place and the people and their activities in her letters. This was somewhere I knew through reading about it. In a way it felt like I'd stepped into the world of a favourite book. But Ma's questions now were the ones she'd asked in her letters that I'd avoided answering, things about my family and background and past life.

She didn't mean them to be difficult, I knew that. She wanted to know all about this person that had been added to her family. They were still questions I didn't want to answer, afraid that the answers would cause problems for Perry, afraid they wouldn't want me around once they knew all about me. In my head I realised that was silly; after all, everyone at House St Peter now knew and it hadn't made any difference. But I still didn't want to risk it.

Perry knew why I was being evasive. "It's okay," he said. "You can tell Ma anything you want. Or not. It won't make any difference."

I looked at him disbelievingly and then, taking a deep breath and holding his hand tightly, I told Ma the answers to what she had asked. It was the first time I'd told anybody out loud about my past. About the slave orphanage, the way I'd been treated and the beatings. About stealing, and fighting, and running away. About being a nestling and about the hunts. Even with Perry I'd only shown him my memories, not used words. When I had finished, Ma wrapped her arms around me and held me close. "You're safe now," she said. "We're your family and you belong with us."

I felt like I'd come home. Ma left me and Perry together for a moment while she went to fetch something. I curled up close to Perry, getting my mental breath back. Ma came back with a small box. "I've had this since my daughter died shortly after she was born," she said. "But now I'd like to give it to you."

I opened it carefully. Inside was a silver bracelet, just a simple one but beautiful, with three wavy parallel bands of blue stone set in it and a small green stone at either end of the blue lines.

"Technically, Deep River – that's this farm – is a High House pledged to House Tennant," Perry said. "The blue lines are its logo and the green represents House Tennant." He looked up at his mother. "This was Jenny's?"

Ma nodded, lifted the bracelet out of its box and fastened it round my wrist where it sat just below the Trader sign marking my skin. She stroked a finger over that mark. "These are just ordinary jewels," she said. "But I'd be really happy if you'd agree to wear it."

I felt honoured and overwhelmed and, like with my Trader bracelet and my St Peter necklace, I thought I'd never want to take it off.

"Now, off you go," Ma said. "Perry said you need to visit Pastor Thomas, and I've still got some chores to do."

I suspected that was just an excuse and that she needed some time alone. Giving me the bracelet clearly meant as much to her as it did to me.

***

It was only a short walk to the pastor's house and the church. We ambled along a dirt track, broad and flat, wide enough for two carts to pass although we saw no one else on the way. Both sides of the track were lined with hedges interspersed with the occasional tree, green leaves fluttering in a slight breeze, causing dappled shadows on the path.

"Perry?" I asked. "Why don't your parents have a telephone of their own?"

I knew telephones tended to be the prerogative of High Lords and the wealthy but I was sure Perry's family fell into that category.

Perry grinned at me. "Officially, or the real reason?" he asked.

I shrugged. They were different?

Perry answered anyway, "Officially, not many people round here have them, so they'd make little use of one. Ma doesn't want anything that sets them apart from everyone else, or marks them as different. And installing them is expensive and that would be a waste of resources."

"And really?" I asked.

"If they don't have a telephone, Lord Neville can't get hold of them quickly or easily. Which means it's much harder for him to place any demands on them." Perry laughed slightly. "Except I happen to know that it was Lord Neville who arranged and paid for the one to be installed at the Pastor's house. It's used by most of the community but the real reason it's there is in case Ma and Pa need it." He grinned at me again. "I don't think they know any of that, so don't let on."

By now we'd reached the church – three buildings, joined together in the shape of a very lopsided capital letter E. The church was the largest part, in the middle, with Pastor Thomas's house (the smallest part) on one side and a community hall on the other. Between the buildings were pretty courtyard gardens with places to sit in the sun. I looked longingly towards the gardens, but the Pastor opened the door to us almost before Perry could knock.

"My Lord Prospero, Lady Leonie," he said. "Come in, come in." He held the door and beckoned us through. "You've come for the telephone, no doubt," he continued, pointing to an internal door. "It's just through there. Do you know how to use it? Yes, yes, of course you do."

Perry nodded. "Yes, I do. And please, Pastor Thomas, it's just Perry and Leonie. No need for titles."

"Of course, of course. And just Thomas, please. Now, will you both be making the call?"

Pastor Thomas looked at me and I shrunk behind Perry, shaking my head. I'd never used a telephone and I didn't really want to learn. I'd much rather leave that to Perry.

"I think Leonie would rather sit in the garden," Perry said.

"Of course, of course," the Pastor said again. "And if you

like, I could show you the church too."

Perry nodded encouragingly at me, so I went off with the Pastor. After all, the church was right next door to his house so I wouldn't be far from Perry. I liked the church; it was much smaller than the Abbey back home but it had the same sort of feeling of welcome and safety. But I liked the garden much better. And I loved the way both church and hall had side walls of sliding glass doors which could open right out onto the garden, making it all one space.

"You're very welcome to come and sit here anytime you want," Pastor Thomas told me. "And the church building is always open if you want to go in there, too."

Perry came to find us fairly quickly, slipping his arm round me and smiling at me. "Lord Gabriel sends his greetings and his thanks," he told Pastor Thomas. Then he grinned at me. "And I've been thoroughly interrogated on how you managed the journey. Benjamin's very pleased."

After making our goodbyes, Perry led me home by a different route. "I want to show you our lake," he said. He sighed happily when we got there. "It's even more beautiful than I remembered."

He was right; it was beautiful. Today, in the sunshine, it was a clear still blue with meadows and trees stretching out on the far side. Out in the middle were wooden swimming and diving platforms. From where we stood, there was a grassy bank leading down to a small sandy shore, and at one end the bank and beach rose to a flat rocky promontory where you could stand and look out over the lake. At the other end, the beach petered out into pebbles and stones, partly covered with shallow water. Someone – male, about my age – was standing in that area, skimming stones across the lake. Perry called out to him; he turned round and I realised it must be Perry's brother, Jonny. He looked at us a little puzzled for a moment and then his face lit up with recognition as he came towards us. "Perry?" he said, his voice a question.

I supposed it was half his lifetime ago that they'd last met which must have felt really strange. Then he looked at me, almost as if I was some sort of exotic alien and his voice immediately became more confident. "You have to be Leonie," he said. "There's no one else round here with hair anything like that."

To Perry's obvious surprise and, admittedly to mine, I laughed out loud at that. I'd disliked my hair – red, curly and uncontrollable – for years. It stood out which had been a problem when I'd been trying not to be noticed. And I'd learnt just before Perry and I had married that it marked me out as a – bastard – child of House Chisholm. But more recently I'd come to like it. Perhaps that had something to do with the fact that Perry loved it, both the colour and the curls. Or that I no longer needed to hide.

Anyway, my laugh made Perry smile. Jonny looked pleased too and it kind of broke the ice between the three of us. I figured I'd get on well with Jonny.

As the three of us crossed the farmyard towards the house, two men intersected our path.

"Leonie," Perry said. "These are my twin brothers, Jack and Eddie."

The men grinned at me, silently. I couldn't see any difference between them. They were even dressed the same.

"Which is which?" I asked.

Perry shrugged. "I don't know. I'm not sure they know. I think they swap."

"Swapping is," said one twin.

"a lot," said the other.

"of fun," finished the first.

I looked back and forth between them, utterly confused.

"Yeah," said Jonny. "They're weird. They always talk like that. When they bother to talk at all. You get used to it. As for which is which, just pick a name. They'll both answer."

One of the twins cuffed him affectionately round the head before the pair of them headed into the house, leaving us by the door.

I followed them with my mind, trying to find some way to distinguish between them. Usually people were individual points when I saw them with my mind's eye, but the twins were more of a blob. And when they moved apart the blob just stretched, so they were permanently joined together. Perry looked at me curiously, so I whispered to him. "They're just one person, sort of. Look at them with your mind."

He did so, and smiled, amused. "I never spotted that before," he said.

Then we both realised at the same time what I had said and what it really meant. "I saw them in my head," I exclaimed. "I can see them in my head!"

Perry couldn't stop smiling and picked me up and swung me round, kissing me soundly at the same time. Jonny sighed heavily and dramatically at our antics. "Get a room," he said.

All three of us were giggling away as we piled into the house and through to the kitchen for the evening meal.

Not long after we'd finished eating, four more people – two men, two women – surged into the kitchen. One of the men, who looked a lot like Perry, headed straight for Ma, kissing her on the cheek. Perry stood up to greet the other with a hug, before the two men swapped places. I watched, bemused again.

Pa must have noticed my bemusement. "Introductions," he said. "Manners, boys." He pointed to the one that was now by Perry, the one who looked like him. "That one's Matt," he said.

Matt stretched out his arms and pulled me into a hug. "Welcome, Leonie."

He released me, but only to pass me to the other brother. "I'm Sam," he said, following Matt's example and wrapping his arms round me. I had to crick my neck to look up at him. He was both taller and broader than Perry, fair instead of dark, and seemed to fill any space he was in. He put me down and looked around, then grabbed the hand of one of the women and pulled her towards us. "This is Lizzie," he told me. "We're handfasted."

Lizzie was only as tall as me; Sam dwarfed her. I nodded hello as the other woman appeared at my side and kissed my cheek. "And I'm Chrissy," she said. "Handfasted to Matt. Good to meet you."

"Shoo, you lot," said Ma, waving her hands at us. "Go sit down over there." She gestured at the seating area. "Jonny, put the kettle on and make some tea and coffee."

Everyone obeyed, but no one stopped talking or laughing. I curled into a corner of a sofa, next to Perry, tucked tightly against him, where I could watch and listen to everyone from a safe place. Strange to think that just over a day ago we were at House St Peter and now I had all this new family. I nestled my head onto Perry's shoulder and closed my eyes, just for a moment.

Perry

Perry sat with his arm around Leonie, revelling in being accepted back into the centre of his family, simply watching them, overwhelmed by all that had happened since they'd left House St Peter.

His mother was clearly overjoyed to have her whole family under one roof even if it was just for an hour or two. Perry felt guilty about having deprived her of that joy for so long, but at least they were here now. His father sat quietly in his armchair reflecting his mother's happiness.

"Useful to have you here," said Matt. "We could do with another hand in the harvesting." He grinned at Perry, challenge in his eyes. "That is, if you think you're up to it. Not gone soft in the monastery."

Perry grinned back. "Oh, I'm up for it. I could beat you any day, even now. But I'll have responsibilities at the surgery, some of the time."

Matt snorted, still smiling. "Good excuse, huh?"

Chrissy nudged Matt and whispered something in his ear that Perry didn't hear.

"Well," Matt continued. "I suppose we do need a doctor and you're probably better than nothing."

"I'm much better than nothing," Perry confirmed. "As you'll find out if I ever need to treat you."

Matt laughed and turned to say something to Sam so Perry returned to watching the others. He vaguely remembered Chrissy and Lizzie although he knew more about them from his mother's letters. They were handfasted to Matt and Sam respectively, living as man and wife, but with a year and a day to finalise that with a formal marriage. The two couples had neighbouring houses, about ten minutes' walk away from the main farmyard. Both women were roughly the same age as Sam; Chrissy was tall and dark and taught at the local school, while Lizzie was blonde and petite.

Lizzie was the local nurse practioner and midwife, and would be working with Perry when he took up the role of doctor round here. He watched her with idle curiosity thinking about the fact that they would be working together, wondering what that would be like and what her level of knowledge and experience was.

Lizzie caught his eye and smiled back. "You know she's asleep, don't you?" she asked quietly.

Until that moment, Perry hadn't realised and he twisted his head to look down at Leonie. "So she is," he said, equally quietly. "I hadn't realised how late it was getting. It's been quite a day and she gets tired very easily at the moment. I should have made her go to bed ages ago."

Sam looked across at Perry who was slightly trapped by Leonie's sleeping body. "Want me to lift her off you?" he asked.

Perry shook his head. "Thanks," he said. "But I think she'll panic if she's disturbed. In a little while I'll wake her just enough to get her to bed."

"She seems so small and delicate," Sam said. "Did she really do all that's reported?"

"I haven't seen any reports, so I don't know what they say," Perry replied. "But probably, yes. What she did was amazing. I've never seen anything like it. I don't think anyone has."

Somewhat to Perry's surprise – he had her down as a quiet follower, not a leader – Lizzie curtailed the conversation then by suggesting it was time they headed home, and the others followed her lead. Once all the goodbyes had been said, and Jonny and the twins had disappeared to their own rooms, he took advantage of the quiet to wake Leonie gently and guide her back to their room.

"Would you like a hand getting her to bed?" his mother

asked.

"I'm fine," he told her with a smile, but she came and helped him anyway.

"Don't rush her in the morning," she said. "Both of you sleep yourselves out. I'll find breakfast for you whenever you're ready. And if we're not ready in time for church, that's fine too."

Perry grinned back at her, shaking his head and pretending to be shocked at the idea of missing the Sunday service. "I think we'd both like to go to church," he said. "I know I would."

After his mother had left, he slid into bed beside Leonie, pulling her into his arms as he let his mind roam back through the day. It wasn't long before he, too, was asleep.

***

Perry woke before Leonie and lay watching her for a while before she opened her eyes and smiled at him. Then she looked concerned, a cute wrinkle appearing between her eyebrows. "I don't remember coming to bed," she said.

"Sorry," he replied. "That was my fault. You fell asleep. I should have made you go to bed much sooner. I just didn't want the evening to end. I haven't been taking very good care of you."

She reached to reassure him, pulling him close and carefully twisting her mind into his. His body responded with desire, her touch electric on his skin. He nuzzled into her neck. "We've plenty of time," he whispered in her ear.

Chapter 13

Sunday

Leonie

Getting washed and dressed should have been easy; after all how many times in my life had I done it? It was finding my clothes that proved the challenge. I knew that most of our things had been sent ahead of us and been unpacked and put away. Logically, I opened the cupboard and looked in – and recognised nothing. I should never have left the packing to Edward.

"Perry," I said, in desperate confusion, "are these my clothes? What do I wear?"

He came to look over my shoulder, still wrapped in a towel from his shower. "Edward's been at it again, hasn't he? Sent you with a whole new wardrobe? Me too, I shouldn't wonder." He reached in, rifling through the hangers and piles, and pulled something out. "This will do just fine," he said, handing it to me.

I looked at it, turning it this way and that. It was a short-sleeved dress in some soft, pale green fabric.

"Trust me," Perry said. "It's warmer here than at St Peter's, and women wear dresses like that more often. Only you'll need some sun cream." He reached for the tub and held it out to me. "I'll do you if you do me."

I looked at him, and he burst out laughing. "Just sun cream," he said. "Behave yourself. I need breakfast."

The dress was lovely when I put it on, loosely fitted to my hips, with a fuller skirt. Perry admired it before finding a top and trousers for himself.

Ma looked up as we walked into the kitchen. "Good morning," she said smiling. "Did you sleep well? You look beautiful, Leonie."

"That's Edward's magic," I told her.

She raised her eyebrows in a question, so Perry explained, "Edward's one of the Brothers, who's made himself responsible for making Leonie's clothes," he said. "Leonie thinks it's the clothes that make her look beautiful. The rest of us know better." He wrapped his arms round me from behind, amorously nuzzling into my hair.

Jonny was just passing through the kitchen and he mouthed "Get a room" at us again.

I didn't think either Perry or his mother noticed, but I did and had to smother a giggle. Ma busily began to offer us breakfast, and Perry moved over to hug her too. He persuaded her to make pancakes – not that she was unwilling. I think she'd have done practically anything Perry wanted, she seemed so pleased to have him home.

"Bacon and pancakes and syrup were always a Sunday morning treat," he told me as we sat down at the table.

"Still are," Ma said. "Are you planning to cook them?"

Perry grinned and stood up again. "Used to be my job," he said and took over at the stove, cooking the pancakes. So that's where he'd learnt how.

Although I assumed they had already eaten, much earlier, before seeing to the necessary chores on the farm, Jonny and the twins and Pa all wandered back in, bit by bit, to sit down at the table and eat.

"That's perfectly normal," Ma said to me. "Breakfast happens at least twice most mornings, and this lot seem to know instinctively and home in as soon as any food is on offer."

Although Ma was in charge, she wasn't doing it all. Everyone knew their role and fulfilled it without getting in anyone else's way. Even Perry slotted back in as if he'd never been away. Watching Perry cooking, laughing, joking with his family, I could see he was really happy and relaxed, the worries of the past few weeks forgotten. He'd been like this in the early weeks of our marriage, before our visit to House Eastern. I hadn't realised how much the accident there had affected him, nor how much his worries had affected me. With him happy, I could relax and start to enjoy my new surroundings too.

***

We headed to church in one big group. I held onto Perry's top, afraid I would lose him among all these people. He very gently disentangled my fingers from his clothing and held my hand tightly. "I won't let go," he said softly and he didn't.

Pastor Thomas started the service by welcoming me and Perry. Everyone turned and looked at us so I shuffled just a little closer to Perry. No end of people there had been praying for us. I guessed it was because of Perry, who must have all sorts of roots and friends and relatives here. I found that thought very troubling. It kept coming back to me all through the service, making me realise how little I really knew about him.

At the end of the service everyone decanted into the hall for refreshments. Ma and Pa got swept off by people wanting to talk to them, and there were so many people hovering, wanting to catch up with Perry. I felt trapped; the urge to escape, to run, started to rise within me, and the world seemed to go blurry. I suspected I might have started to go pale again; fortunately Perry spotted it.

He pushed me gently through the crowds towards some chairs. "Sit here," he instructed. "I'll get you a drink."

Feeling very bewildered by everything – there still seemed to be so many people around – I did what I was told.

Perry turned to Jonny. "Could you stay with her please until I get back?"

Jonny nodded and sat down beside me, but only moments later an elderly lady turned up in front of us. "Shoo!" she commanded Jonny, waving her stick at him.

He tried to stay, bravely defying her. "Great Aunt Lettie, Perry told me to—"

But she didn't let him finish. "Be off with you, I want to speak to Leonie. You can go tell Perry I've sent you away, that should be long enough."

Probably Perry should have sent Jonny for that drink but he did have a tendency to do now and think later. Unable to disobey, Jonny disappeared after Perry, and the lady, obviously Great Aunt Lettie, whoever she was, sat down in his place. Everyone else seemed to give us a wide berth which was a real bonus.

"So," she said, "you're this Leonie then?"

I nodded and she carried on, "Slave brat, runaway, Trader girl, what are you now?"

Her tone was curious and somehow I wasn't surprised that she knew what I'd been. I answered almost without thought. "I'm me. I always have been."

"Ha!" she responded. "Good answer. Maybe the boy has more brains than I give him credit for, picking you. Now look at me."

She stared straight into my eyes, her own eyes slightly

glazed. "Hmm," she said. "You're going to recover and quickly, but it's not going to be easy. It will happen though, hold onto that. Do you understand me?"

I nodded, not sure that I did.

She let my eyes drop. "I don't suppose you do, but it's probably better that way. You mean well, at least."

Perry appeared beside us, without my drink and looking more flustered than I'd ever remembered seeing him. Before he could speak, Great Aunt Lettie did, "So, boy, you've arrived. Sit!"

She gestured at a chair with her cane, and much to my amazement – and amusement – he sat, without a word. She carried on, "Seems you've picked well with this one. More sense than I thought you had. Didn't think you had any when you chose the monastery but perhaps it did you good."

I could see Perry trying to decide whether to be amused or annoyed but Great Aunt Lettie didn't give him much of a chance either way. "Young couple like you should be breeding," she told him. "Lots of strong healthy children. Get her well and get on with it." She reached for her cane and stood up with a final command to Perry, who was now blushing. "She's tired now. Take her home, and don't leave her alone again."

With that, she stomped off, though I'm sure she winked at me first, when Perry wasn't looking in her direction. Perry had turned towards me. "I didn't mean for you to be left alone, I'm sorry." He continued before I could answer, or defend Jonny, "Was she right? Are you tired?"

I nodded, but he barely waited for that either before he carried on, "Come on, let's get home. Are you okay to walk that far?"

He hovered over me, an arm round me as I stood up, using

his body to guard me from others. I expected it to be difficult to leave the building – understandably everybody still wanted a piece of Perry – but Perry just focused on getting us out, and Sam helped by distracting people.

Once home, we sat quietly in the garden and I might have dozed, resting comfortably against Perry. It certainly didn't seem long until the others all got back. Matt sat down next to Perry and they started chatting about people I didn't know, but Jonny had brought his girlfriend, Emlee, along and they sat on the ground near us. I slipped off my seat to join them.

Emlee smiled at me. "I love your hair," she said. "Mine's just so straight and boring." She rolled her eyes to emphasise the point.

I didn't think her hair was boring; it was shoulder length, straight and a glossy dark brown. Jonny ran his hands through it. "I think it's beautiful," he said.

"Eeww. Get a room," I protested, in a passable imitation of Jonny.

Then, suddenly, the three of us were laughing together, friends. From this lower position, I could see Matt, lounging in his chair, with a drink on the ground beside him. He kept reaching for it without actually looking and mostly he was teasing Perry about leaving home to join a monastery and then coming home with a wife. I figured that needed some revenge. "Jonny," I whispered, nudging him to look in that direction. "Are you good at telekinesis, like Perry?"

He nodded, getting the idea instantly, moving the glass just away from wherever Matt was reaching. We tried to contain our giggles, but Perry spotted what was going on – he'd have felt Jonny's use of his Gifts anyway – and nudged me gently with his foot. "If I didn't know better," he said quietly, "I'd think that was you up to mischief."

I looked up at him with my best innocent look and he burst out laughing. Someone behind him took a photo and he looked back over his shoulder. "If you've captured that look, I want a copy. Several, probably," he told the man with the camera.

Perry's reaction alerted Matt, who worked out what was going on and recaptured his glass. He drained it and then, laughing, he threw it at Jonny, who caught it without even looking, still laughing himself. I didn't think Jonny needed any inciting to mischief. I could have a lot of fun here.

The man with a camera was Lizzie's father. Ma wanted a photograph of her whole family together, and apparently he was a photographer. Ma pretended to cuff both Matt and Jonny as she organised us all into a group photo but they both ducked. I thought she'd just want a picture of her family, her six boys, and she did get a group shot of them, all laughing together. But what she really wanted – and got – was everyone, including Lizzie, Chrissy, Emlee and me.

I had a tremendous feeling of belonging, being part of a family, far more than I'd ever expected. We all sat round the big kitchen table for the midday meal. It was piled high with so much food I didn't know how it would all get eaten.

"Just help yourself," Ma said to me. "Everyone else will. You'd be amazed how fast this will all disappear."

I looked at her a little dubiously but Perry just laughed and loaded my plate alongside his own. Everyone else seemed to be talking, all at once, passing dishes, laughing, joking. I couldn't keep up with any of the conversations. And then things started going fuzzy, blurred and swirling around me like they had yesterday. Somebody called Perry's name from a long distance and all I could do was hold tight onto him.

Perry

Perry sat at the middle of one side of the kitchen table, enjoying being surrounded by his family. His mother was at the far end of the table, and he smiled to himself when he realised she was watching all of them, rather than paying any attention to her food.

"Perry," she called. "Leonie…she's falling…"

Twisting sharply he used both his body and his telekinetic ability to catch Leonie, and then lift her into his arms as he moved away from the table. Even as he did so, he was frantically trying to assess her medically and was relieved by his findings. Both Lizzie and Ma came round the table to join him and followed him as he carried Leonie to their room in search of somewhere more peaceful.

"She's going to be fine," he told them as he sat on the bed, still holding Leonie on his lap – not that he had much choice given the strength of her grip round his neck. "She just needs to sleep."

Ma sent Lizzie back to the kitchen to reassure the others, and to ensure that dessert was served. "But save some for Perry and Leonie for later," she instructed. She reached over and stroked Leonie's head. "Something set it off, didn't it, love?" she asked gently.

Leonie lifted her head off Perry long enough to answer. "Such a family," she said. "Everybody belonging together."

"And you didn't feel you belonged?" Ma asked.

"No, I do belong." Leonie buried her head in Perry's shoulder again, and he rocked her gently, holding her close.

Ma looked at him, bewildered. "Isn't that a good thing?"

He smiled at her over Leonie's head. "Oh yes, very good

indeed," he confirmed. "Just far too much for her to take in."

"She should get into bed, she'll be asleep in moments."

"She's all but asleep now," he agreed.

"'M not," murmured Leonie but that didn't remain true for very much longer.

Perry continued to hold her close while Ma watched the pair of them. "You can't be everything to her, you know," she said gently. "The two of you are too close, too entwined. You need to manage time apart, lead your own lives as well as your life together."

Perry looked up. "I know you're right, but I don't know that we can, not now. What I did, to keep her alive, there are consequences. It's not as simple as all that. Being apart…it's difficult. And we might have so little time left together. Every time I say goodbye or goodnight…it could be the last time."

"No one ever knows how long they have," his mother replied. "But that doesn't mean you shouldn't try. And we are going to make this work."

Perry grinned at his mother, well aware he was outclassed. "Thanks," he said.

Despite that, he didn't venture further than the next room while Leonie slept. His family came to join him for a while, before the younger members headed off to the lake for the rest of the afternoon.

"We'll join you when Leonie wakes up," he told his brothers.

***

Perry was reading when Leonie emerged from the

bedroom. He put his book down and held his arms out to her. She snuggled up next to him on the sofa.

"Feeling a little better?" he asked, smiling at her.

She nodded. "Much better. Where is everyone?"

"They've all gone down to the lake. If you want we can join them when you're ready."

"Okay," she said, but her voice was quiet, almost subdued.

"We don't have to go," he replied. "I thought you'd like it there."

She nodded. "I would, but…"

He smiled, sure he knew what the problem was. "There's so many of them, is that it?"

She nodded, and he carried on. "It's a much bigger space and they'll be off doing different things, swimming, sailing, whatever. It won't be nearly as overwhelming."

Her eyes lit up. "Swimming? Can we swim?"

He knew he should never have mentioned that. He stroked her face with one finger. "I'm sorry," he said. "I'd love to say yes, but I really don't think swimming would be a good idea today, not after what happened at lunchtime. But we'll go back to the lake tomorrow and swim then, okay?"

"Promise?" she asked.

"I promise. Come on."

He got up and she reached for his hand and came with him, willingly enough.

He stopped them about half way to the lake. "I think we should check out your ability to perceive people," he said. "You won't be able to sense anything this far away, but we'll stop and check every hundred metres or so from now."

He touched her mind gently to watch as she tried to perceive the presence of others. Despite that connection, it was her eyes that alerted him to her success, filling with excitement as she looked up at him. "I can see them, I can see them. Not clearly but I can see them," she said, the words falling over themselves as she spoke. She turned away from him and ran down the track to try again, and he followed, equally excited. Now they were closer the images were clearer.

"That's Jonny, by the edge of the lake," she told him. "And the twins are sort of on the water."

"They'll have a boat out there. And they do have names, you know," he told her, but he was grinning as he said it.

"Jack and Eddie are in a boat on the lake," she said, slowly and carefully, mocking him, and smiling with mischief. "And the others are all sitting on the beach, but I can't tell who is who, I don't know them well enough yet, except Chrissy is the closest to us."

He was puzzled. "So how can you tell Chrissy?"

"She's pregnant. Can't you see that?"

He shook his head in wonder. "In all these years, I never thought to look for pregnancy that way." He studied Chrissy carefully with his mind. "But you're right. Can you tell how far along?"

Now she shook her head. "Not accurately, but I'd guess about six weeks. And she'd have to be about twelve weeks before I can tell boy or girl."

He wrapped his arms around her and kissed her gently,

pleased that his strategy had worked and she was much more animated. "I don't think anyone else knows," he said. "We'd better keep it secret, too."

They headed on towards the lake, finding the others much as Leonie had perceived. Jonny was standing where they had first seen him yesterday, throwing stones into the lake. Leonie looked up at him. "Can I go do that with Jonny?" she asked.

He understood her attraction to the water. "Of course," he replied. "You don't need my permission. But no swimming today, we'll do that tomorrow."

He watched her as she ambled over to Jonny, his feelings conflicted. Certainly he was pleased that she was being independent just as Ma had said they needed to be. But he was slightly lost without her, and almost, but not quite, jealous of Jonny. Perry shook his head to dismiss those thoughts and sat down on the beach beside Matt, his eyes still on Leonie.

"Leonie not talking to us then?" Matt asked with a slight grin.

Perry shook his head, smiling. "She just finds everyone at once a little scary. And Jonny and Emlee are more her age anyway."

He suspected also that Leonie was drawn to Jonny because his stance and separation from the others suggested that he was hurting somehow, but he didn't voice that.

"Emlee had to go home early today for something. That's why Jonny's in a mood," said Matt. "And anyway, we're not scary."

"Just how old is Leonie?" Chrissy asked.

"She's eighteen," Perry replied, well aware that Matt had

just lifted a drink to his mouth.

"Eighteen!" Matt spluttered, drink going everywhere. "Eighteen! Only eighteen? Does Ma know?"

Perry nodded, grinning.

"And you're still alive?" Matt continued.

"Obviously," Perry said, still grinning. "Though I have been duly…reprimanded."

Matt laughed. "Are you going to swim?" he asked, gesturing at the lake.

Perry shook his head. "Not today. I told Leonie not to, so it seems a little unfair if I do."

"What sort of a husband are you, telling your wife what to do?" Matt was still teasing, but now there was an edge to his voice.

"I didn't tell her as her husband, I told her as her doctor. And I'd expect you to do what I told you as your doctor, too."

Chapter 14

Jonny

Jonny heard someone approaching from behind him but he didn't look round. He didn't want to hear from one of his brothers about how he should stop moping and join in now Emlee had gone home. Sure, he missed Emlee when his brothers were all paired off, but actually he was thinking about Perry. He didn't have many personal memories of Perry. His earliest memories dated from around three or four years old, by which time the teenage Perry had been spending significant periods with Uncle Neville. Then Perry had gone off to college and by the time Jonny had been a teenager himself, Perry had already been a monk, elevated to an almost holy status in his mother's family stories. He might be the son who'd got away, but he was the one who had defied Uncle Neville, even if he'd also rejected Ma's plans for him. For most of his life, Jonny had been somewhat in awe of this remote and mysterious being, and actually meeting the human behind the stories was very strange.

The approaching person appeared at his side with a timid hello, and he looked round to see it was Leonie. He smiled at her. Whatever else he thought about Perry, he'd certainly picked his wife well. Leonie was a lot of fun. She held up a flat stone, and then skimmed it out over the water.

He nodded approvingly at her skill. "Bet I can make one skip more times," he said.

"No cheating. No telekinesis," she told him firmly.

"Is that what Perry does?"

She nodded. "Sometimes. If he's losing."

He laughed at that before skimming his own stone. They were pretty evenly matched in skill, and had several turns each before there was a scuffling noise behind them. He looked round. Perry and Matt were rolling on the ground, wrestling, with the others just watching.

Leonie was off like a shot, running straight for his fighting brothers. He had to stop her before she got hurt.

"Sam," he shouted as he raced after her. "Stop them. They're upsetting Leonie."

His longer legs and arms aided him and he caught her within a few strides. She fought him as he held her away from them, with more strength than he'd expected, struggling to get away from him.

Then suddenly Perry had disengaged himself from Matt, and was right beside them, taking Leonie from him. Perry held her closely, speaking softly, trying to reassure her and calm her down. "It's okay, love," he said. "No one's hurt, it was just play fighting, like puppies in a litter."

Leonie pulled back from him, fear turning to anger in her voice. "Even puppies fight for a reason!" She poked him in the chest. "You were fighting because you are way too competitive, and you're the firstborn and after so long away you've got to reassert your position, and you," she turned on Matt, "you were fighting because he forced you to take that position and you're still mad, but you love the farm and now you're afraid he's going to reclaim it." She paused for breath as they all stared at her, speechless. "And it's so stupid because Perry is firstborn, that's a fact that can't change, and he's never going to want the farm because it would make him miserable and Matt loves it and Perry's a doctor anyway not a farmer."

Clearly exhausted by the outburst, she leaned back into Perry's arms.

"Wow," said Sam into the stunned silence. "Well said, Leonie. Looks like you've married a wildcat there, Perry."

"My wildcat," Perry said gently to Leonie.

She looked up at him. "Why are you grinning at me?"

"Because you yelled at me," he answered. "You're absolutely right, of course. There's something I need to do. Can you stand?"

She nodded as he stepped away, but to Jonny she looked like the slightest breath of wind would knock her over, so he moved closer behind her and took her gently by the elbows. She leaned against him gratefully. She felt so fragile he thought if he moved he'd break something. He couldn't believe that only moments ago he'd been struggling to hold her as she'd fought to escape him.

He watched as Perry walked over to Matt who was dusting himself down, still looking stunned by Leonie turning on him the way she had.

"Matt, I am so sorry," Perry said. "I didn't think about how my actions would affect you. Can you forgive me?"

Matt looked at him, brows furrowed. "Yes," he said slowly. "I guess I can. You're still my brother, after all."

Perry nodded. "And I give you my word that I have no interest whatsoever in inheriting the farm, nor will I ask for support from it. Will that do, or is there some other way I can convince you?"

"That'll do," said Matt.

The tension left Matt's body, shoulders dropping, as he and Perry hugged. Then Matt turned to Leonie and swept a deep and formal bow. "My Lady Leonie," he said. "My apologies for upsetting you. Would you permit me to escort you on the way home?" He held out his arm to her, but she looked uncertainly between him and Perry, still leaning on Jonny for support.

"It's up to you," Perry told her. "He may be a bit of a ham actor, but he means what he says."

Jonny grinned to himself at that comment. Perry had Matt summed up. After another moment's hesitation, Leonie stepped forward and took the offered arm. Matt smiled at her and started talking quietly to her as they walked. Jonny ambled along behind Perry and Lizzie.

"Perry, when I knew you and Leonie were coming, I read up on what had happened and what was likely to happen, and what medical support she might need, just to be ready," Lizzie said. She rested her hand on Perry's arm. "Perry, I am so sorry, so very sorry. Until then, I hadn't realised what was most likely to happen."

Jonny listened harder, wanting to know what on earth Lizzie was talking about.

"She's beating the odds so far," Perry said, but his voice sounded odd, sort of choked.

"Episodes like at lunchtime don't help, do they?" Lizzie asked.

"Well, yes and no. If something happens…" Perry took a deep breath. "If she dies, it will be as an immediate consequence of some episode like today, though that was a very minor one. But each one that she survives increases her chances long term and her chances of surviving the next one."

Leonie was likely to die? She was that ill? Jonny knew she'd been injured, but he'd assumed her recovery was just a matter of time.

"Have you shared this with anyone?" Perry asked Lizzie.

She shook her head. "No, it didn't seem fair without talking to you first. Have you?"

"Ma and Pa know, that's all. Leonie doesn't and I'd rather she didn't. You can tell Sam if you want, if you need to talk about it. I don't really mind people knowing, I'd just rather Leonie didn't."

In Jonny's opinion, Leonie ought to know, but he was eavesdropping himself, so he'd have to keep it secret too. Somehow, having a wife that might die, such a loss ahead of him, made Perry seem a lot more human, a lot less remote.

Chapter 15

Monday

Leonie

We were allowed to sleep in again the next day. When we eventually wandered into the kitchen, Ma and Lizzie were sitting at the big table.

"Good morning," said Ma with a smile, standing up to sort out some food for us. "Hope you slept well."

I nodded. "Yes, thank you. But I hadn't realised it had got so late."

Ma put a well-laden plate down in front of me. "Don't worry about that," she told me. "You're to carry on sleeping as much as you need. I'll wake you if and when I think it is necessary. But you"– she turned to Perry – "you can start getting up with the rest of us and make yourself useful until Leonie is awake."

Perry just grinned and took it. He was as happy to be home as Ma was to have him there and quite amenable to her plans. In fact, Ma and Lizzie had things pretty much planned out for both of us. Perry was to work on the farm each morning until I was ready and then we could have the rest of the morning together.

"We can explore the countryside and the town and go swimming, things like that," Perry told me.

After the midday meal, I was to sleep again – I wouldn't find that hard going by current experience – while Perry either visited patients or held a clinic, or some other medical duty. Lizzie had that all organised for him. Once I woke, I could go meet him and we'd be free again to do what we chose. Perry's idea was that we'd use some of that time to practise developing my Gifts, maybe even ask Jonny and Emlee to join us because the same exercises would be good training for them. And when I fell asleep after the evening meal, Perry could spend time with his family, or a couple of times a week he'd hold an evening clinic, leaving me with Ma and Pa.

"It'll be good for both of you to have some time apart," Ma said.

I knew she was right really. I knew we both needed to have our own lives here, just as we'd had at House St Peter before the accident. It was just that the idea of doing new stuff with new people in strange places and without Perry scared me. What helped was the thought that it would be good for Perry too. If it was something he needed, then I guessed I'd just have to find the strength to do it.

Today we were going to walk into town together, have a look round, see where the medical practice was based and what facilities it had, and then go swimming. We set off shortly after breakfast. I already knew the route as far as the church but after that it was all new to me. Perry started pointing out places and landmarks to me again. It turned out that the church, train station and school were all on the farm side of the town, which obviously worked out pretty well for Deep River Farm.

"The town is called Deep River, too," Perry said. "And with our farm being the High House, all the businesses, farms and the like round here are pledged to it. And my father represents them to my uncle at the Great House."

I looked at him curiously.

"Yes," he agreed, "it should probably be my mother or perhaps both of them, but my mother won't talk to Uncle Neville so my father does it."

The town itself was much smaller than the one around our

Abbey at House St Peter, although this was clearly another rural community. There was one main shopping street, and one at right angles to that which had places like the medical practice, a dentist, an animal doctor – services rather than retailers. The rest seemed to be houses, low shaded buildings with verandas, well spread out on large plots, much of which were turned over to vegetables or chickens, perhaps the odd pig. Transport seemed to be by horse, or horse and cart, or on foot. Perry said there were many other farms within about twenty miles of the town, all of which looked to Deep River as their centre.

Lizzie met us at the medical practice and showed us around. Most of the medical stuff went over my head so I set myself the task of moving away from Perry, slowly venturing further and further away, opening doors at random. I got a little caught up in it and eventually found myself on the roof. It was a flat roof, and, like the hospital at home, it was set out as an herb garden. Only this one wasn't anything like as well tended. It badly needed weeding and pruning and tidying up, and some plants were more than ready to be harvested. I found a box with some tools in and set to work gently doing what was necessary. It was very pleasant out there in the sunshine and I must have been working for more than half an hour before Perry came to find me.

"There you are," he said.

He sounded relieved, although he must have known where I was and that I was happy through looking for me with his mind. Lizzie stepped out from behind him. "What a difference you've made in such a short time," she exclaimed. "I haven't really known what to do for the best here. Our last doctor used to look after it and I don't have the experience."

I shrugged. "It's easy really, mostly weeding and pruning. I enjoy it. But these plants…" I pointed round at them. "These all need harvesting and then treating in different ways to preserve them or make the most use of them."

"Would you consider taking on looking after this garden?" Lizzie asked me. "It wouldn't be too much for you?"

I looked at Perry eagerly. "Could I? Would that be okay? I'd really like to."

He smiled at me happily. "I think that's a great idea. I'll help if you need me to, but you can be in charge of it. There's a room downstairs that Fred – he was the doctor here when I was growing up – used to use for drying and preparing herbs. You can use that, too."

I turned back to Lizzie, still all excited. "And if you like, I'll show you what needs to be done for when we go home."

She smiled too and nodded. "I'd like that."

For now, I just picked what was most urgently in need, and took it down to Fred's still room which was pretty well equipped. A quick look suggested the best thing I could do would be to dry what I had harvested, so I hung them up in bunches before Perry and I left. We didn't stop at the lake to swim on our way home or we'd have been late for lunch but Perry promised we could swim later in the afternoon.

I told Ma all about the herb garden and my plans, so excited the words tumbled out before my brain could get them straight. Ma listened and understood and made suggestions. Despite my enthusiasm and excitement I was yawning and nearly asleep before the meal ended. Ma packed me off to bed. "You stay here and finish eating," she said to Perry. "I'll make sure she gets into bed before she falls asleep."

He looked a little reluctant, but he did as he'd been told. So did I.

"Don't worry," Ma told me. "There'll be someone nearby all the time. I'll be no further than the kitchen and you'll be quite safe."

I knew I would, really. I could trust Ma and I had to get used to Perry not being there all the time. I closed my eyes and slept.

Perry

Left alone at the table, Perry leaned back in his chair. Logically and intellectually, even medically, he agreed with the plans and routine Ma and Lizzie had set out. But emotionally, he was still incredibly uneasy about not being close to Leonie at all times.

Earlier he'd been so involved looking round the medical practice that it had been some time before he'd realised Leonie was not right beside him. He liked like the thought of her looking after the herb garden, though he suspected that was at least partly because it meant she was more likely to be nearby when he was working.

He thought the answer to his uneasiness at being apart from Leonie was probably to distract himself with other activity as much as possible, just as he'd been distracted at the medical practice. That would be simpler tomorrow when he would be working while she slept.

He got up from the table and he wandered out aimlessly into the farmyard. The twins had a small stable yard to one side of the main yard and he went over there to see what horses they had.

That yard was quiet too, the horses also dozing after lunch but he found the twins in the tack room busy cleaning harness. They looked up, smiling.

"Got horses,"

"for you"

"and Leonie."

"Come see."

They took him through the stable block to show him the dark bay mare they'd chosen for him. He was a competent horseman, which his brothers knew, and a good enough judge of horses to realise they'd had chosen him a very good mount. "She's beautiful," he said, stroking her neck and starting to make friends with her. "Thank you."

"Called Sadie."

"Yours for"

"this summer."

"How well"

"does Leonie"

"ride?"

Perry looked at them in astonishment. There was still so much he didn't know about her. "I've never seen her ride," he said. "The few times we've been on horseback together, she's ridden in front of me. She seems comfortable around horses, though."

"Two to"

"choose from."

"Willow if"

"competent rider."

"Floss if"

"nervous."

"Can I see both?" Perry asked.

The twins nodded and showed him both horses. He hoped Leonie was a competent rider because he was certain she would prefer Willow, a pretty dun mare. The twins went back to their harness cleaning, and Perry ambled over to the main yard where he found his father in the barn.

His father smiled at him. "Not quite sure what to do with yourself, where you fit back in?" he asked.

Perry shook his head, grateful for the understanding, and they sat together on the pile of hay bales there.

"She's quite something, your lass," his father said. "I hear she gave you and Matt an earful yesterday."

Perry grinned at the memory. "She certainly did. But I needed it. She makes me look at so many things differently, more clearly."

"At least you and Matt got things sorted between you and I'm happy with that. Do we need to formalise things, get it written down?"

Perry shook his head. "I don't. But I'm more than happy to if Matt does."

His father accepted that. "Now you need to sort things out with Neville," he added after sitting quietly for a time.

"He's said there's no hurry, we can visit and sort things when Leonie's stronger."

"We messed you up good between us, didn't we? Me and your Ma and Neville?"

Perry shrugged. "It worked out in the end. I've needed

these years at St Peter's, they've been good for me. Matt will do much better here than I would and Lilyrose will do better as Neville's heir. And I have my role as a doctor and I find that fulfilling. The only thing I regret is hurting people I care about."

"It wasn't one sided, it wasn't just you. Our actions hurt you too. It's no excuse but we got pretty messed up when Jenny died. And then Neville tried to stake a claim to you and he had Lilyrose but we didn't have Jenny...it all escalated and you got caught in the middle. We weren't really thinking about the impact on you, and we should all have known better."

They sat quietly together again. Perry understood that he had been forgiven for the hurt he had caused but also that he had been asked for forgiveness, which he had given. The matter was at an end. Eventually, Perry spoke again. "Jenny's why I wanted to be a doctor so much," he said. "I needed to find a way to reduce the suffering."

"She might only have lived a couple of hours but she had a big impact on all our lives," his father agreed. "I saw your mother gave Leonie Jenny's bracelet. I reckon that's a good thing for both of them." He stood up. "Come on," he continued. "This barn won't tidy itself. You can make yourself useful until your lass wakes up."

It wasn't long until Leonie herself appeared, running across the yard into the barn and throwing herself into Perry's arms. He swung her round, hugging her closely.

"You said we can go swimming now," she reminded him.

"I did," he agreed, smiling at her excitement. "Are you ready? Have you had something to eat since you woke up?"

She hadn't, so he made her return to the house for a drink and a snack before he would let her swim. It still wasn't long before they were heading down to the lake together. She was halfway into the water, with him close behind, before she turned towards him with a look of shock on her face. "It's cold," she said. "I didn't think."

"It's not that cold," he told her, a little surprised. "It's been warmed by the sun all day. It'll be fine when you're in."

She shook her head. "I know that. It's just that...before...I always heated it."

He didn't understand, and she tried to explain further. "I used my mind. To warm the water around me a little. Just till I got used to it."

He was astounded. "How on earth? Can you remember what you did, while I watch?"

She nodded so he linked his mind into hers and watched her memories. Whilst she could no longer activate that Gift, he could see what she had done. "You used something similar to pyrokinesis – fire lighting – to heat the water," he said. "I've never seen that before. I can't do it. I've never been able to do anything in that area. We're going to have to put up with the cold."

She nodded her agreement and, moving quickly, slipped further into the water and started swimming for the platforms in the middle of the lake. After a moment he followed her, catching up shortly before she reached them.

"Will I be able to do it again?" she asked him and he could only hear the loss and sadness in her voice.

"It doesn't matter," he hastened to reassure her. "You're still you. I love you no matter what."

"But do you know?" she persisted.

"No," he admitted. "I don't know. No one does. We just

have to wait and see."

To distract her – and himself – from such thoughts, he challenged her to a race. With or without her Gifts, she was far more at home in the water than he was and he was hard put to keep up. They spent the rest of the afternoon swimming, splashing, and sunning themselves on the central platforms, before returning to the house later, tired but happy and relaxed.

Chapter 16

Tuesday

Leonie

Light played across my eyelids. Without opening them, I decided I was awake and rolled over towards Perry. His side of the bed was empty, not even warm. My eyes shot open and I sat up. Where was he? Where was I?

I took a deep breath, calming the rising panic. I was in our room, it was morning, and Perry would be working on the farm somewhere. I reached out with my mind and there he was, not too far away. I guessed he was out in a field somewhere, with his brothers. And that blob of light was Ma, in the kitchen. I leapt out of bed to get ready for the day. I was so pleased to be able to tell where Perry was that I didn't stop smiling the whole time I was washing and dressing. Perhaps I would get all my abilities back.

I headed into the kitchen to find Ma and some breakfast. While I ate, Ma started to pack a basket with drinks and snacks. "They're harvesting up in one of the fields," she said. "When you're done we'll take this up to them."

There was a slight whimper from the corner where the dog basket was, and Ma went over. I followed her and stared at Amber. For once her eyes were open and she looked back at me. She looked so miserable I couldn't be frightened of her. Instead, I astonished myself by wanting to make her feel better. Ma squatted down to be more on a level with the dog so I followed her example. Gently, Ma introduced me and Amber to each other. Amber just held still as I touched her and then progressed to stroking her head.

"She was always Perry's dog, you know," Ma said once I was comfortable stroking Amber.

I looked at her in surprise. "I didn't know. He never said."

She nodded. "They were inseparable when he was a teenager, and she was little more than a puppy, but of course he couldn't take her to college. Jewel was Michael's and the two of them worked as a pair, but Amber was Perry's through and through. She used to get so excited whenever he came home."

"So why is he ignoring her now?"

"He told me he doesn't want you to get attached to her because he thinks you'll be upset when she dies."

I stared at her as I worked this through. That didn't make sense; Perry would expect me to avoid Amber, just as I had been doing. "You mean," I said slowly, "Perry is using me as an excuse not to be friendly with her because she's going to die and it'll make him worry more about me dying and he's afraid he won't be able to cope?"

Ma grinned back at me. "You're a sharp one, aren't you? Yes, I guess that's what I mean."

"He's daft," I said then realised I was talking to his mother.

But she just laughed. "Men can be like that," she said. She carried on with a different track. "Are you worried about dying?"

That was blunt but I'd already found I could talk to Ma. I shook my head. "I know they all – Perry and Andrew and Benjamin and everyone – think I'm more likely to die than live after all that happened, but the only thing that worries me is how much Perry would hurt. I thought I was dead, but God was there so I know that's going to be alright."

"We'd look after Perry, you know," Ma said.

I nodded. "I know. Lots of people would. But he'd still hurt."

It was her turn to nod. "That goes with loving someone. He thinks you don't know that you could die."

I grinned back at her. "I know that, too. But I'm not going to die. Great Aunt Lettie told me that, on Sunday."

"And you believe her?"

I suddenly realised that I did. Ma seemed to think that was perfectly reasonable; Great Aunt Lettie apparently had a reputation for predicting these things accurately when she deigned to predict them at all. Turned out she was descended from Traders so she probably had the Sight.

Ma finished packing the basket of elevenses and asked if I was ready. Impulsively, before I could regret it, I asked if we could take Amber.

"If you can persuade her to come," Ma replied. "It certainly won't do her any harm." She rummaged in a drawer and passed me a lead. "Amber doesn't need this, but it'll mean you both know who is in charge."

I didn't know how to persuade a dog so I just clipped the lead on and told her we were going to find Perry. It seemed to do the trick; she got up slowly and padded along next to me.

It wasn't that far to where they were harvesting, maybe a ten minute walk. They were up on the hillside, slightly above us so we could see them as we approached. It was already warm and they'd all stripped their shirts off to work but I just had eyes for Perry. I loved watching him whatever he was doing – working or reading, moving or still. Here in the fields he looked capable and happy, like he knew what he was doing. But somehow he didn't look like he fitted in quite as well as he did back home. Perhaps it was just what I was used to. I was surprised he'd taken his shirt off. He had scars across his arm and back and ribs, a result of a very bad nightmare, and he usually kept them covered because he was ashamed of all that was behind them.

Perry waved and came to meet us, shrugging his shirt back on and putting his arm round me once he reached us. "You've been okay, then?" he asked, and as I nodded he noticed the dog at our feet. "Ma!" he said reproachfully, indicating Amber.

I nudged him, showing him the lead I held. "It was me, Perry. I brought her, and now she's feeling better."

He took my head in his hands gently, looking concerned. "She's old, Leonie. Nothing can change that. She's going to die, soon, and I don't want you to be hurt."

I knew he thought he was trying to protect me, but I wasn't distressed by those who died after a good life, not like those who died without a real chance. Perry didn't understand; I hadn't been looking to prevent Amber dying, so I tried to explain. "But she's sad and now she's happier. She deserves that, doesn't she?"

"Yes," he said, smiling slightly. "Yes, she does."

He bent down and petted her properly for the first time, which left her pretty much overcome with pleasure. "So," he said to me, "you've faced up to your fear of dogs just to make this one a bit happier for a few days. You are amazing." He stood up. "You didn't do it for the dog, did you?"

Well, no I hadn't but I hadn't expected him to spot that, either. Before I could get my head together to answer he bent and kissed me. There were whistles and catcalls from his brothers but he just made a dismissive gesture at them – I assume it was a reasonably polite one, especially in front of their parents – and carried on. Then he slipped his arm round my waist and together we wandered over to join the others, Amber following happily.

He got teased by his brothers as we sat down, I guessed

that's what brothers did, but it was all good humoured. I gathered they'd been teasing him already, not expecting him to be as physically fit as he was. I supposed it would be easy to think the monks just sat around praying and singing but it wasn't like that at all – although Perry had told me that could also be exhausting. Benjamin had said to me once that our bodies are a gift from God so we have a responsibility to look after them well. Andrew had pointed out that praying and walking went very well together and being active was very much a part of everyday life for both House and Order. Back home Perry's domestic chores were in the gardens and he did a lot of physical stuff there, like digging. He definitely made a point of keeping fit; I'd wondered if it was a form of compensation for the abuse he'd put his body through in his student days but decided that didn't matter.

Amber flopped down beside him, resting her head on his leg and he fondled her head and ears absentmindedly. She looked pretty happy at all the attention and Perry was clearly relaxed about it, so I guessed that'd all worked out. Ma quietly said, "When you lose those you love, the trick is to love more, not to avoid hurt by loving less."

I didn't know whether that was to me or Perry but it made a strange kind of sense.

The waggon was nearly full, so I went with the twins to help harness the draft horses to it. That was something I'd done many times with the Traders; they seemed surprised at how familiar I was with it. They asked how well I could ride, which was another thing I learnt with the Traders.

"Got a," one said.

"horse for," said the other.

"you to"

"ride this"

"summer. Called"

"Willow. Show"

"you later."

For now, we headed the horses and waggon back to where the others were sitting. Perry came and slipped his arm round me, pulling me slightly away from his brothers who were whispering together about something.

"What are they whispering about?" I asked him.

He pulled me close, his eyes full of wicked amusement. "Matt asked where you learnt to handle draft horses, so I told him it was probably with the Traders. He knows the rumour about Trader women being the best lovers, and he's sharing it with the others. Now they are deciding whether they can tease me, us, about it, or whether my recent vocation means I am so innocent that there'd be no point because you're the only woman I've slept with."

That was too much for me and I burst into giggles, and Perry joined in.

"Are you going to tell them?" I asked him, once I got my breath back.

"No," he said, considering. "I know that God has forgiven me for all the wrong I did then, but I'm not proud of it, and my mother would be very disappointed in me if she found out. Besides, whilst everyone back home knows, or finds out pretty quickly, it's quite nice being here with no one knowing."

I could understand that; one of the things I'd liked about becoming part of House St Peter was that it was a clean start, no one knew about all the things I'd done in the past. Of course I'd told Perry everything before I'd married him, that was only fair. Then everything had come out as a result of the accident. I was still coming to terms with the fact that everybody knew, but even more so with the fact that it didn't change how they felt, any more than it had changed how Ma felt when I'd told her. If Perry wanted to keep his more disreputable past quiet that was fine by me.

He grinned at me, eyes still lit with amusement. "Just how quickly did you find out, anyway? And from who?"

I smiled back. "If I tell you when, you'll work out who, and the other way round!"

He worked it out from that comment alone. "Less than twenty-four hours, then. That first day, with Edward, then probably more from Pedro over the next few days." That was spot on but he continued, "All those years a monk and the first thing they tell you about is my wild years as a student."

It sounded like there was some bitterness in his tone, so I reached up to stroke his face. "The first thing Edward told me was what a good doctor and monk you were. The wild thing only came up when we were talking about nightmares. Which made me feel a lot better, that someone else had them as bad, I mean."

"Glad I could help," he said, his voice much happier.

He bent his head and kissed me, to more catcalls from his brothers. We turned back towards them to go and help but then another thought worried me. "Won't they mind, about me and the Traders, I mean? I know Ma didn't but what about everyone else?"

He shook his head. "Traders are held in very high esteem round here and there's a fair number who've settled here, for one reason or another. Trader caravans often pass through. I can remember them camping in one of our big fields for a rest day when I was a child. You never know, you might even have come here once."

I shook my head, I'm sure I would have remembered that, though my memory had been playing all sorts of tricks on me since the accident. That reminded me of something that had been troubling the back of my mind since we'd got here. "Perry, I don't know where I am! I don't know how I got here!"

The panic rose, trying to close my throat as I thought about it.

He was very calm. "This is Deep River Farm and High House, where I grew up, pledged to House Tennant. I brought you here on the train."

I shook my head, the panic building further. "No, no, I know that. But I slept all the way. I don't know how to get home. I don't even know which way home is!"

After I joined the Traders I'd developed a mental map of where I was and where I'd come from and where I'd been, and now there was a great patch of fog swirling around in the middle of it. Perry looked around quickly to get his bearings and then pointed. "Home, House St Peter, is in that direction."

The swirling settled down and I could breathe again. He held me closely for a few moments. "Better?" he asked.

I nodded.

"Good," he said. "Later I'll find a large map and we can trace the journey, get it all in perspective, if that'll help?"

I thought it might, but for now I was okay, and we headed back towards the farmyard with the waggon. As we reached the farmyard, the twins appeared on either side of me.

"Want to"

"meet Willow?" they asked.

They led me over to their stable yard and disappeared into the stable block for a moment or two. Then one of them reappeared leading a beautiful buckskin mare, her hide almost gold in the sunlight. She had large, intelligent eyes, a black mane and tail, and black legs up to her knees. She butted me gently with her muzzle as I stroked and petted her. "She's absolutely lovely," I told whichever twin it was.

"Saddled," he pointed out and offered me a leg up. I was in the saddle before I thought to look round for Perry. He was mounted too, on a bay mare, a little taller than Willow.

"This is Sadie," he said, patting her neck. "We can ride for a bit if you'd like. There's somewhere up behind the farm I'd like to show you."

I followed him out of the yard and onto a grassed track between hedges and trees, wide enough for us to ride abreast. It was so good to be on horseback again. I'd ridden in front of Perry once or twice, but I hadn't ridden properly since I was with the Traders. If we went too far I'd pay for it tomorrow, but it would be worth it. Perry grinned at me. "I didn't know how well you could ride," he said. "Did you ride a lot with the Traders? Did you have your own horse?"

I shook my head. "I did ride a lot, but most riding horses were trade goods, so it was often a different horse every time."

"Well, Willow's yours for the summer, so you can get used to her."

I grinned back at him. "Faster?" I asked and nudged Willow into a canter ahead of him. He caught up but Willow was fast and more than held her own against Sadie as we raced along the track. We slowed down as the track rose steeply for a moment and then led through the trees into a clearing.

"This is what I wanted to show you," Perry said, riding across to the far edge of the clearing and stopping. We'd climbed higher than I'd realised and the track dropped away in front of us, steep but navigable. Spread out in front of us like a map or a child's building toy was the farm and the town.

"There's the rail track," said Perry, pointing. "You can see a train coming in. I thought this might help you work out where you were."

"It does," I told him. "It's an amazing view. Look, I can see the church and the lake. And is that Ma, in the garden, hanging out the washing?"

"I think it is," he said, leaning forward to get a better view. "And I think we'd better head back or we're going to be late for lunch."

He urged Sadie forward down the slope and I followed, my nimble and sure footed Willow having no problem with the descent.

Chapter 17

Early July

Leonie

Our days started to develop a pattern. Amber and I would take the mid-morning basket out to wherever Pa and the brothers were harvesting – now I could see Perry clearly with my mind I could always find my way, so that took a job off Ma. Then Perry and I would come back and either ride, or walk or swim. If it was a swim or a short walk, Amber would come with us and, for a while at least, she seemed to have a fresh lease of life. In the afternoon, after I'd slept, I'd go and meet Perry at the medical practice and work on the garden or in the still room until he was ready. Amber often came with me then, too, and there was nearly always someone heading into town from the farm for some reason, to keep me company on the walk. It took me a long while to realise that wasn't a coincidence.

Once Perry had finished work, we'd meet up with Jonny and Emlee somewhere – often by the lake – for a session working on our Gifts. Then we'd head back to the farm for a meal and an evening with family, although some evenings Perry would head out again for a clinic.

Tonight was the first time he'd be doing an evening clinic. Lizzie and Sam, Matt and Chrissy all joined us for the evening meal first. Perry and Lizzie started discussing medical stuff, both getting deeply involved in the conversation, almost to the point of stopping eating. Ma rapped her knuckles on the table. "Do you mind?" she asked. "No gory details at the meal table, please."

Jonny laughed. Perry looked more amused than told off. "Sorry, Ma," he said. "I'm too used to eating with other medics."

He and Lizzie set off for town as soon as the meal was over.

I helped Jonny and the twins clear up and then joined Ma on one of the big sofas. We chatted about some of the herbs that I was growing at the clinic and how they could be used in cooking, as well as medicine. She fetched a big reference book off the shelf and we pored over it together. Then I yawned.

"Bedtime," Ma said, closing the book. "Off you go. I won't be far away and I'll check in on you from time to time."

Obediently I headed off to our rooms, climbed into bed and fell asleep quickly.

***

The Them swarmed around my bed. I leapt to my feet, standing on the bed, bouncing slightly, higher than the Them for once. "Go away," I snarled. "I have no Gifts."

As they swayed towards me I remembered that wasn't true. With elation I grabbed for the power. It swirled towards me – and sputtered out. Drat. Maybe I had weapons? I grabbed for a pillow to see what would happen. Still a pillow. I swung it at the Them anyway and they fizzled out as it approached, reappearing when it had passed. I was sure that if I could have seen their expressions, they'd have looked smug. They glided over to the door. No, no way. They were heading towards my family. No way would I let them get hurt. I had to lead the Them away. Swinging my pillow, I leapt off the bed and plunged through the middle of the Them to get to the door first. We had our own door to the outside world and I raced for that, hurtling out into the farmyard. Yes! The Them were following. "Come on, then, you bunch of horrors. Catch me if you can."

There was a path ahead, well lit, and I raced down it, the Them chasing me, moving safely away from my family. Now what did I do? I couldn't wait for Perry to rescue me. I had to deal with this myself. In front of me was the Abbey. The Abbey? Here? How the...? I didn't care. The Abbey would make the Them disappear and keep me safe until Perry arrived. I shot through the door, across the building and curled up, hidden in one of my favourite places, panting slightly with relief and exhaustion.

Perry

Once the clinic was over, Perry and Lizzie walked back to the farm together.

"From my point of view, that went well," Lizzie said. "I think we've finally dealt with most of the people who've just come out of curiosity about the new doctor. This evening was more about people who really did need some form of treatment."

"I agree," Perry said. "Most of the things I had to deal with were very similar to what I've treated in clinics back at House St Peter."

He looked up as they approached the farm yard. It looked surprisingly busy for this time of night, with people everywhere and the big external lights switched on. His stomach churned. Had something happened to Leonie?

Ma saw them come through the gate and hurried over. "Perry, it's Leonie, she's missing. We can't find her!"

The panic rose from his stomach at the thought of losing Leonie and he took a deep breath to try to quell it. Outwardly he worked to remain calm. "How long?"

"Less than thirty minutes," Ma replied. "I've been checking on her about every half hour, last time she wasn't there." She continued to fret, wringing her hands, moving from foot to foot. "What good are Neville's guards if she can just disappear like this?"

He strove to reassure his mother as well as himself. "They'll be here to protect her, not restrict her. She's most likely sleepwalking and she's really good at not being noticed. Can we turn off the lights and stop shouting for her? Awake or asleep they'll scare her and make things harder."

Lizzie ran towards Sam to get him to comply. Perry took another deep breath. "Okay, I'm going to take a few minutes to look for her. If she's close – and she will be – I'll spot her."

Barely aware that most people in the yard had turned to watch him, he closed his eyes and started to reach out slowly, searching with his mind. He concentrated hard on the glow that meant Leonie, trying not to panic as he reached further and further without spotting her. Shortly, he opened his eyes, staggered slightly as he lost his balance with the change in perspective, and bumped into Sam who had returned with Lizzie. "Sorry, Sam. I should learn to sit down before I do that," he said absently, and then turned towards Ma. "Ma, when are the Shields switched on at the church? It's not all the time, is it?"

Surprised by the question, she took a moment to answer. "No, they're too expensive to run. There's a sensor, they come on when someone is in the building, except that Pastor Thomas can override it. He'd switch them off if it was only him there."

"So there'd be no reason for them to be on now?"

She shook her head, puzzled. "No, there'd be no one there at this time of night."

"That'll be where Leonie is then. The Shields are on right now."

People converged on Perry and then, with a whine, Amber twisted through their legs to sit at his feet, pawing his leg. Automatically, he reached to pat her.

"She started whining," said Ma. "And then when we realised Leonie was gone, I shut her in the kitchen so she wouldn't be in the way. But she was trying to tell me, wasn't she?"

"I'll come with you to get her," said Sam.

"Me too," added Jonny.

"And me," said Lizzie.

"Thanks, but no," Perry told them, thinking that she would be scared enough anyway without a whole party going to find her. "Ma, will you come with me?" he asked. "And we'll take Amber. Lizzie, Leonie's likely to have grazes, scratches, nothing that won't wait till we get back, but can you get ready what we're likely to need to clean them, please? And a dose of inhibitor, just in case. Sam, she won't be up to walking back, can you get one of the twins to hitch up a horse and come after us, please?"

"I'll do that," said Pa. "You set off. I'll catch you up shortly."

They walked fast, Amber running ahead and doubling back for them. Without thinking, Perry whistled for her, using the commands they had been familiar with years ago. Immediately, Amber came back to heel remembering all he had taught her then.

"How can you be sure Leonie is at the church?" Ma asked.

"She has to be, I can't see her anywhere else. That area is blocked by the Shields which is how I could tell they were on, and it's the sort of place she'd make for, if she were scared and sleepwalking."

"She hasn't run away from us? Or someone taken her?"

He shook his head, surprised at the question. "She won't run away. And I don't really know why Uncle Neville's so worried about keeping her safe. I don't know of any particular danger. I'm sure we'll find her at the church."

Indeed, as they came close they were greeted by Pastor Thomas looking round the main door. "Thank goodness," he said. "I'd no one to send for you, and I didn't like to leave her."

"She's here?" Perry couldn't hide the relief in his voice; he had not been nearly as confident as he had suggested to his mother.

"Yes, yes, come in."

Amber wriggled past them, heading straight for the altar table at the front of the church.

"She's underneath the altar table, isn't she?" Perry asked Thomas.

"Yes, how did you know? She just headed straight there."

Perry hurried up the aisle towards the altar, closely followed by Ma and Thomas. Amber had stopped in front of the table, whining quietly. Thomas reached to lift away the cloth that covered the altar table to the floor. Perry caught his wrist to stop him.

"Sorry," he apologised, "but Leonie will be both asleep and very scared. If we disturb her suddenly her instinctive reaction will be to attack."

"How do we get her then?"

Perry gestured for them to sit down, which they did on the floor behind the altar, leaning against the back wall. "We get her to come to us," he said. He called her name. "Leonie, you're safe now, I'm here and it's time to go home. You're safe to come out."

Nothing happened for a moment or two and then Leonie slipped out from under the cloth and straight into Perry's waiting arms. She curled up tightly against his chest and was to all appearances still asleep. Perry felt the tension leave his body now he had her safe. Amber flopped against his leg, equally relaxed and relieved.

"As easy as that was it?" Thomas asked.

Perry grinned back at him, knowing his relief would be showing clearly in his face. "Not really," he confessed. "It doesn't always work even for me."

"What happens then?"

"Mostly, I just risk being attacked. She's usually okay once I can get my arms round her and hold her close."

Thomas shook his head slightly. "These nightmares are a terrible thing. I've seen lads, grown men really, pale and shaking, absolutely terrified by them."

Perry agreed. "They're a side effect of developing Gifts; the power takes your worst fears and experiences and twists them into nightmares to torture you with. It's possible to stop them with drugs or Shields, but then the Gifts don't develop – some people choose that."

"Is there nothing you can do to ease it?"

"Not really. We give students a mild inhibitor and sedative after any nightmare, just so they can sleep and recover, but there's not much else we can do. The nightmares ease once the Gifts have developed. It's just tough for Leonie right now because she's recovering faster than they'd normally develop, and she was very Gifted, and there are some horrible experiences in her past, so it's all more intense."

Thomas nodded, understanding. "She'll be feeling cold. I'll go find a blanket for her."

Perry took advantage of his departure to check Leonie gently for injuries. He found nothing to concern him, other than a long ragged gash in the outer edge of her left foot, which he felt could wait until they got her home.

Ma had more questions for him. "What happens now?"

"Ideally, we hope the nightmare is over and we try to get her home, get that foot treated and get her back into bed without waking her. That way she might not remember anything about tonight."

"Is that likely? What happens if she wakes?"

"No, it's not very likely. If she wakes she'll remember what's happened and she'll be distressed at the trouble she's caused. I'll probably have to give her something to help her sleep again."

Ma looked at him carefully. "Why do I get the feeling that there's another possibility and it's even worse?"

He grinned, still euphoric at retrieving Leonie. "Because there is, and it is worse, and it's the most likely. We usually try and avoid it by actively waking students but I really hate to wake her when there's a chance of getting away with it. But if I don't, somewhere, something will tip her back into the nightmare. It will be worse, she'll be scared, it'll be difficult to wake her from it, she'll be uncooperative in anything we try to do. When I do manage to wake her, she'll struggle to sleep again without help, and tomorrow, when she remembers it all, she will be distraught."

Pastor Thomas arrived back with the blanket at about the same time as Pa arrived with the horse and trap. Perry wrapped the blanket carefully around Leonie, and, with the help of Thomas, managed to stand up with Leonie still in his arms. They made their way out of the church, and settled comfortably in the trap, Leonie still safely wrapped in Perry's arms, Amber nestled at his feet. He found himself very reluctant to let go of Leonie, even to allow someone else to help him.

"These nightmares sound much worse than what you had before you left, and what Jonny has now," Ma said on the way home. "I just have to wake Jonny, perhaps make him a hot drink, and he settles down to sleep again. You were much the same at his age."

"That's just the first stages, they get worse. And they start earlier for females."

"Did they get worse for you?"

"Oh yes, much worse. There are those who claim my nightmares and sleepwalking were some of the worst the college had seen in twenty years or more. Until Leonie came along, she holds that honour now."

"Were you scared, like Thomas described?" She rested her hand on his arm, looking into his face, worry creasing her brow.

His reply came slowly, concerned about the impact this might have on his mother, and on his father who was listening closely as he drove. "Yes...yes I was. I've been that person running from some unknown terror, fighting, or cowering in the corner."

His mother shuddered. "I don't like to think of that. Was there someone there for you?"

"Always. Just because our people suffer it doesn't mean they have to suffer alone. And now I'm often the someone there for others."

Pa put in a question, "I get the impression that Leonie has often suffered alone?"

"Yes, she has. There's rarely been anyone there for Leonie. Her Gifts and nightmares started very young, and they've caused all sorts of problems for her. She was always afraid she'd hurt someone, she used to try and find somewhere to sleep where no one was around, like in the woods, up in the hills. And when she came to the college it was worse for her, because she was afraid that she'd have a nightmare and we'd find out she was a girl masquerading as a boy. And of course that's exactly what happened. After that, we could be there for her, but she struggled with accepting that and trusting anyone."

Pa nodded. "Trust takes time. You can't change the fears of a lifetime in a few weeks."

Ma's next question was more hesitant, "Will this happen to Jonny?"

Perry had to be honest. "Almost certainly, he seems very Gifted. And maybe to Emlee, too."

"And there's nothing we can do?"

He sighed, sure that the honest answer would not be one that Ma would like. "Sometimes, if there's someone you're close to, that you trust absolutely, they can ease the nightmares for you just by being there. Once we were married, and we shared a bed, Leonie's nightmares pretty much stopped. She didn't have any from our wedding until after the accident."

"You're not suggesting that Jonny and Emlee sleep together!" Ma was shocked as he had anticipated.

"No, I'm not. I'm just saying that sharing a bed with someone you trust, just to sleep, is the best way we've come across to make things easier."

Privately, he thought it likely that Jonny and Emlee were already having sex, though perhaps he should credit them with more restraint than he'd had.

"Was there someone like that for you?"

Ma'd had to ask, hadn't she? And he'd have to answer. He grinned at her again as he tried to decide just how honest to be. "You're going to be even more shocked. There were a couple of girlfriends who did have that effect, but mostly, well, do you remember Andrew?"

Ma nodded. "I remember. He became a monk, too."

"That's right. He could always stop or ease my nightmares, and I could do the same for him, though his weren't as bad. We've spent many nights sharing the same bed, to our mutual benefit."

Ma wasn't quite speechless. "But you didn't... You're not..."

Perry was amused. "We just slept, Ma, that's all it takes, just sleep."

"And Lord Gabriel allowed this?"

"He doesn't interfere in the private lives of students. Once we joined the Order, though, that was different. He separated us then."

"But what about the nightmares?"

Again, he took his time replying. "When I joined the Order, I felt such a sense of peace, and relief and of burdens lifted. I put my trust in God, and He was and is always there for me, and for me that eased the nightmares. It was the same for Andrew, too. And we were older by then, which helped."

His mother's voice was barely a whisper as she said, "Jonny won't... I can't lose another child..."

His father reached a hand back to her in support. Perry was deeply remorseful. "I'm sorry, really I am. And everyone is different. Just because I did something doesn't mean Jonny will."

She reached up to ruffle his hair as she had often done

when he'd been a child. "I know you are, and it's okay. I understand it was what you had to do. And at least Leonie has brought you back now."

"Yes, she deserves the credit for that. She wanted to come so much this summer anyway."

"Didn't you want to come?"

"Yes, I did. I have all along. I just didn't want to face up to what I did to you."

She ruffled his hair again. "Silly boy. You're always wanted here, don't you know that?"

He smiled at her and nodded, finally accepting that he was forgiven. "Thanks, Ma."

They had reached the farm; Pa drove through the open gate and pulled up outside the house. A gaggle of people burst through the front door to greet them, eager for news. Sam reached up to lift Leonie down from Perry's arms, and without thinking he relinquished her. As Sam turned towards the house, and others gathered around her, the effect on Leonie was immediate. She started struggling, fighting Sam and lashing out at those nearby. Perry looked towards his mother. "Option three," he said, and then vaulted over the side of the trap to follow Sam into the house.

He caught up with them in the kitchen, Leonie still struggling but Sam not having much problem holding her firmly and avoiding flailing arms and legs.

"She's still asleep," Perry explained to Sam. "I don't know what's going on in her nightmare, but it can't be good." He looked to the person behind him, which turned out to be Matt. "Can we clear everyone out of here, please? I think everyone's making her more scared. Just Sam and Lizzie stay for now."

Matt nodded and started to organise matters, although they went little further than the sitting area of the kitchen. Perry reached towards Leonie to take her from Sam. This time his touch woke her and she fell into his arms from Sam's, clinging to him, unaware of anything or anyone else. He scooped her up and sat her on the kitchen work surface, her head buried in his shoulder, and his body between her and the others in the room. He worked at making sure she was fully awake to break the nightmare, whilst still trying to calm her fears, talking to her and trying to get some response. Lizzie brought him a glass of juice and he managed to get Leonie to drink a little of it.

He spoke to her again, a little louder, intending a message for Lizzie too. "I think you may have hurt your foot. Lizzie's just going to check and clean them."

Leonie clearly understood; she curled into a tighter ball, lifting her feet and tucking them against him so Lizzie couldn't reach them. He was firmer with her. "If you don't let Lizzie look at them, I'll have to let go of you to treat them myself."

She understood that, too, and reluctantly stuck one foot out round him where Lizzie could reach. Admittedly, it was her right foot, rather than the injured left one, but he supposed it was a start. When Lizzie had finished with that foot, Leonie didn't exactly proffer the other one, but she didn't object when Lizzie reached for it and started cleaning it, too.

"It could do with stitches," Lizzie mouthed at Perry, where Leonie couldn't see.

"Later," he said. "Just clean it for now."

He gestured to her to add some of the sedative inhibitor drug to Leonie's juice and then persuaded Leonie to drink the rest of it. He felt it take effect as her body relaxed into sleep against him, and he lifted her off the surface into his arms.

"Now," he said to Lizzie, "if I sit down and hold her, which will keep her calm and asleep, and Sam holds her foot still, can you just stitch that cut?"

They were soon arranged with Perry sitting on the sofa, Leonie on his lap, Sam next to him with Leonie's foot held on his lap and Lizzie kneeling beside them stitching. Everyone else made themselves comfortable around them.

Sam grinned. "The last time we did anything like this, it was an injured lamb," he said.

Lizzie laughed. "I end up stitching nearly as many animals as humans. It's not very different."

Perry laughed too. "Am I going to end up treating animals, too?" he asked.

"I shouldn't think so," Lizzie told him. "It's mostly either Sam who asks, or when I'm visiting, people ask because I'm there, and it's convenient."

She finished treating Leonie's foot and bandaged it. As soon as she and Sam let go, Leonie pulled her foot back, without waking, and curled more tightly into Perry.

"You're going to need a hand getting up," Sam told him. "Will she wake if you pass her over to me?"

Perry thought it worth trying now she was deeply asleep. As he did so, he discovered her hands were tightly gripping his shirt so he slipped out of it rather than try to disentangle her. He was still a little surprised that Leonie settled comfortably into Sam's arms, staying relaxed and asleep. Both Sam and Lizzie looked curiously at the scars on his ribs, arm and shoulder.

"Seen them before, out in the fields," Sam said. "How'd they happen?"

"Argument with a window, while I was having a nightmare," he told them.

"Are injuries pretty common then?" Matt asked. "Does Leonie have scars too?"

Perry shook his head. "Injuries are pretty rare, at least bad ones. Leonie's scars are mostly from being badly beaten as a child." He nodded towards Leonie, where the hem of her top had ridden up at the back as Sam had taken her. "You can see just a little there."

Matt looked over and swore. "Sorry," he said. "Someone beat our Leonie badly enough to leave marks like that? How could anyone beat a child like that?"

"There are people out there who even hunt children," Perry said shortly. "That happened to Leonie, too." Struggling to handle his own feelings about it, and needing to touch Leonie to reassure himself, he lifted her off Sam. "She needs to go to bed," he said. "Ma, you can tell them what they need to know."

There was a babble of voices behind him as he headed for their room.

Chapter 18

The Next Morning

Perry

Perry sat at the kitchen table, trying to study medical notes for the visits he was supposed to be making later that day. He couldn't concentrate. No one had gone out harvesting that morning; everyone had found jobs around the house and yard, waiting for Leonie to wake, desperate to see that she was okay. Perry kept watching Leonie with his mind so that he could get back to her the moment she woke. He turned a page of his notes. Awareness of Leonie flared across his inner vision.

Before he could react to the knowledge that she was awake, Leonie burst into the kitchen, coming to an abrupt halt when she saw everyone there turn to look at her. Horror dawned across her face as she began to work out what must have happened.

"What did I do?" she whispered.

He started towards her. "Nothing, you did nothing."

She brushed past him, running for the door into the yard. Lizzie went straight after her.

Urgently Perry called, "Don't chase her. You'll scare her."

His voice died away as he realised he was too late. But Lizzie stopped at the door, calling out to Sam who was standing in the middle of the yard talking to someone. Almost without looking, Sam stuck out an arm as Leonie passed, catching her and sweeping her up off the ground. She flailed at him with arms and legs but he took no notice, simply holding her so she could get no purchase and cause no damage. She looked at him in astonishment. Perry could hardly hold back a laugh at the look on her face as he headed out across the yard towards them.

"Ah, Perry," said Sam as he reached them. "Would you like your wildcat back?"

"Always," he said.

He lifted Leonie down to stand in front of him, her head against his chest and his arms tightly around her. He started whispering to her to reassure her while Sam and the others drifted away to leave them in peace.

Leonie

I leaned against Perry in despair. "I can't do this," I said. "Perry, I can't do this."

"Maybe you can't," he said. "Not alone. But we can, together, and with God's help."

I shook my head. "I'm going to hurt someone. I'll end up forcing you to choose between me and your family and that's not fair."

"Always you," he said softly. "Don't you know that? It'll always be you."

"But you shouldn't have to choose," I wailed.

"I won't have to. You won't hurt anyone. There's no danger."

He didn't understand. "I could. It's too big a risk."

"No, you won't. You don't understand. Trust me, you won't."

How could he be so sure? He guided us over to a bench, sat down and pulled me onto his lap. "Have you ever hurt anyone during one of your nightmares?" he asked. "Even back when they were at their most powerful?"

I thought back. I'd done lots of damage, but people? No, I'd never hurt anyone. I'd tried to avoid that at all costs.

"See?" he said. "Your strongest gift is your awareness of where other people are. Andrew and I worked that out, way back, just after Christmas. You see further and more clearly, more accurately than any other perceptor I know. It's how you were able to locate people well enough to pull them out of the ruins. And it's the Gift that came back, easily and quickly, with no trouble. You might try to scare people, to frighten them away, but you never hurt anyone and you never will."

I tried to take that in. Could I believe him? Perry had never told me anything but the truth. Sometimes he failed to tell me things I could have done with knowing, but what he did tell me was always true. If I trusted him – and I did – I could believe him and stop worrying. Taking a deep breath, I exhaled and then relaxed against him. "It's all going to be okay?" I asked him.

"It is," he said. "It's going to be fine."

I sat there, thinking over all that had happened since I'd first met him. It had been a traumatic time for both of us. He'd been utterly unfazed by my past, where many would have walked away. He'd come after me whenever my fear had caused me to run and each time given me the strength to continue. He'd shown me his faith and his family and made both mine. And despite all the dangers, he had never left me either deliberately or by dying as so many had before him. I twisted so I could see him, in some sort of wonder. He smiled, stood us up and guided us back into the house and through to the kitchen, keeping his arm around me.

He sat me down by the table and started to put a plate of food beside me, little things like pieces of fruit and cheese and toast. I ate them without thinking, just watching him. He sat down on the end of the bench next to me, facing me and lifted my bandaged foot into his lap.

"I'm just going to check this while Lizzie's still here," he said, starting to remove the bandage.

I barely heard him; I was still watching him as if I'd never seen him before. "Perry," I said slowly.

He looked up from what he was doing and smiled.

"Perry," I repeated. "I love you."

The smile that spread across his face was like the sun rising after the darkest, scariest night I could imagine. "I know," he said. "I've always known."

He let go of my foot, reached out and pulled me onto his lap, his arms around me, and our lips met. The rest of the world disappeared; there was just me and him and I didn't want or need anything else. Eventually, the world came back. Even then, he didn't let go of me.

"Lizzie," he said, without looking round. "Can you come and check this foot for me please?"

She pulled up a chair and lifted my foot onto her lap instead. "It looks fine," she said after a moment or two. "Clean and healing, no sign of any infection."

Perry tilted his head to have a look and nodded. "Very neat stitching," he said.

That made me look, too. I turned back to him in amazement then stared at my foot again. "There are stitches in it," I said, turning my gaze to him again.

He was clearly amused, almost laughing. "I know. You've seen stitches before, surely?"

Of course I had; I'd even put quite a number in, but that wasn't what astonished me. "But they're in me!" I said.

His face twitched as he struggled not to laugh. I supposed my face was a picture.

"Now you have a family," he whispered, just for me.

Now I had people who cared. I relaxed against him and he held me a little closer, a little tighter. He told Lizzie not to bother bandaging my foot again, he'd do it later and after a while she left for her work and Ma got on with her chores in the kitchen.

"I need to check you haven't any other injuries," Perry said quietly.

I shook my head. "Nothing hurts," I told him.

"Doesn't matter," he said. "I'm still going to examine you."

He stood up, lifting me up in his arms and carried me back to our room. He did examine me, thoroughly and gently, his fingers whispering over my skin. By the time he had finished, my senses were electric with his touch and my body was aching for more. I put my arms around his neck and pulled him close. He grinned wickedly, well aware of the effect he'd had on me, which had been exactly what he'd intended, and then gave me everything my body had been asking for.

Chapter 19

July

Gabriel

Sitting at his desk, Gabriel caught himself humming, "The High Lords came in two by two," as he realised each visiting High Lord would bring their heir or other close family member. He laughed to himself at his own parody of an ancient childhood rhyme about the Biblical story of Noah and the ark. In one version of that story the animals entered the ark in sevens and he thought that might be even more appropriate given each High Lord would bring a retinue as well.

Lord Neville of House Tennant arrived first, bringing with him his daughter, Lilyrose. The similarity to her cousin in her colouring and features was clear, but she was barely taller than Leonie. Dressed today in the formal clothes of an heir to her House, she looked far too delicate to be the tough soldier and able deputy to Lord Neville that rumour described her as.

"Left Brin in charge," Neville said. "Thought Perry might relate better to him if there were any problems."

"Are you expecting any particular problems?" Gabriel asked, suddenly a little concerned.

"No, not exactly," Neville said. "But, well, you tell him, Lilyrose."

Lilyrose might have looked delicate but her voice was composed, confident of her subject as she said, "When we were considering security for Perry and Leonie's journey and visit, our sources suggested there was just a little too much interest in where they might be. I suppose visiting House Tennant was a fairly obvious possibility. Naturally, we increased our security both at our borders and directly around Perry and Leonie. Brin coordinated it and made contact with them; I don't think either of them realised how closely they were guarded. Certainly they reached Deep River safely and we have adequate protection around them there."

She paused for breath. Gabriel thought how musical her voice sounded. Although higher, it reminded him of Prospero's voice and he wondered if she was as musical as he was and if they'd inherited it from the same ancestor. He returned his concentration to what she was saying, certain now that the rumours about her capability were true.

"I also used our intelligence sources to track the interest in them as much as possible. There were three distinct threads. Firstly, Traders and Settlers which I discounted. They form part of our information network and I assume they also form part of yours. The second thread was from the Assassins."

She looked at Lord Gabriel to assess his reaction.

He sighed. "Yes," he said. "My sources took me there too. And Leonie has a tracker implanted, which seems remarkably similar to those used by the Assassins, though neither Leonie nor Prospero know that. We deactivated it after the incident."

He had wanted Benjamin to remove it at that point, but Leonie hadn't been anything like strong enough. When they had first found the tracker, months ago, he had chosen to leave it in place and operational, concerned that any action would alert whoever had placed it there. After the incident at House Eastern he had figured that any interested party was now well aware of Leonie's circumstances. He had hoped that deactivating it might allow them to move Leonie without the knowledge of others. Clearly that had not been the case.

Lilyrose was less concerned about the Assassins. "They know they aren't permitted on House Tennant land," she said.

"And anyway, Leonie is not yet twenty one. She's safe enough from them. My concern is with the third strand. That took me back into House Lindum. I think the real danger could be there."

"My sources suggested Chisholm, not Lindum," Lord Gabriel said, alarmed. "Lord Leon actively tried to protect Helena. He doesn't want Leonie dead."

Neville butted in. "That's as maybe," he said. "Lilyrose is right. It led us back to Lindum and, what's more, into the Great House. But no further than that."

"Any faction in either Lindum or Chisholm could want Leonie dead or alive depending on whether their priority is to protect their House or take over the other one, or whether there's some other motive we haven't fathomed," Gabriel conceded. "Both Lindum and Chisholm will be here later, probably with their heirs. At least Leonie is safer not here."

"I'm still impressed you got them both to agree to meet at all," Neville told him, and the conversation moved on to details of the formal meeting.

James

James looked up as Leon, High Lord of House Lindum, walked into his office at Taylor House. "Father," he said. "I didn't know you planned to visit today?"

"I'm heading to a meeting at St Peter's. Come with me." It was more of an order than an invitation. "That'll make this trip look like it's about Taylor House."

Intrigued, James joined his father on the journey. It wasn't long before he began to worry that this might have been a mistake. They were a small party and their journey took them straight from their own lands onto the lands of House St Peter. James and Lord

Leon rode together, out of earshot of the rest of their retinue.

"In your work with House St Peter, have you come across Prospero, from House Tennant? The one who just got married? Whose wife was involved in that incident at House Eastern?" Lord Leon asked James quietly.

That question seemed innocent enough, and James answered freely, "Yes, he's spent quite a lot of time at Taylor House. He was here only a few weeks ago, bringing in some nestlings his wife had found near the Abbey."

"Did he bring his wife? Have you met her?"

Now that was far more dangerous territory, thought James. "No," he answered. "He didn't bring her. Lord Gabriel said she shouldn't miss classes or work or something. He said he'd bring her next time."

"Have you seen the pictures? From House Eastern? Know what she looks like?"

Feeling as though he was walking along a tightrope, James answered carefully, "Those pictures weren't very clear. I could see she had red hair."

He hoped the allusion to the Chisholm link would distract his father. Some of the things James knew and had done in the past could get him into a very difficult situation should they be discovered. And yet, despite everything, he'd always had a good, if somewhat distant, relationship with his father. He didn't want to have to deceive him any more than he already had.

Lord Leon cleared his throat. "Hmph. Well. You might as well know. You'll find out soon enough if you haven't heard any speculation already. This meeting is about her. She's Helena's girl."

James looked at him, astounded. Not at the information, which, as he had been shown Perry's favourite – and very clear – picture of Leonie, came as no surprise whatsoever. Leonie looked just like Helena. No, what astounded him was the fact that his father was openly admitting it.

Fortunately, Lord Leon seemed to interpret his reaction as astonishment at the news and carried on speaking. "I knew the child's body wasn't hers. Didn't tell anyone. Thought that if someone wanted her dead she'd be safer if everyone thought she was. Couldn't find her, though, and couldn't look hard without giving the game away. When you wanted to set up Taylor House, I supported you so I could use it to look for her."

Now James was truly astonished. That had been his own purpose for Taylor House but he'd kept it secret from his father – and everyone else – ever since its inception. He'd passed it off as charitable work, suitable for a youngest son who had no hope of inheritance and no real role in the function of the Great House. But the question at the forefront of his mind was, "How? How did you know the body wasn't hers?" James had known himself that the child's body wasn't Leonie's, of course he had, but he'd not been able to say for fear of what the consequences might have been. If his father knew this, what else might he know?

"Kept an eye on them," said Lord Leon, sounding a little embarrassed. "Couldn't do much or often but I did what I could to make things easier without Augusta knowing it was me. Had some pictures of the child as she grew." He paused and then, sounding even more embarrassed, he added, "It's not treason if I do it. How can I possibly act against myself?"

James was all but speechless, which probably saved him from confessing his own activities. Hidden in his luggage was a gift he'd promised Perry for Leonie. Its very existence was a danger to him – at least if anyone else recognised it, which Lord

Leon would. But from the moment he'd realised who Leonie was he'd needed to give it to her. Until his recent meeting with Perry, it had been safely hidden at his own home; since then he'd kept it with him or at Taylor House. It would have been safe enough left there, but he'd been unable to resist the possibility that he might be able to see Leonie and give it to her.

"How can you know their Leonie is Helena's child? Couldn't she be someone else? There's no real shortage of Chisholm offspring." James was certain himself, just from the picture that Perry had shown him, but it was the obvious question to ask.

Lord Leon winced at the open mention of Chisholm. "Eleanor showed me a picture. There's no doubting it once you've seen her. But they say they've done a DNA test which proves it, and they've no reason to lie."

James was silent again, his mind whirling as he tried to work out what he would say or ask next if he was innocent in all this, if he didn't know what he knew, if he hadn't done what he'd done. Fortunately, his father took his silence as shock and incomprehension and volunteered what other information he knew, which didn't add much to what James had already heard from Perry.

The one additional piece of information, which brought James considerable relief, was that Leonie and Perry were not currently at House St Peter. It had suddenly struck James that Leonie might recognise him. True, she'd been just a small child when they'd last met but there was a strong possibility that she would remember him. And if that happened in public, before he'd had a chance to get to her privately, then he was probably done for. Desperate as he was to see her again, he was also deeply relieved that Perry had not brought Leonie to Taylor House a few weeks back.

Edmund

Edmund, youngest son to Lord William of House Chisholm, was sure he'd made a serious mistake joining his father on the journey to House St Peter. Chisholm lands bordered those of House Lindum, but on the opposite side to House St Peter. As crossing Lindum was out of the question that meant a long journey round, with a large retinue of guards. Edmund was finding the journey uncomfortable, although this particular conversation had been rehashed many times.

"I don't believe Jaim ever did anything without you knowing about it. You must have known about the Lindum girl. Why didn't you stop him?" William snarled at him.

Edmund knew from experience that he had no need to answer. Not that he could or would, anyway. There were things he knew, things he'd done that he had no intention of sharing with anyone, ever. Jaim had been his twin, long dead now, but Edmund's loyalty was still to his brother above everyone else. Well, almost everyone else.

Lord William continued, "This Leonie, she's going to turn out to be that Lindum slut's brat."

Edmund winced at the words and the tone, but his father's tirade continued, "Gabriel didn't confirm it, but why else would he drag me there? There's already rumours going around. She's going to be Lindum's heir and he'll use her to take my House. And all because your brother couldn't keep his hands off the girl. And you didn't stop him."

Now he turned directly on Edmund, "I thought she was dead. You said she was dead. You said you'd seen her body."

Edmund gave his usual defence. "I did see a body. A red headed girl, the right age, in the right place. How was I to know if it wasn't the right child? It's not like I saw her every day."

No, he hadn't seen her every day. But he'd seen her often enough.

"You should have found a way to make sure. That child's cost me a son and now she'll likely cost me my House."

"She cost them their heir. And St Peter's got her now, not Lindum. And I hear she may yet die anyway," Edmund said mildly, hoping to placate his father.

His father just glared at him and refused to speak to him for the rest of the journey. Edmund found that a considerable relief.

Chapter 20

Gabriel

Gabriel greeted his guests as they entered his private dining room for the evening meal. He was grateful that the Lindum and Chisholm parties had not crossed paths until they were within the boundaries of the Abbey campus, weapons lodged with the Porter. At least, those weapons they carried openly. He wasn't naïve enough to think they'd surrendered everything, nor would he insist upon it. Building some level of trust was going to be essential to the success of this venture.

The diners included not only the parties from Lindum and Chisholm, but also Tobias and Leah, leaders of the local group of Settlers. They'd brought Ethan, Merchant for the Trader caravan Leonie had been with. And Eleanor had invited a number of senior members of House St Peter, too. Benjamin was there as head of the hospital, Lady Sarah as head of the college, Sister Elizabeth from the convent and Brother Richard, as Gabriel's deputy.

As his hostess, Eleanor showed the guests to their seats. She'd chosen a circular table to avoid issues of precedence, but she'd placed Lindum and Chisholm as far apart as possible and interspersed members of House St Peter between the visitors.

Ellie was across the table from him. *"So far, so good,"* she said, telepathically as the first course was served. *"At least they're all eating together. When did that last happen?"*

"Generations ago," he answered.

Shields were an area where he'd taken Ellie's advice. "We'll have Defender and Container Shields on, naturally," she'd said. "But not the Dampener. Telepathy may be useful to us."

"Won't they object?" he'd asked, meaning his guests.

She'd shaken her head. "No," she'd said. "Tennant and the Traders won't care. Lindum and Chisholm won't be able to object. If they ask for more Shields either they're saying they don't trust you to be an unbiased mediator, or they're suggesting they've got something to hide. Neither will risk that."

Certainly Eleanor would be making the best use of telepathy. He looked round at the servers – Andrew, Chloe, Joseph, Beth – they were all definitely telepaths. Fran he didn't know well, but she was Gifted, so almost certainly a telepath. And Aidan was a telepath too, although perhaps a strange choice? No, like Andrew he was excellent at languages. No doubt they'd all be reporting any discussions they overheard to Ellie. He smiled to himself; Ellie had been stacking the deck in his favour all their life. He should have known she'd be on top of this, too. She was seriously devious. He should probably speak to her about it, but then again, he found her abilities so useful he didn't really have a leg to stand on.

Leonie's name was mentioned and he pricked up his ears, ready to intervene in the conversation if necessary. Ethan was asking Benjamin about the girl's health. Fair enough; Ethan considered himself in the role of father to Leonie. His caravan's route might mean that he was mostly out of contact but that didn't absolve him of the responsibility. It was understandable that he'd want the latest information on her well-being. Gabriel tuned in to the discussion and noticed that Leon, James, William and Edmund were all doing much the same, whilst trying to look as though they weren't.

"She's doing very much better than any of us expected," Benjamin said. "We wouldn't normally expect someone to survive what she did at House Eastern. And, of course, she's not out of the woods yet."

"But she's clearly well enough to travel, as she's not here?"

asked Ethan. "I was hoping to see her."

"We felt it was better for her to convalesce elsewhere," Benjamin said. "I have a hospital full of very curious doctors and I didn't think that was fair on her," he added with a grin.

"But she will recover? And she has proper medical care, where she is?" Ethan sounded very concerned.

Benjamin tried to be reassuring. "Her husband's with her, and he's an expert in these areas. She couldn't get better treatment. As to whether she will recover and how fully, we don't know. We'll just have to wait and see."

Ethan accepted that was the best he was going to get and moved on. "What's she like now? As a person, I mean?"

He glanced around the table at those who knew her most recently.

Leah answered first, "Quiet and very private, still."

"Determined and independent." That was Tobias.

Now everyone had given up the pretence of not listening and the conversation encompassed the whole table. Gabriel spoke next, giving those of his House implicit permission to join in. "She can be impulsive at times but always with the best of intentions. And she's very perceptive. It's practically impossible to keep secrets from her."

Except it wasn't, was it? He had certainly kept secrets from her; still did. William snorted quietly. Of course, the Chisholms were known for being impulsive. William's own cautious nature was quite unusual in that family.

"Very giving and caring. She'll help anyone who needs it," volunteered Sister Elizabeth.

Gabriel hadn't thought she knew Leonie that well.

Sarah took up the theme. "She's hardworking, very quick to learn. And she absorbs information like a sponge."

Now it was Richard's turn. "She finds it very difficult to be looked after, to be the recipient not the giver. Prospero's a very good match for her. He's teaching her to accept that she's loved."

And that was another surprise for Gabriel. He'd thought that Richard had very much disapproved of his own actions, of his adoption of Leonie, and of what had been happening between Leonie and Prospero over the last few months. And he'd certainly got the impression that Richard thought Prospero should not have left the Order, let alone married Leonie.

Benjamin spoke next. "I think she's brave. A lot of the time, at least to start with, she was scared of what might happen, or what she didn't understand. But always, she faced up to it."

Eleanor finished it off. "When she feels safe and relaxed she's full of mischief and laughter."

Now it was Leon's turn to snort quietly. "That pretty much describes Helena and Augusta," he explained. "Such a pair of mischief makers, even as small children."

Edmund had been pretty quiet throughout the meal, but now he spoke. "What's her life been like? Since we all thought her dead?"

William glared at him. Clearly he didn't like such independent action on the part of his son. Gabriel realised that William and Edmund were probably the only two around the table who didn't know broadly what had happened to Leonie since Augusta had died.

Gabriel decided to answer before anyone else did, just to

ensure he could keep the story consistent and the atmosphere tranquil. "We don't know where, nor how she got there," he said, making sure his voice was very calm, "But she was in an orphanage somewhere and then she ran away and became a nestling. I think she was one for several years before hunters chased her straight into Ethan's caravan. They rescued her and she travelled with them until they reached the town here, perhaps a couple of years ago."

Ethan nodded. "Maybe a little more. My Headwoman was insistent she remained here so we left her with Tobias and Leah when we moved on."

Gabriel took up the story again. "She masqueraded as a boy to become a student here. Eventually – and I regret to say it took us several months – we discovered her deception and I chose to take her as my ward."

"So she had a pretty bad childhood then?" Edmund asked. "At least until she met you." He nodded towards Ethan.

In yet another surprise for Gabriel, Benjamin answered before he could. "Leonie's one of the most resilient people I've come across. She doesn't see her childhood as bad, she just thinks that things happened, both bad and good and she dealt with them. Just because more bad things happened than good, doesn't make her life bad, not for her. Most of the time she was actually pretty content, living in the moment, accepting that this was just how things were and getting on with it." He paused for a moment before he added, "The thing that really upset her was when someone she cared about left her or died. She's afraid that'll happen again."

Everyone was silent for a moment, each contemplating Leonie's losses, each remembering their own dead. And then the servers broke the tension and the silence by clearing the plates and bringing the next course. That'd be Ellie, managing and manipulating the situation again, thought Gabriel.

"You didn't recognise her when you saw her?" William asked, noticeably more curious and less sullen than he'd been earlier.

Gabriel shook his head. "We certainly weren't expecting to find her. Like everyone else, we believed her dead," he said. "Of course, we assumed the Chisholm ancestry from her hair, but I wasn't aware that you'd lost track of any of yours so I didn't think much of it."

"I wasn't aware I'd lost track of one either," William interrupted dryly.

Gabriel continued, "It really wasn't until Benjamin did a DNA test as part of a medical for Leonie that we spotted the connection. But that is an issue for tomorrow and not tonight."

However reluctant the visitors might have been, the members of House St Peter took Gabriel's hint and the subject changed, with several separate conversations developing around the table. The rest of the meal, and indeed the evening passed without incident. Gabriel heaved a huge sigh of relief when all parties finally dispersed to their own rooms for the night without any actual bloodshed.

Chapter 21

Gabriel

As Gabriel gave the final blessing at the first service of the day, his stomach twisted again with nerves. He glanced over at where Lord Neville and Lady Lilyrose were sitting. Given Neville's disparaging comments when Prospero had first joined the Order, their presence at this service was unexpected, to say the least. Should he join them for breakfast? No, he'd given all his visitors the opportunity to take breakfast in their own quarters, just as he normally did. He would take breakfast privately, if he could manage to eat anything. Then he'd pray again, just as he had been since the dawn, even earlier than normal.

An hour later, he stood in the central courtyard with Sister Chloe awaiting the transcopter bringing the High Lord of House Eastern, Lady Anna-chesska. As it hovered overhead, he struggled with some unpleasant memories – and from the look on Chloe's face she was struggling too. They were perfectly used to the comings and goings of transcopters but this was the one that had brought Leonie and Prospero home from House Eastern just a few short weeks ago. Gabriel would never forget the look of loss and pain on Prospero's face, nor the sight of Leonie, pale and all but lifeless in his arms.

He pushed the memories to one side to welcome Anna-chesska. As far as he knew, she was the only attendee who had no claim on Leonie but the precipitating events had taken place within her House. He'd felt strongly that she should be included in these discussions.

They walked side by side to the meeting room, exchanging pleasantries, Chloe following along behind. Gabriel pushed open the door to the meeting room and gestured for Anna-chesska and Chloe to go ahead. That gave him a chance to glance around the room. Everyone else seemed to be there; those who'd sat down now stood up to welcome Anna-chesska.

He, Eleanor and Chloe had chosen a circular table again. Lords Leon and James were directly opposite Lord William and Lord Edmund. Neville, Eleanor, Leah and Tobias sat between them on one side. Ethan and Lilyrose were already on the other side, with a space for Anna-chesska and Gabriel.

Gabriel started the meeting with prayer; whatever anyone else might believe, this was his House and this meeting would need all the help it could get. He watched the reactions of his guests as he invited them to pray. The Traders and Settlers bowed their heads, bodies relaxed, comfortable in prayer and Neville and Lilyrose reacted in a similar manner. William and Leon were both ramrod straight in their seats, bowing their heads on stiff necks, just enough to avoid disrespect. James and Edmund glanced down at the table, looking anywhere but each other, both fidgeting, unable to keep still, clearly uncomfortable, their minds anywhere but prayer.

Gabriel took his time, trying to align himself with God's will, and found it provided him with much needed calmness. He hoped it had done the same for the other attendees, although their body language suggested perhaps not. Nonetheless, they had to begin somewhere.

Briefly, he outlined what was public knowledge of the situation surrounding Leonie's birth, the little they knew of her life since Augusta's death, and the events leading up to their identification of her as Leonie Lindum. He asked Lord Leon to describe finding Augusta's body and that of the child.

"If the dead child wasn't Leonie," growled William, "then who the he...who on earth was she?"

Lord Leon shook his head. "At the time there was no reason to suspect that the child wasn't Leonie. Red hair, right age, right place. We didn't carry out any further identification."

"Well, it must have been someone. And one of mine too, no doubt." William turned on Gabriel. "How do I know that this Leonie you've found is the real one, not some imposter?"

"The medical details are beyond me," Gabriel said. "And no doubt you will want to make your own tests in due course. However, I can call Brother Benjamin in to go over his genetic tests if you wish."

Neville spoke up, "The medical details may be beyond most of us. Why don't we assume for now that Brother Benjamin's findings are correct and work on that basis."

"Hmph," William snorted. "Suppose I can't really doubt a monk."

"In that case," Gabriel said, "what we must discuss is not the past, but Leonie's future and how that impacts on all of us."

"If she is Jaim's, as everyone assumes, then, biologically, she's my daughter." Edmund had been silent to this point but now his statement dropped explosively into the discussion.

"Legally, she's my daughter." Even Gabriel was surprised by the speed and vehemence of his own response.

"As she is definitely Helena's then she's my heir," Leon snapped back at Edmund almost at the same time.

"And it is my caravan, my people, who have cared for her. We fostered her. She is one of us, my daughter." Ethan was not slow to point out.

Neville was slower to respond but he too staked a claim. "She is married to one of my heirs. That makes her Tennant, too."

Leah spoke slowly and deliberately, her voice soft but

commanding, "We have all made a claim to the girl but none of us own her. Let her choose her own allegiance, her future path. That is not relevant. What is important here is what we do as a result of her existence. Like it or not, she has already bound together every House and Clan represented here and probably some that aren't. Do we build on that to our mutual benefits, or do we throw away all that she represents?"

"I cannot risk the safety of my House," William replied sharply. "I have a responsibility to my family. If she chooses Lindum they could use her to challenge for my House."

"Why would I want your House? My own is enough for me," Leon retorted. "And anyway, it's the same for me. If she chooses Chisholm, you could use her to claim my House."

"I'd rather reclaim the Badlands. But how can I trust you? A Lindum?"

"Perhaps a treaty, then," Neville suggested carefully. "A mutual non-aggression pact between each of you, her and whichever House she chooses? Binding in perpetuity on heirs too, of course."

William turned on him. "And you would sign something like that? She could choose your House, too."

"Not only will I sign it," Neville declared, "I will pledge the time and resources of my House to working out the terms, if you will both agree to it in principle."

Leon exchanged glances with William and sighed. "We have been enemies for such a long time. I'm not sure the original reason is even known, now. It's a big step. And it will be a lot of work to get my people behind it."

"You've already made more progress than generations before you. How long since Lindum and Chisholm sat to talk in the same room? That doesn't even happen when the Council of High Lords meets."

"I should include my heir in any discussions, but I will if Lindum will. And subject to agreeing the terms of any treaty," William capitulated more rapidly than Gabriel had expected.

"Very well," agreed Leon. "Then I will, too. Subject to the same conditions."

Slowly he extended his hand across the table to William. Equally slowly, William reached out and, for the first time in centuries, Lindum and Chisholm shook hands in agreement. Gabriel sat back and watched as Neville took over the meeting, not yet discussing terms, merely starting to sort out the process by which they would hold such discussions.

That matter well in hand, Gabriel suggested the meeting adjourned for half an hour or so for comfort, and for refreshment which was provided in the next room.

"Gabe," Eleanor called telepathically. *"Edmund's just behind you. I think he wants a word privately."*

Gabriel turned towards Edmund, using his body and position in the room to block the view of others. Edmund looked pale and distraught as he opened his mouth to speak. "It was me," he confessed quietly, his words a rush. "I was the one who placed the other body there. My father doesn't know."

"Ellie," Gabriel called. *"I need more time."*

"No problem," she answered and she guided William out of the door, apparently deeply engrossed in their own conversation. In his turn, he guided Edmund into the privacy of his own office and shut the door.

"No one will disturb us here," he said. "Lady Eleanor will

take care of your father. Sit down and tell me all about it."

Chapter 22

Edmund

Edmund had barely slept, and nor had he been able to eat that morning. As the meeting progressed he had become less and less able to concentrate, his mind filling with images of Augusta as he had last seen her, and the child's body, lying dead beside her. Despite all his resolutions, his loyalty and his vows to his dead, he could no longer hold in what he knew. Safely in Lord Gabriel's office he sank into a chair without looking.

Now he'd finally told someone, the words came quickly and easily. "The child – Leonie – I loved her. From the moment I first saw her, I loved her. I had to help them. What else could I do?" He looked up at Gabriel before he continued. "There was a remote place, high on the border between our Houses, where I used to meet Helena after my brother died and before the baby was born. Augusta knew it too. When she ran with the baby, she thought I ought to know and she waited for me there. I found her. I wanted her to go somewhere safe but she wouldn't leave Lindum lands. She wouldn't have been safe on our lands of course, but I could have found somewhere. I should have insisted more." He paused again, taking deep breaths as the painful memories flooded back. "She had somewhere to hide out. I visited when I could, helped as much as I could. And then one day – one evening rather – I found Augusta dead and Leonie missing. I searched for her, in case she'd wandered off, but all the signs suggested she'd been taken. I wasn't thinking straight. I thought if I could make it seem as if Leonie was dead then perhaps she'd be safer, of less value to anyone, they might release her and I could find her. I don't know why I thought that; it doesn't make sense now."

Again he looked up at Gabriel, pleading for understanding.

"You would have been very upset," Gabriel said gently. "It's no wonder you weren't thinking straight. Where did the other child's body come from?"

"We'd buried her that day. One of my nieces. She'd been frail since birth but she was about the same age. It was so easy to substitute her, so convenient. At the time I felt like it was meant."

At the time, he'd been terrified. He'd been in his late twenties and seen plenty of dead bodies, but still, finding Augusta like that had shaken him. It was clear to him that she'd been assassinated; he'd seen the signs before but he hadn't realised just how much danger she'd been in. Then the increasingly panicked search in the dark for Leonie in the slim hope that she'd only wandered off but knowing all the time that really, she'd been taken. Eventually, he'd given up searching, the wind and fine cold rain cutting at his face like glass shards as he'd retreated back to the hut, his thoughts in turmoil. That was when the plan to substitute a body for Leonie's had started to develop in his head. If she'd been taken by the Assassins, they'd protect her until she was adult but somewhere out there would be their client, the one who wanted her dead. If he could make it seem as though Leonie had died of natural causes – and that was made public – the client would have to accept that and pay the Assassins. Neither client nor Assassin would be able to object without their own identity becoming public. Once paid, the Assassins wouldn't care that Leonie was still alive. And if she was still alive, then he had a chance of finding her.

Little Jessie had been buried that day. She'd been the right age and had died of natural causes. And she'd been red headed, like Leonie. Augusta had lived very reclusively with Leonie, so practically no one had known what Leonie looked like and the chance of being caught out was very low. He hadn't been able believe he was doing it, disrespecting Jessie, desecrating her grave, but he'd moved as if in a dream – no, a nightmare. The darkness and wild night had helped, but truly it had been remarkably easy. The return journey, back to Augusta's hut, in dark and wind and unseasonable freezing rain, with Jessie's lifeless body in his arms had featured in his nightmares for many years; even now once or twice a year he would wake, shaking, shivering and sweating, haunted by his memories. It wasn't the only nightmare either – the day his twin brother had died tormented him too.

"I took her body back to Augusta's hut. I tried to make it look as though the child had died and Augusta had killed herself in grief," he told Gabriel. "And they were found and eventually it was made public that they were dead."

The story out, Edmund sat quietly, empty, resting his head in his hands, eyes closed, unable to work out what to do or say next. The office door burst open and someone charged in, shutting the door again in the face of whoever had been trying to stop him. Edmund didn't look up, incapable of facing anyone else.

"Whatever he's told you," the newcomer said, "we were in it together. I am just as much to blame. I knew about the body. We were both there."

Edmund wasn't sure whether the noise he made was a laugh or a sob. He opened his eyes and raised his head. "Thanks, James," he said. "I wouldn't have told him about you."

"I know," Lord James said quietly, as he sat down beside Edmund. "That's why I came. We're in this together. We always have been."

"So," Lord Gabriel said, leaning back in his chair, "Lindum and Chisholm have been working together for fourteen years? And here I was, congratulating myself on getting you under the same roof."

James laughed and even Edmund had to smile. "Eighteen years," he said. "We both helped Augusta practically from Leonie's birth."

Gabriel smiled too. "Everybody is surprising me today, one way or another."

Edmund turned to James. "What happened to Taylor?" he asked. "I mean, I realised about Taylor House, obviously, but what happened to the original?"

James moved slightly to reach into one of his pockets, pulling out a small drawstring bag. "I kept him safe," he said, handing the bag to Edmund.

Carefully, almost reverently, Edmund opened the bag to find the little toy zebra, still wearing the outfit Augusta had made for Leonie's fourth birthday. He stroked it gently with one finger, as he tried to get his emotions under control, while James explained to Lord Gabriel. "Taylor belonged to Helena when she was a child. Augusta thought Leonie should have something that belonged to her mother. You never saw Leonie without him. He went everywhere with her. That's how we knew she'd been abducted because Taylor was there on the floor. She'd have never just run off and left him there, however scared she was."

"Leonie should have him back," Edmund said.

James agreed. "I thought that from the moment I knew who she was. That's why I brought him with me. And then, on the way I thought, what if she recognises us? It's been a long time and she was very young, but she might remember. And my father will certainly recognise Taylor. I think we're both in trouble and we need to face it together."

Edmund was quite certain they were in trouble.

"Both your Houses would consider your actions treason," Lord Gabriel said. "Should either of you need it, you may have a place in my House. However, I doubt it will be necessary. Lord James, I think you will find your father sympathetic. He did all he could for Helena. Lord Edmund, I don't know how your father will react, I'm afraid, but I suspect he will want to avoid any scandal."

"My father helped them too," James admitted. "He told me yesterday. He did it secretly, even Augusta didn't know it was him. He didn't know about us, I'm sure he didn't from the way he told me."

Acknowledging that with a nod, Lord Gabriel continued, "As to whether Leonie will remember you, I don't know the answer to that either. She has memories of Augusta, but she's neither shared nor have we seen any recognisable memories of either of you. That may mean nothing; she has had forgotten memories triggered by new events before and you may fall into that category."

"So what do we do now?" Edmund asked, still feeling unable to function coherently.

Gabriel took his time in replying. "It's up to each of you what you tell your High Lords and when," he said eventually. "If you wish me to mediate such a meeting, I will. Although you've both kept this secret for so many years I am sure it will come out in the end and it's perhaps better if you volunteer it before that. But if you wish to keep this secret, so will I."

They discussed it for a short while but quickly came to the conclusion that Lords Leon and William should be told, immediately.

"But just them," Edmund insisted.

"Very well," Gabriel agreed. "I'll ask Lady Eleanor to arrange matters. I will tell the others that the issue of the child's body has been explained to my satisfaction and is not relevant to the rest of our discussions."

"And Taylor?" Edmund asked.

"I'm quite prepared to offer sanctuary to Taylor, too," Lord Gabriel said, smiling at the concern he had for a small soft toy. "But I think you should be the ones to return him to Leonie. Until then, I can keep him safely here, if you wish."

He got up from his chair, walked over to the office door and opened it. "Chloe," he called, "Lord James has something for Brother Edward to keep safely. Please arrange that and tell Edward it is vital this is kept both secure and secret. Thank you."

As Chloe and James left, taking Taylor, Edmund rose to follow them but Gabriel called him back. "A moment more, if you please."

Edmund sat down again, surprised.

Gabriel looked at him. "Substituting Jessica's body for Leonie was one thing," he said, "but that wasn't the only substitution going on, was it?"

210

Chapter 23

Gabriel

When Edmund had finished his second, halting confession, Gabriel sighed and looked at him. "I think you need to tell the others this too, don't you?" he asked gently. "Are you ready, if I get them in here?"

Edmund nodded mutely, so Gabriel spoke briefly to Eleanor, telepathically.

"What's happening?" she asked him.

"I'll tell you later," he said. *"Truly, Ellie, you wouldn't believe it. You couldn't make this up. For now, can you get William, Leon and James in here please?"*

The three men came into his study, Leon leading the way, relaxed and curious, James sheltering behind him a little, clearly cautious and nervous. And William tramped in after them, frowning, someone who appeared naturally grumpy. Gabriel admired Eleanor's skill at manipulating people and knew he would be lost without her.

"What's all this about then?" William asked gruffly.

"Lord James and Lord Edmund have some information that they wish to share with you both," Gabriel said, gesturing them all to seats.

He didn't think Edmund was going to manage to speak, but James took the lead and started to explain what had happened fourteen years ago, and the background to those events. As he finished, Edmund seemed to pull himself together. "There's a bit more yet," he said. "James doesn't know this." Slowly, stumbling over his words, he explained the rest of what he had just confessed.

Both High Lords were stunned into silence for a moment and then Lord William swore, mostly at Edmund. Loudly and graphically, until he remembered where he was and lapsed into silence with a mumbled apology to Gabriel. Then he stood up and marched towards the door. "Come on, Lindum," he said. "Let's go and talk peace treaty. At least that I can understand. Honestly, the younger generation..." He turned back to the two younger men, both looking stunned. "Well, aren't you coming?" he asked. "You did a good enough job of looking after her to start with. You'd better come and finish the job off."

"Bit of a change of tune, isn't that, Chisholm?" Lord Leon asked as James and Edmund scrambled up to follow them.

William shrugged. "There's no real doubt who she is, not now, not after that. She's my flesh and blood and I take care of my own. Always have. So do you. And Edmund. Guess I didn't do too badly with him. Your James, too. Figure there must be some good in you Lindums after all."

With that, he stomped back into the main meeting room. The others followed, Leon looking amused, James relieved, and Edmund still too stunned to do more than follow the crowd. As they sat down, Leon whispered to James, "We'll have words later about all you've been keeping from me, but well done, my son, well done."

Now James looked as stunned as Edmund. Gabriel kept his own amusement to himself, and tried to concentrate on Lord Neville, recapping the arrangements for the peace treaty. To his surprise, Lady Anna-chesska spoke up. "There's no likelihood of Leonie choosing my House, although it would be open to her. But I would still like to be a party to this treaty and I suspect there will be others also. Is that acceptable?"

That was something we hadn't considered, Gabriel thought, though he welcomed the idea. They decided to sort out the details of the treaty as already agreed and then make it open to any other House that wished to participate.

Peace treaty sorted, for now anyway, Gabriel had another issue to address. "Lord Neville and I, through our intelligence sources, are fairly certain that Leonie is the subject of an Assassin's contract," he said. He held his hand up for silence as the others in the room started to respond. "Yes, I know she is in no particular danger for now, given her age, but we will have to sort this out. Someone has instituted this contract and until we know who and deal with it, she will not be safe. Lord Neville and I are investigating but there is also a danger that some House affiliated with either Chisholm or Lindum may see action against her as a way to build favour with either of you."

"Where is she now?" William demanded, looking around as if he might spot her in a corner of the room.

"She's on my lands, and well-guarded," Neville told him. "She's safe enough from Assassins. But that's not the point. She's not safe from whoever commissioned this contract and there is still the issue of who substituted the other child's body and why."

Gabriel interrupted at that point. "I'm satisfied that the issue of the other body is merely a red herring and not relevant. I'm not at liberty to say more. We need to concentrate on who wants her dead."

Neville looked at him, eyes wide and brows raised, but Gabriel held his gaze and Neville silently accepted his word.

"Was the incident at Eastern directed at her?" Leon asked, breaking into their silent communication.

"We don't think so," Lady Anna-chesska said quickly. "Her presence was not expected; indeed quite the opposite. I do not think those responsible had any connection with this. Everything suggests they are simply a militant anti-adept group." She shrugged. "Of course, they could be manipulated by others, but there is no evidence of that."

"So we can rule that out as a red herring, too," Leon confirmed. "I will say that I have never wanted her dead. She makes matters complicated, but I would never want that and will not support any within my House or allegiances who does." He looked around the room to emphasis the point. "Not that there aren't plenty who do," he conceded.

William agreed with him. "I won't deny that I was relieved to hear of her death, when we thought the child was her. It would be convenient if she hadn't been found. But I never sought harm to her. If this comes from within my House, or my underlords it is not with my blessing."

Neville leapt on their clear alignment. "Can we agree that you will both make public the fact that she is under your protection? That you will take action – together – against anyone who harms her?"

Again, agreement.

Later, as the attendees left what Gabriel considered a highly successful meeting, he offered up a quick prayer of thanks, and then realised he had one more issue to deal with.

"Neville," he called, and Neville turned back towards him. "Someone will need to tell Prospero and Leonie about Leonie's heritage and how she needs to choose her House allegiance."

Neville nodded. "I'll do that. I need to meet with Perry anyway and it'll be a lot sooner than you'll see them."

Of course, that meant that Gabriel had to confess to Neville about blocking Prospero's memory.

"It'll come back as soon as you start to tell him," he warned Neville. "He'll be furious about it and what I kept from him."

Neville grinned. "Don't you worry, I can handle Perry."

***

The pageantry started with the first service of the morning. Each House brought its colours – its House flag or banner – to the Abbey to be blessed. They might have come to St Peter's incognito with those banners furled and stored, but they'd each brought them, all the same. The historic purpose of such colours, from ancient times, way before the Devastation, was to form a rallying point for troops, a way to identify and locate your side. Gabriel supposed their resurrection in modern times showed their enduring practicality for that purpose.

James and Edmund led the procession into the Abbey as flag bearers. No one seemed quite sure whether this was promotion or demotion, punishment or reward for their actions but the two of them were smiling as they did so, flagpoles held out in front of them, angled so the full banner was revealed. Until that point, seeing them side by side, Gabriel had never realised just how similar their House logos were. Of course, they hadn't hung or been seen together in generations, so perhaps that was understandable. Both were the same flower but Chisholm's was drawn as an outline, black lines on a white background. The Lindum flag had a white background too, the flower formed from solid blocks of red with no outline. Really, they could be superimposed to make one flag.

James and Edmund were followed by Leon and William, walking together, then Lilyrose with the banner of Tennant, partnered by young Simeon, hastily roped in from the Settlers to carry Merchant Ethan's colours. Simeon managed to look both nervous – understandable given the company he was in – and so proud he could burst at the same time. Interestingly, those colours were for the Traders as a whole, unadorned by the additional insignia of Ethan's caravan. Finally came Ethan himself and Neville.

Each flag bearer knelt, turning their flagpole horizontally across their body to present it to Brother Richard, before moving to make space for the next. Richard accepted the banners and laid them in turn across the altar table in front of Gabriel. Once all had been received, flag bearers and High Lords alike all knelt before the altar table – stiffly, in the case of Leon and William, with the fluidity of youth for Lilyrose and Simeon. As he stretched his hands forward to bless both people and banners and the Houses they represented, Gabriel wondered if they knew or understood the symbolism of what they were doing.

It didn't matter, he decided. Presenting their colours like this symbolised submission to a higher authority – in this case, God, and God certainly knew. And when Richard lifted their colours and returned them, that was commissioning each to go forward with whatever mission the higher authority had for them. Whether they knew it or not, God was using these people to further his purpose.

And then the departure, after breakfast, all gathered outside the main door of the Abbey, a moment in history to remember. Lindum, Chisholm, Tennant and Merchant Ethan were to ride together across St Peter's lands to Taylor House. From there they would travel across Lindum lands to Chisholm and symbolically on into Chisholm territory. After that, the party would split, each to their own homes, but with plans to meet again to work on the peace treaty and make arrangements for formal visits.

Several groups developed – James and Edmund laughing and still brimming with the euphoria of burdens put down, communicating itself to their mounts who were prancing, the House colours rippling above them in the breeze. Lilyrose and Simeon were near them, and only slightly calmer with their banners, though in Lilyrose's case it was natural exuberance and in Simeon's, nervousness. A more sedate group had formed with the High Lords and Merchant Ethan, their horses standing calmly as they mounted and passed last minute instructions to their staff. And a larger, more widely spread group of those extra staff and guards each High Lord had brought with them, Lindum and Chisholm, each eyeing the other warily and separated by Tennant. It would take time for them to come to know and trust each other, no matter what their High Lords ordered.

When everyone was mounted and ready, guards in place, horses stilled, all turned towards Gabriel who lifted his hands in final blessing. James and Edmund wheeled to lead the way, flanked by Lilyrose and Simeon, in a clattering of hooves and a clanging of harness, leaving behind a silence almost bigger than their presence.

Eleanor appeared quietly at Gabriel's side. "We did it," she whispered. "Well done. The world is changing."

Chapter 24

Mid July

Perry

For Perry, the days at Deep River were reminiscent of those never-ending happy summers of childhood. Not the uncomplicated happiness of just a few weeks earlier, but a more intense feeling, framed by the knowledge that it could be torn away from him at any moment. Every morning, he'd start work as enthusiastically as any of his brothers, and then slow down as he kept looking out for Leonie. Sometimes she'd be running, as eager to reach him as he was for her arrival, Amber flitting around her feet. Other times, she'd be ambling along lazily, her thoughts drifting, with Amber bounding ahead.

Each day, he couldn't wait to greet her, dropping his tools and hurrying towards her as soon as he spotted her. He'd reach out to touch her, almost afraid she was a mirage, and then pull her close, smelling the sunshine on her hair, stroking the warmth of her skin. Matt teased him mercilessly, the twins ignored them, and Jonny shook his head and sighed dramatically. Sam was silent, watching them with a look that said Lizzie had told him everything.

In the afternoons, Perry would listen out for the distinctive sound of her feet on the stairs as she passed his consulting room on the way to the roof garden. Once free of that particular patient, he'd be unable to concentrate on the next until he found Leonie in the garden or still room, her skin now scented with whichever herbs she was using.

Today he slipped his arms round her from behind, nuzzling her neck. "You smell of outdoors and sunshine and happiness."

"Get back to your patients," she said but she turned in his arms to kiss him, sliding her hands round his neck and into his hair.

"I've only got a couple more to see," he said. "How long will you be?"

"No longer than you, if you get a move on," she replied, but she was smiling as she sent him back to his work.

He hummed happily to himself under his breath as he ran back down the stairs, counting days in his head. They were more than a third of the way through the first one hundred days since the accident. Leonie was doing so well. Could he dare to hope that she now had more chance of recovery than not?

Once he'd finished the clinic they walked down to the lake, hand in hand, to meet Jonny and Emlee. Leonie danced along, in time to the music that was still running through Perry's head. Jonny and Emlee were there already, engaged in Jonny's favourite pastime of skimming stones across the lake but they turned and came quickly across the beach.

They sat, the younger three making a loose semi-circle facing Perry, Emlee in the middle and Leonie slowly inching closer to Perry. Jonny leaned forward, eager to participate but both girls slouched, looking at the ground and running the sand through their fingers. Perry reached for his bag and brought out about a dozen soft fabric cubes which he placed in the middle of the circle.

Emlee looked up. "They're like the bricks my baby brother plays with!"

"I suppose they are," he said. "They're also very good for practising telekinesis."

"Girls can't do that," she protested. "I can't."

"Maybe, maybe not," he replied. Beside him, Leonie was slouching further, not looking up, apparently concentrating on the sand still running through her fingers. He looked away from her and carried on. "It's perfectly possible for girls to be Gifted in telekinesis, even if it's rare. Leonie was and I think it's likely she will be again." Out of the corner of his eye he spotted Leonie drop the sand and straighten up. "You can only find out by trying, and we're beginning to think that just trying makes your mind more receptive to it and more likely to succeed. And if not, just making the effort will help strengthen your other Gifts."

He slid towards Leonie, wrapping an arm around her, pulling her close to him as he spoke. "Now, Jonny, I know you're good at this, so you should practise precision and accuracy. Try to see how tall a tower you can build with these blocks. Emlee, pick one and try to move it. In a moment, I'll watch you and be able to see how close you are to succeeding."

He turned his attention to Leonie. He'd brought her to Deep River in part to get her away from those who would remind her of all the skills she'd lost; now he worried that working with Jonny and Emlee was doing the opposite. He twisted his mind into hers just as he wrapped his arms round her, moving to sit behind her, his head beside hers, looking over her shoulder. He whispered in her ear. "It's going to be okay, you know. And you don't have to do this if you don't feel up to it."

"'M okay," she said. "I just can't do it."

"Try, please? For me?"

He felt her try, sensed the activity in her mind like a flame trying to travel along a broken fuse. "So close," he said. "You're nearly there, believe me. Go on trying while I just check on Emlee."

He kept his mind twisted into Leonie's while he touched

Emlee's mind. Here again he could see the activity like a travelling flame. "You're nearly there, too," he told Emlee. "A few more sessions and you'll be moving the blocks."

An explosion of colour hit his mind, blocking his physical vision. Instinctively he jerked his contact away from Emlee and created a tight mental Shield around himself and Leonie. When he was able to open his eyes, just a couple of seconds later, Jonny and Emlee were both staring at him, eyes wide and mouths open in horror.

"You both okay?" he asked.

They both nodded but he brushed a flicker of his mind across theirs anyway to be sure, even as he turned most of it towards Leonie. She was limp in his lap, eyes closed. As he reached to search her mind a Shield snapped down, cutting him off.

No, no, no. Not this.

He forced himself to remain calm. "Emlee," he said, his voice trembling a little with the effort. "You're the fastest. I need you to go back to the farm and warn them." He fished in his pocket. "Here, take these keys. Tell Ma what's happened and tell her to get my drug chest out – she knows where it is. I need her to find the strongest liquid pain killer I've got, and a syringe. Okay?"

Emlee looked at him with wide, scared eyes and he knew he needed to reassure her.

"It's going to be okay," he said, far more certainly than he felt.

She nodded and set off running.

He turned to Jonny. "I need you to hold Leonie. I know what to do, but I need someone else to hold her."

Jonny nodded, his eyes almost as wide and scared as Emlee's had been, but he moved to take Perry's place behind Leonie's limp body. "What's happened?" he asked, finding his voice at last.

Perry took a deep breath. "When you practice your Gifts, your brain develops and strengthens the connections that allow you to use them. Leonie's brain has grown them too fast and they've kind of short circuited and created a Shield. She's stuck one side of it and we're the other."

"Does that happen often?" Jonny asked, fear seemingly turning to curiosity.

Perry shook his head. "I've only ever seen it once before. But don't worry, I know what to do."

That was almost true anyway. He knew the theory. And that he had to act fast. Faster than they could have got to the hospital even if they'd been at House St Peter.

"All I have to do," he said to Jonny, trying to sound reassuring, "is break the Shield from outside."

"Is that even possible?" asked Jonny. "Will it hurt?"

"Yes, it's possible. It won't hurt when I do it, but it will start to hurt later. Leonie'll ache everywhere and probably run a temperature. We've got a very difficult couple of days ahead."

And that was an understatement but he pushed the subsequent thoughts away to concentrate on the here and now. "Ready?" he asked.

Jonny nodded. Perry reached towards Leonie's mind and almost laughed out loud with relief. The sooner you act, the easier it is, he'd been told and that was certainly true. And maybe it helped that Leonie couldn't shield strongly yet, or that his own mind had been partly linked with hers when it happened. He could see exactly what he needed to do. With his mind he pushed *this* way, then twisted like *that*. The Shield shattered. Leonie sat up abruptly, pulled free of Jonny's arms, and threw herself against Perry. He caught her, buried his face in her hair and held her close for a moment.

Then he was all medical urgency, checking her pulse, her breathing, her temperature. "Talk to me," he said. "How do you feel? Do you hurt anywhere?"

"I'm okay," she replied. "I was stuck but you found me. I don't hurt."

Now his urgency translated itself to movement as he stood up and pulled her to her feet, an open mouthed Jonny following their example.

"Come on," Perry said. "We need to get home."

Chapter 25

The Next Morning

Leonie

I was walking down to the lake with Perry. I could feel the sunshine on my face, and hear the music in his head. Then I was in my own bed, the early dawn light just creeping through the curtains. I could feel Perry in the next room and I had to get to him, so I lunged across the bed and through the door. He was asleep, sprawled out on the couch and I squatted by him, staring at his face.

"Don't wake him," Ma said behind me. "He needs to rest. He's been watching you half the night."

I turned and stared at her. What did she mean? Why would he be watching me? Why was he asleep on the sofa and not in our bed? I shrugged. It didn't matter. If Ma said he needed rest and not to wake him, then I would obey that, and I would protect him from anyone else. I climbed onto the chair opposite and sat there to watch him.

Each time someone approached, I growled at them and lunged towards them. I didn't need to do more; they backed away. I couldn't let them near in case they woke Perry. Hot and cold fire was licking across my skin but that didn't matter because Perry needed me to protect him. Eventually he opened his eyes and then he was instantly awake and in front of me, pulling me up into his arms. "Leonie," he said. "You should have woken me. You're too hot."

His arms touched my back and I flinched as the fire intensified. He spun me around, pulling my robe off my shoulders. "Oh, Leonie," he said, his voice was full of pain and sympathy.

He pushed me towards the bedroom, taking my robe from me and making me lie on my front on the bed. Gently he spread something on my skin; it was thick and cool and the fire disappeared as he touched me. He was singing quietly, too, so I closed my eyes and listened. As the fire went away, I slept. And I dreamt.

Perry

As soon as he was sure Leonie was asleep, Perry turned towards Lizzie who was standing by the bedroom door. "You should have woken me," he said, his voice reproachful.

"I couldn't," Lizzie replied. "Ma told her not to wake you, so she chose to guard you. I couldn't get near."

"No, I don't suppose you could," Perry agreed resignedly. "The fever will be confusing her, and when she gets like this she has difficulty remembering our language so she wouldn't have understood you anyway. I just feel bad she's suffered because I was asleep."

"Is that rash on her skin some sort of allergic reaction?" Lizzie asked.

"She reacts to practically everything," he said, unable to keep the frustration out of his voice. "This must be to what I gave her to ease the pain and her temperature and help her sleep. There seems to be more and more stuff I can't use. At least this cream seems to be working."

"You were singing to her, to calm her down. Sam does that with frightened animals."

"I know," Perry said, feeling a little embarrassed. "As well as singing and talking to them he radiates calm and reassurance. I found myself trying it with Leonie once and it works, so I keep doing it when I need to."

"Pa said Leonie was a bit like a wild animal. She's totally devoted to you and she just tolerates the rest of us for your sake." Lizzie lifted her hand to her mouth, clearly regretting what she'd said, but Perry grinned at her. "He's said that to me, too. But he's wrong. It might have been like that right at the beginning, but now she loves everyone here for their own sake, not mine."

"We love her, too, you know, not just as your wife."

"I know, and so does she. She's just not used to it, that's all."

"What happens now?" Lizzie gestured at Leonie.

"Ideally? Textbook? The worst of the pain should be over. For the next twenty-four hours she should sleep a lot, her mind will be working on repairing itself and her temperature should come right down. In about twelve hours it should be close to normal, and within a couple of days she'll be fine." He paused, and then decided Lizzie at least should have the full story. "On the other hand, if her temperature doesn't come down, or worse still, rises over the next few hours, that's a sign that her mind and body aren't coping with what's happened. There's a couple of drugs I could try then, but my options are getting more and more limited and they can have nasty side effects. I don't want to use them until I have to."

"But they will definitely work?"

Perry shook his head. "Not necessarily. Sometimes they do, sometimes not."

"And if they don't?"

Perry looked at her steadily and spoke very evenly. "If Leonie can't pull through on her own, and if the drugs don't work, then we've run out of time."

"Oh, Perry," she said, lost for words.

"We're not there yet," he said as much for himself as to reassure her.

He checked Leonie's temperature every hour. Each time it rose. He resisted the temptation to fling the thermometer across the room in frustration and placed it back in his case. It was far too soon to use any drugs. He opened doors and windows to get a cool breeze across the room, and looked up as his mother came into the bedroom.

"Lizzie had to leave," she said. "I came to see if I could help."

"Towels, Ma," he replied. "I need cold, damp towels and ice. Have you got ice? Lots of ice?"

She nodded then left again, before returning just a few moments later with a pile of towels and a tub of ice. Together they wrapped the ice and placed it around Leonie, attempting to cool her down. He checked her temperature again and shook his head. "Down a little, but not enough," he said. "At best we're just reducing symptoms. It's not really getting to the root of the problem and there's nothing else I can do."

Ma patted his arm. "You're doing the best you can. That's all you can do."

"Do I give her medication or not?" he asked, voicing the thoughts that had been tormenting him. "She'll recover best if she can manage without. If I give it too soon, the side effects can be terrible and delay her recovery. If I leave it too late, it won't work."

"Relax," Ma said. "You'll know when it becomes necessary, if it does. If you aren't sure, don't do it. Now, just stay with her and I'll be back shortly."

He nodded and turned back to Leonie. She was fitful and restless, drifting in and out of sleep, struggling to understand what was happening and unable to communicate easily how she felt. He sat beside her on the bed and she crawled up onto his lap. "Perry," she whispered. "Make it better."

"I can't," he told her. "I'm sorry. There's nothing I can do, yet, that won't make things worse. You've got to fight this off for yourself."

He didn't know whether she'd understood, but she nodded, closed her eyes and curled her body into his. He held her like that, letting her sleep – peacefully for now – in his arms, undisturbed, although he could feel her temperature rising again. He stroked her head, hoping against hope that they weren't approaching the end and trying to pray.

His mother came back in and sat beside the bed. "It's not looking so good, is it?" she asked.

"No," he agreed. "Not right now, it's not."

They sat in silence for a while before he spoke again. "I held her like this, just a few weeks ago, a couple of days after the accident. It was touch and go whether she'd live or die then."

"She fought to live, then, or you'd not be here now."

"I know. I love her so much, I want her to live, I don't want to be without her. But am I doing the right thing? Should I be fighting to keep her alive, when really she should die? Knowing when to stop treatment's important too."

"I think you're doing the right thing. Giving her every chance to live," Ma stated.

"Did you ever think about Lazarus? Jesus raised him from

the dead. Do you think he was pleased, or really annoyed about being deprived of getting to heaven earlier? Am I depriving Leonie?"

Ma smiled. "I've never thought of Lazarus being annoyed," she said. Her smile dropped and her voice became more serious, "I'm pretty sure Leonie's idea of heaven is being with you. Besides, she doesn't want to die and she doesn't intend to. She told me that the other day, the first time we came up to the field, where you were harvesting."

That encouraged Perry. "Did she? I didn't know that. I didn't know she thought she still might die."

"No, you've both been keeping quiet about that, to protect each other I suspect," Ma continued. "Last time, how did you help her, what did you do?"

"I talked to her. I told her how much I love her, I told her of all our plans for the future, about coming here, meeting everyone, all the things we'd do together, having children…" His voice broke and he couldn't carry on.

Ma stood up and rested her hand on his shoulder. "Why not try that again? It worked before."

Quietly, she slipped from the room. It took a few moments before Perry could find his voice again, but then he started talking to Leonie softly, just as he had before.

"Perry," she said sleepily in response, trying to lift her head.

"It's okay," he told her. "Stay asleep, it's good for you. I'll be here."

She settled more comfortably against him and, as far as he could tell, continued to sleep peacefully. He was almost sure that, even if it wasn't dropping, at least her temperature had stopped rising. He decided to let her sleep for a couple of hours. She was quieter, not so restless, her skin less flushed. He hoped that meant she was winning, that she was recovering.

An hour later, she started mumbling without waking. She thrashed and turned on the bed, her skin flushed again and sweat coating her face. She opened her eyes, sat up and lunged for him, clinging to his arm, clearly terrified and trying to tell him something he just wasn't getting. She pointed around the room and then spoke carefully, putting all her effort and energy into forming the word. *"Them."*

Suddenly, he understood. "You saw the Them. You were asleep, dreaming."

She shook her head. "Now."

"You can see Them now?"

She nodded.

"They're not really here," he told her gently. "You're imagining things." He could tell she didn't believe him. "That does it," he said. "You're terrified. I'm not having that. We're going to go into the other room and get something to make you feel better. The Them won't follow us."

She came with him, willingly enough, but refused to let go of him as he tried to sit her down while he prepared the medication. At that moment, Jonny opened the main door. "Pastor Thomas is here," he said and disappeared, leaving Thomas standing on the threshold.

"I'm sorry," said Thomas, looking round hesitantly. "Is this a bad time? Only I bumped into Lizzie and she said Leonie wasn't well and I came to see if there was anything I could do?"

"It's no worse time than any other," Perry told him with a sigh. "If I can get Leonie to sit down I'm just going to give her something to help her."

"Perhaps I can help then," Thomas said. He looked at Leonie. "Come and sit by me, child, while Perry gets what he needs."

Leonie stared at him so intently that Perry wondered who, or possibly what, she was seeing. To his surprise, she released her grip on his hand and sat down quietly beside Thomas, whilst Perry studied the options he had for treating her. There were three possibilities; the best he ruled out because he knew she would react badly to one of the components. As for the other two, it was a question of which side effects would be the least worst. He picked one, prepared the dose and took it back to Leonie.

Perry hadn't been able to make out the words, but Thomas had been speaking quietly to her and she certainly seemed calmer. He took her arm to inject the dose, prepared to hold her with his mind if necessary but she stayed still and calm. Once done, he sat down beside her and she climbed onto his lap resting her head on his shoulder.

"Would you like me to pray for you now?" Thomas asked.

Leonie lifted her head a little and nodded, before settling back down. Perry found the time of prayer reassuring and comforting. As Thomas finished, Leonie started to shake and shiver.

"Shall I fetch her a blanket?" Thomas asked.

"No," said Perry both relieved and thankful. "Not yet, thanks. This is the drug starting to work. It's going to work. She's finally cooling down."

Ma came through the door, carrying a tray of tea and cakes.

"I'm so sorry, Thomas," she said. "Jonny only just told me you were here."

Thomas smiled. "There's no need to apologise. And thank you for the tea."

"Ma," Perry said, his voice jubilant. "It's working. The drugs are working. She's going to be okay."

Ma just smiled at him. "See," she said, "I told you so. I said you'd know when to use them." She turned back to Thomas. "Would you like to stay for dinner? It won't be that long."

"That's a very kind offer, Mary," he replied. "But I suspect Perry hasn't eaten properly while Leonie has been ill – through no fault of yours, I'm sure. Why don't I sit with Leonie while you all eat, and I'll get something later?"

Ma accepted his offer before Perry could decline it. Outmanoeuvred, Perry agreed gracefully, knowing that Leonie was now likely to sleep for at least twelve hours if not longer. Ma left him and Thomas chatting for the time being, Perry wanting to hold the sleeping Leonie for as long as he could. Curious, he asked Thomas what he'd been saying to Leonie.

Thomas smiled a little. "I thought I heard her use a couple of Trader words," he said. "I know a little Trader – well some Bible passages, a couple of Psalms – so I was just reciting those. Does she speak Trader?"

Perry nodded. "She's fluent in it, but it's not her mother tongue. When she's sick or stressed she has difficulty with this language, I hadn't thought to try Trader – well, actually I don't speak it well enough for it to be useful."

"So what is her first language?"

"I don't know. I don't recognise it, but then languages

aren't really my thing. We hadn't got round to tracking it down properly. Even she doesn't know where she comes from, so that's no help."

Chapter 26

Leonie

The early morning light crept through the curtains as I stretched and opened my eyes. My head felt clear and as though the strands of my mind were finally weaving back into place. I scanned the house; everyone was still asleep or just starting to stir. I sat up carefully, so as not to disturb Perry who was asleep beside me and tried to work out what day it was.

I remembered being by the lake with Jonny and Emlee, attempting to move blocks with telekinesis. That had been late afternoon. We hadn't made home before my whole body had started aching and hurting. Walking had become so painful Perry had picked me up and carried me. Then the next thing I remembered was waking to find him asleep on the couch. That had been early morning, so I guessed that was the morning after we'd been at the lake. But this couldn't be the same morning so it must be the next day.

I had all sorts of hazy memories and I wasn't sure what order they'd happened in. I'd known that as long as I held on to Perry, as long as I could touch him, then I'd be safe. But I was sure Perry had told me I'd had to fight someone and that didn't make sense. There'd been bandits attacking our caravan – no, that must have been a dream of Trader times. Katya's voice, talking to me, reciting words and poetry, had to have been a dream too but it seemed so real it could have happened yesterday.

And Lord Gabriel had been here. He'd told me to sit quietly and let Perry do whatever he had to, which of course I'd obeyed. I remembered that clearly – but surely he'd have been far too busy to come here? He certainly wasn't here now, or I'd have spotted him when I'd scanned the house. As I puzzled over all of this, Perry opened his eyes and then reached to touch me.

"Leonie," he said. "Your skin's cool. How do you feel?"

I started to say that I felt fine, and that I was just thinking that he looked pretty hot, but he'd raised himself on one arm and turned to pick up the thermometer and his blood pressure machine. I submitted to his actions, knowing he'd feel much better with facts and figures to confirm how I was.

"Excellent," he said, smiling widely as he put the equipment down again. "Come here." He pulled me down so we were lying with our arms around each other. "I was so worried about you," he continued quietly, stroking my face and hair. "I thought you might die. I can't face the thought of being without you."

I wriggled so that I could take his face in my hands, and in the process he ended up on top of me, braced on his elbows either side of me.

"I'm not going to die," I told him softly.

"You'd better not," he said and buried his face in my neck, trying to regain control of his emotions.

His shoulders were shaking so I just held him, stroking his back until he lifted his head. Despite his distress, the feel of his body over mine, his skin touching mine, sent shivers of desire through me. I slid one foot along his calf and over his thigh until my leg was wrapped around him. Then I delicately touched his mind with mine at the same time as my lips touched his. He responded eagerly and then pulled back. "No, Leonie, you were so sick yesterday," he protested.

I ignored his protests and ran my fingers into his hair and down his neck, as far along his spine as I could reach. He shivered with pleasure and I knew he wouldn't be able to say no to me.

***

Afterwards, we lay wrapped together, the early light still coming through the curtains, and listened to the faintest sounds of the farmyard just starting to awake.

"You," Perry said, "sometimes use sex to make us both forget our worries and feel better."

"So?" I asked sleepily against his chest. "It works."

"Yes, it does," he said frowning, "But when I... I got in such a mess, before, doing that."

"Well, yes," I yawned. "But that's because it wasn't with me."

That made him laugh and he pulled me closer and rested his cheek on the top of my head. "Very true," he agreed.

"And anyway," I told him, sleep making me relaxed and incautious, "that was about you running away. This is about us helping each other."

"True again," he said slowly. He might have gone on but I yawned again, all but asleep. "Sleep well, my wildcat," he said, and – for once – I obeyed him.

***

Next time I woke, Perry was gone. A quick search told me he was in the kitchen and Jonny was in the next room. I climbed out of bed, grabbed a robe and went out to investigate.

"Hi," Jonny said. "You look a lot better. I thought you were going to die."

"I'm not going to die, not yet," I told him. "Why does everyone keep thinking I'm going to?"

He grinned. "You didn't see the way you looked day before yesterday. Or yesterday for that matter."

Maybe he had a point. I dismissed that. "Anyway, where is everyone?"

"Ma insisted Perry have some breakfast. And he said you wouldn't be interested in food today, the smell might even make you feel sick so he went to eat in the kitchen rather than here. So I said I'd stay here in case you woke and needed anything."

"I don't need anything," I said. "I feel fine."

But he was right about food. Even the thought made me feel a little queasy. To distract myself, I picked up one of Perry's soft blocks – they were sitting in a pile on the table – and threw it at Jonny. He caught it and threw it back, and this time I caught it.

"You know you did that without using your hands, don't you?" Jonny asked.

I looked at him in amazement. I just hadn't thought about it. "I did, didn't I?" I said happily and picked up a whole bunch more to throw at him.

The whole thing degenerated into a sort of indoor snowball fight. We both used hands or telekinesis, whichever was more convenient, and jumped on, over and hid behind the furniture, laughing like crazy. We must have made a lot of noise because Perry and Ma appeared in the doorway, Jonny and I ducking down behind the arm of the sofa, giggling nervously. Perry looked so serious that I grabbed for a handful of blocks – mentally, they were too far away to actually reach with my hands – and threw them at him.

"Enough," he said and stopped them all mid-flight, holding them there in mid-air.

I sometimes forgot how strong and impressive his Gifts really were because he didn't use them to their full extent very often. Without even looking he directed the blocks back to the table, arranging them in a neat and tidy pile. I challenged him for control of one of them but I lost. He didn't even waver in his control of the others.

"I said enough. You're not strong enough for that," he said coming towards me.

"Yet," I told him defiantly. "But I will be."

He put his arms around me, and placed his mouth by my ear. "I'm looking forward to it," he whispered, his voice full of both happiness and hope.

Ma couldn't have heard him because she spoke from the doorway. "Come on, Perry," she said. "You saw what they were doing. Isn't that something to be happy about? Wasn't it worth the last couple of days for Leonie to be able to do this today?"

He turned back towards her, keeping me in his arms. Now he was all smiles. "Definitely," he said. "But I'd still rather it wasn't all quite so dramatic, quite so risky."

I tugged at his sleeve and he turned back to me. "I'm sorry, Perry. Really I am. I didn't mean to worry you."

"It's okay," he said. "None of this is your fault. Never think that. What you did was right."

But it was my fault, really, wasn't it? I'd chosen to do what I did, expecting to pay the price myself, willing to do that, accepting it. I'd expected to die, and to leave behind all I loved. I had known Perry would suffer, but he'd chosen that too, knowingly, when he'd told me how to do what I did.

And then I hadn't died and I hadn't paid the price and now it seemed it would be paid, at least in part, by the suffering of so many of those I now cared for. My actions had consequences for them, consequences they hadn't chosen, a price they hadn't agreed to pay. And they'd accepted that, willingly, because they loved me. That thought alone was almost too much for me.

When I'd acted at House Eastern I'd done so for that moment alone. I hadn't thought about the future. Now the reaction was spreading out like ripples in a pond, beyond my control, beyond my ability to take the consequences, which were reaching so many other people. How could I make choices, take responsibility for my actions, when I didn't know what the consequences could be?

Chapter 27

Late July

Perry

"Are we still going ahead with your wedding?" Chrissy asked, out of the blue.

Perry looked up sharply from his meal. How could he have forgotten about the plans for their second wedding this summer? The whole point was so that his family could be there, having missed the original service. He glanced at Leonie, who had dropped her cutlery and was staring at Chrissy wide eyed, hand to her mouth.

"Only, we'd planned it for the middle of next month, and everything is still in place," Chrissy continued.

This might be just what Leonie needed. She'd recovered quickly from what happened at the lake but she'd seemed a little subdued...no, more preoccupied. It was nothing he'd been able to put his finger on, nothing she'd been able to explain, nothing he could see in her mind, and it worried him slightly because he didn't know quite what it was or how to deal with it. A distraction could be just the answer. He smiled at Chrissy. "I think that would be great," he said. "Don't you, Leonie?"

She nodded enthusiastically, but then her brow creased. "Only I didn't bring my wedding dress," she said, her voice sad.

"You can have a new one," Ma said from the far end of the table.

Leonie looked round at her, shaking her head. "A different one wouldn't feel right."

Perry hastened to reassure her. "Don't worry. I'll phone Chloe tomorrow, from the surgery. She'll have it here within a couple of days." And then to distract her a little he said, "I thought some of the buttons went missing anyway?"

"Oh, no," Leonie said innocently. "Edward gave me some replacements and I mended it."

He pretended to hold his head in his hands. "I suppose you told him why you needed them?" He knew he hadn't needed to say that.

"Of course," she said. "But he guessed anyway."

And then she looked at his mother – his mother! – and said, still with her best innocent look, "It has lots of little buttons down the back and Perry can be terribly impatient."

Everyone round the table burst out laughing, and even Perry had to smile, although he also shook his head and buried his face back in his hands, knowing he was blushing. When he looked back up, Leonie had turned the innocent look on him and he became absolutely convinced she was back to her normal self.

***

Leonie was dancing along beside him the next morning as they crossed the yard to the house on their way back from the fields, full of plans for their day. Ted, who delivered the post, was at the door as they reached it, talking to Ma. He grinned at Perry. "Your Ma doesn't get nearly so many letters with you here," he said. "But there's one for you today."

He handed over the thick formally addressed envelope before making his goodbyes. Perry twisted the envelope back and forward in his fingers, sure he recognised the handwriting and reluctant to open it. Leonie was far more curious. "Go on, open it. What is it? Tell me!"

He slid his finger into the envelope and pulled the contents out, unfolding them where Leonie could see too. An invitation – or was it a command? – to visit Lord Neville at Castle Tennant. Despite all the reassurances he had been given by Lord Gabriel, he found himself hesitant, very reluctant to obey. "You still need to sleep so much," he told Leonie. "I don't think you're strong enough yet."

"Am too," she said, with one of those defiant but innocent looks he'd learnt to associate with trouble. "It's not far. And I'm sure I'll be able to rest if I need to. You're just trying to put off going."

His mother looked over Leonie's shoulder at the formal invitation, written on heavy cream paper. "One way or another," she said, "I think we're going to have to invite Neville to this wedding. So it would be best if you met with him and sorted things out before that."

He stared at his mother, speechless. She thought they should go? She was going to invite Uncle Neville to the wedding? Despite the decades' old rift between them? Then he caught sight of his father, standing behind his mother, winking at Leonie from where Ma couldn't see. Figuring he wasn't going to win now, he gave in. "Okay then," he said to Leonie. "But we'll go by train. You're certainly not strong enough to ride over, and camp out on the way like I used to."

Leonie grinned at him, her eyes dancing with mischief and excitement. "I like trains," she said. Then her face fell a little. "What do I take? What do I wear?"

He shrugged, smiling to himself. Were women all the same when it came to clothes? "It doesn't matter," he said. "Much the same as we wear here. If we were going to need anything formal, he'd have said."

Leonie looked at him doubtfully, then dragged Ma off to

their room for better advice.

Leonie

I decided not to challenge Perry on his reluctance to visit Lord Neville until we were on the train and he could no longer get out of it. Once the train had left the station I turned towards him. "So," I said. "You don't want to go and see Lord Neville, do you?" I didn't give him a chance to come up with an excuse. "And don't tell me you do, because I know perfectly well you don't. And I want the real reason not some half-truth you think you can get away with."

He sighed. "Uncle Neville is my High Lord, and I am his heir. One of them, at least. When we meet, I have to bow to him, acknowledge him as my overlord. And that means I'm saying that he was right, what I did was wrong, joining the Order. And I'm not sure I can."

I thought about that for a moment. "Can't different somethings be right at different times?" I asked. "Like it can still be right to have joined the Order then, and right to bow now? Just because one thing becomes right, it doesn't make a past thing wrong."

He smiled at me. "You always make me look at things differently," he said. "Thank you. That helps."

But now I had another worry. "Do I have to bow to Lord Neville?" I asked.

"No," Perry said. "I don't think you count as an adult."

"I'm not a child," I retorted automatically, glaring at him.

Perry smiled. "Oh, I know," he agreed with a wicked smile. "And here in Tennant, you're an adult at sixteen anyway, whatever

Ma thinks. But, despite being married to me, you belong to House St Peter. And because you were adopted by them before you were eighteen, as far as House allegiance and High Lords are concerned you're not an adult until you're twenty one."

"That's not fair."

"It is what it is," he said. "Different Houses have different policies and they each respect the others' rules. But it means you don't have to bow to Lord Neville."

I wasn't sure how I felt about that but Perry had said something else that intrigued me. "What do you mean about what Ma thinks?" I asked.

"Ma's mother died when Ma was about two and her elder sister Elise, who must have been in her early teens, took over mothering her. But Elise married around seventeen or eighteen and died young, in childbirth. Ma felt abandoned, both by her own mother and by Elise. If Elise had been considered a child until she was twenty one or even older, she'd have still been around for Ma, and probably wouldn't have died so young. So Ma has strong views on not marrying young which she made sure we were all very well aware of. And I think she blames Uncle Neville for arranging the marriage, too."

"Is that why Sam and Matt have waited to get married?"

"Probably," Perry agreed. "Though she seems to have made an exception for you."

I was sure that had far less to do with me than the fact that our marriage meant Ma had Perry back.

***

It wasn't a long journey to Castle Tennant and Brin was waiting for us at the station. I vaguely remembered Brin meeting us last time we arrived here. That seemed a very long time ago now, although really it was just a few weeks.

"Hi, Brin," Perry said, and they clasped forearms and clapped each other on the back. Then Brin turned towards me and bowed. "My Lady Leonie," he said. "Welcome back to Castle Tennant." He straightened up and was silent, staring at Perry.

I was puzzled for a moment – was I supposed to say something? Then I realised Brin and Perry were using hand and body symbols to communicate – and I understood them. I'd used them when I was on guard duty with the Traders. And I knew there was one gesture that could mean 'Please may I comment on what you're talking about?' or 'If you don't shut up and let me speak I'll come over there and make you', depending on exactly how you used it. I used that one to see what would happen. I may have – inadvertently, of course – used the stronger version.

It was worth it for the effect. Both Brin and Perry turned towards me, mouths dropping open. I shuffled slightly behind Perry in confusion. I'd acted impulsively and not really expected such a strong reaction.

"No, I didn't," said Perry out loud.

Suddenly I realised the other element of their communication. Perry was a telepath even if Brin wasn't and there was a way to use that. Brin would think what he wanted to say and Perry could read it in the top of his mind. Right now Brin's thoughts were written across his face – he'd just accused Perry of teaching me their hand signals.

Understanding how I was feeling, Perry pulled me closer to him, his arm around me, although that also had the effect of bringing me forward from my sheltered place a little behind him. He looked at me, brows arched in a question but I answered before he could speak, looking back and forth between him and Brin,

"I've done my share of guard duty. It's much the same," I said.

It was clear Brin was now thinking I was too small, too delicate, not a chance I'd be a guard. Perry turned to Brin, grinning at him. "I wouldn't want to be on the wrong side of Leonie," he said. "She's a lot more dangerous than she looks."

Some time, and soon, I planned to find an opportunity to teach Brin the error of his thoughts.

"Anyway," I said, tugging at Perry's arm to get his attention, "you were talking about things that affect me without including me. How many times do I have to tell you? That's not on."

"I'm sorry," he said. "We were just discussing the safest method of transport from here to the castle."

Now I remembered Brin had been there as a bodyguard when we'd first arrived.

"Is it dangerous? Are we in danger here from something?"

"I'm not worried about safety," Brin said hurriedly. "More about an over enthusiastic welcome."

That made sense. Perry had had a position here; he would have been well liked and missed during his time at House St Peter. Of course people would recognise him and want to welcome him back.

"We should walk, then," I said. "If people want to welcome Perry, they should be allowed to and he should be where he can speak to them easily."

Ethan had taught me that; if you're welcomed respond in kind. It pays off.

"Um..." Perry said. "Possibly not so much me as you.

You're something of a hero after House Eastern."

"Urgh!" I said, my opinions changing rapidly. "Can we teleport?"

Brin stifled a laugh. "What's right for Perry should be right for you, surely?" he asked.

I was so going to give him what for as soon as I got the chance. In the end we rode, which was Brin's preferred choice, although Perry insisted that I rode with him, sitting in front of him, his arm around me. I didn't argue; I felt safer that way too. Brin did argue. "If you're not a competent rider, I think you should ride with one of my men, not Perry," he said.

I hoped that chance to give him what for came soon or I'd lose patience. Perry stepped in. "She's as good a rider as me," he said. I wasn't sure that was true but it was nice to hear him say so. "I'd just feel better with her next to me."

Brin shrugged in agreement and led us towards his men and the horses. There were people waving and calling out to us all along the short ride through the town, so I tried to smile and wave back. One or two came over to Perry – I spotted Brin's men subtly controlling who could reach us – and they said 'hello' and 'welcome back' and he was all smiles too, greeting them by name, leaning down to shake hands. They shook hands with me, too.

We approached a wide-arched entrance with crowds passing freely through. On the other side was a large open space, a plaza, a market place surrounded by workshops and offices and food vendors, hustling and bustling as people went about their day-to-day activities. I spotted the area where Traders and Settlers did their business, fulfilling contracts, taking orders and selling goods. The current caravan's pennant fluttered above them in the breeze; obviously I knew the symbols for every caravan but this wasn't one I'd met before, nor one with anyone I knew. I just kept turning my head from side to side, trying to see everything I could.

Perry whispered in my ear, "Lord Neville likes everyone to think of the castle as theirs, rather than his."

We rode straight through to another archway in another wall. The next courtyard was smaller and quieter but still busy.

"Administration and offices, all the things necessary to run the territory," Perry told me this time.

We cut diagonally across this courtyard and through yet another archway although this one had gatekeepers who waved us through. One of them smiled up at Perry. "Welcome home, sir," he said.

Perry leaned down to shake hands. "Thanks, Pete. It's good to be back."

I wondered if Perry meant that. Despite his worries on the train his arm was relaxed around me and there was no sign of tension in his voice. And when I twisted into his mind, I felt anticipation rather than reluctance.

People came running to take our horses, again greeting Perry with pleasure, so we dismounted and Brin's men melted away. Perry clearly knew exactly where to go, but he kept his arm around me and we followed Brin to yet another arched entrance way although this one was much smaller and had armed guards. Again we were waved through and, as we entered this space I just stopped short in surprise. That brought Perry to a halt and he looked back at me and then at the scene in front of us. "Beautiful, isn't it?" he said. "Another thing I'd forgotten."

How could he have forgotten this? I knew there were blanks in his memory as a result of things he'd done in the past, and I knew there were things he preferred not to think about, but to forget this?

We were in a formal garden—low hedges, flower beds, decorative herbs, paths and avenues bordered by shrubs. In itself it was exquisite. But it was laid out to direct your view to a large house behind it, perhaps three storeys tall, symmetrical and simple but elegant. The house was stone built and glowing almost golden in the midday sunshine.

Brin was halfway towards the house before he realised we'd stopped. "Come on," he called. "Uncle Neville will be waiting for us."

We hurried after him through the entrance into an imposing hallway. I couldn't stop looking around but Perry headed off to one side of the hall.

"No," said Brin, beckoning in a different direction. "He'll be in the veranda room, not the office."

Actually, he wasn't in either; as Brin spoke a man strode across the hall towards us. He carried himself with confidence, well built, grey haired and I'd have placed him in his sixties. He looked enough like both Perry and Brin for me to realise that this had to be Lord Neville. Perry turned towards him, and for a moment they both stood absolutely still, staring at each other. I could feel the charged atmosphere between them. And then Perry bowed his head and went to kneel before this High Lord but before he could complete the movement Lord Neville had taken him by the arm and pulled him back up. "No need for that, m'boy," he said. "Welcome back."

He embraced Perry who was broadcasting stunned surprise though maybe only I felt that. After a moment Lord Neville released him and turned to me, smiling. "You must be the very beautiful and talented Lady Leonie," he said. "Welcome as a child of my House, flesh of my flesh, blood of my blood. The freedom of my House and Lands is yours."

I didn't know what to say to that and Perry was no help, still looking stunned. Fortunately, I was saved from having to say anything as Perry got hit by a whirlwind. She was perhaps a fraction taller than me, maybe just a little older, all arms and legs and long black hair tied up in a high ponytail. He did the only thing possible which was to wrap his arms round her in a big hug and lift her off the ground.

"Perry," she said – and her voice was as much a whirlwind as the rest of her. "I've missed you."

"Missed you, too, Lil'Lil," he said.

She went to kick him on the shin but he just dodged, laughed and held her at arm's length for a moment before putting her down. Not a good move from my perspective because then it was my turn to be hit by the whirlwind.

"I've been longing to meet you. Welcome to Castle Tennant," she said, hugging me.

"My daughter, Lilyrose," Lord Neville said. He sounded like he was trying to be disapproving of her behaviour but all that came through was his pride in her.

Brin leaned over sideways to pat her on the head. "Hey, Lil'Lil," he said, grinning widely.

In one swift move, she hooked her foot round his ankle and jerked his leg from under him. He landed – hard – on his backside. I couldn't help laughing at the look on his face, nor could Perry, and even Lord Neville was smiling.

"She doesn't take kindly to that nickname," he explained to me. "But it's never stopped these two. Honestly, bunch of hooligans. To think the future of my House depends on one of these three!" But he went on smiling the whole time and he was still smiling when he turned to Lilyrose. "Take Perry and Leonie and show them their room," he said. "Brin, can I have a word please?"

Chapter 28

Leonie

Lilyrose did what she'd been told and showed us the way to our room, chatting nonstop, her ponytail swinging from side to side as she bounced along ahead of us. We went up an imposing flight of stairs from the hallway and then Perry started going one way but she called him back. "No," she said. "You're over here. You're in the Sapphire Room, not your old room."

He raised his eyebrows at that but didn't say anything as she opened a door and showed us in. I wondered where we were supposed to sleep because it was arranged as a sitting room. Fortunately, before I could say anything and look silly, it became clear that this wasn't just a room but a suite of rooms – sitting room, bedroom, bathroom, dressing room – and even the bathroom was huge.

"Lunch is in about twenty minutes in the veranda room," Lilyrose told us. "I've assigned you a maid and a valet, but I'll introduce you after lunch. Till then, I'll leave you to get settled."

Then she disappeared.

"Perry! A maid?" I wailed, thrown by all that had happened that I wasn't familiar with.

He didn't answer, and I turned to find him standing blankly in the middle of the room, still looking stunned. My immediate thought was that he needed reassurance, that right now he needed me. So I twisted my mind into his, wrapped my arms around him and pulled his head down onto my shoulder, running my hand into his hair. "It's alright," I said quietly. "I'm here. It's going to be okay. We're together. We'll deal with whatever, together."

He took a deep shuddering breath, and I felt some of the

tension leave his shoulders. Then he raised his head and wrapped his arms round me. "I'm okay," he said. "I'll be okay. I thought I was fine and then coming back inside the house…" His voice faded and picked up again. "And there's something strange going on and I don't know what and I don't like it."

"Strange?" I asked, puzzled. I hadn't felt any undercurrents of strange, just a lot of welcome and happiness and pride.

Perry pulled me across to a glass door opening onto a small balcony. We were at the back of the house, on the corner of a central block, flanked by two equally elegant wings at right angles, the three elements surrounding a pleasant, quiet courtyard with views into a garden beyond and down to a river.

Perry pointed across to the wing nearest us. "Brin, Lilyrose and I all had rooms along there, with Uncle Neville at the end," he said. "I mean, I know Lilyrose lives here, but Brin and I had our own rooms here too. That's where I expected us to be." He gestured back inside. "These rooms, they were for honoured guests, or visiting High Lords. They're used as a subtle acknowledgement of status. We shouldn't be here, it doesn't make sense. And there are other things that don't make sense, too."

He led me back inside the room and we sat down on one of the sofas while he worked through it all in his head, but also out loud to me. "You know I'm fascinated by where we got some of our customs from, their history and meaning?"

I did – he'd often be reading about it in an evening when we sat quietly together. I nodded, but he wasn't really looking for an answer.

"Well, I was introduced to that by Uncle Neville. He knows the symbolism of our customs inside out and back to front. On one level, the fact that he stopped me kneeling to him could be meaningless. There was no one to see, he might have guessed it would worry me and so it was thoughtful. On another level it was deeply symbolic and he won't have missed that. And the phrases he used to you, they were deeply symbolic, too."

They were? I hadn't realised. I just thought they were empty phrases, formal words and I hadn't known what to say in response. Again Perry didn't need anything from me, he just continued, "Their meaning depends a bit on context but there were elements from welcoming someone who's joining the House, and the flesh of my flesh bit is only used when acknowledging an heir. And the freedom of the House phrase – that's used either to welcome another High Lord, or in the formal pledging of one House to a higher House."

Now I was seriously concerned. I didn't know anything about any of these and I was afraid I'd let Perry down somehow. "I didn't mean to do or say the wrong thing, or not say what I should," I told him worriedly.

"You didn't, lovable," he said, putting his arm round me to reassure me. "It was him. Depending how you read it, this was either a wildly overenthusiastic family welcome, or he acknowledged me as equal and you as heir, or as equal or even as overlord. And this room reinforces that. And that all doesn't make sense."

Perry paused to think. None of it made sense to me. I'd been feeling reasonably okay about this visit. Brin had turned out to be bit of a pain but I'd find a way to deal with him. I liked what I'd seen of Lilyrose and I hoped that we could be friends. And Lord Neville had seemed far friendlier and more welcoming than I'd expected. It was Perry's reaction that was freaking me out. And the mention of maids and valets.

Perry started speaking again, slowly, as if he was still organising his thoughts. "If Uncle Neville considers you Gabriel's daughter…" I must have made some guilty move that distracted him because he turned and looked at me. "Gabriel thinks of you as his daughter," he said gently. "So it's perfectly reasonable that Uncle Neville does. And if he, Uncle Neville I mean, thinks that we're here as representatives of Lord Gabriel, that might explain most of it."

"Couldn't it just be that he's really pleased you've come back here? And this is how he chooses to show it?" I asked hopefully. I didn't want to think about having the responsibility of representing House St Peter.

"It could," Perry agreed. "It just wouldn't be very like him. He doesn't miss out on the symbolism of actions and customs. But I'd still like to know for sure." He leaned back into the sofa and seemed more relaxed, happier now he'd worked out a possible explanation so I felt better about it too. "And don't worry about the maid and valet," he added, proving that he had been listening to me whatever else had been going through his mind. "They aren't servants, they won't be fussing round us, doing things we could do for ourselves. They're members of the household whose job it is to make sure we can find everything we need, show us where we need to go, and when, make sure we know the appropriate dress code, that sort of thing. I've done it myself for guests here before. It's kind of fun; I always used to enjoy doing it."

That made me feel better, too.

"And," he said, starting to smile again, "I definitely know the way to the veranda room, which is where I think we should be right now."

He did know the way, naturally. It was along the corridor he'd headed down when Lilyrose had shown us the rooms and then down a different flight of stairs from the ones we'd come up. "This end of this wing tends to be just for family," Perry told me.

I found it a little disconcerting that he knew this place so well. I hadn't found his parents' farm off putting in the same way; perhaps that was because this building was so much larger and more imposing. Or was it because it emphasised this whole part of Perry's life from before I'd known him? A part that was so different from my past life and so different from the Perry I knew and the life we'd led together? Could I keep up with what he might have to do here, or would I let him down? I was so lost in these thoughts that I nearly bumped straight into Perry when he stopped to open a door.

The veranda room was on the ground floor at the end of one of the wings. I liked it at first sight. The far wall was made of glass doors that folded back giving access onto a wide-decked veranda which then became part of the room. The whole space was half relaxed sitting area, half dining area and the table was set out for a casual lunch, with serving plates from which we could help ourselves.

Lord Neville, Brin and Lilyrose were sitting in the lounge area. Lord Neville stood up and came towards us, taking my arm in greeting and guiding me towards the table. Again, all I could sense was pride and pleasure, no hint of strangeness or secrecy. He gestured at Perry and Brin. "These troublemakers call me Uncle Neville. I'd be honoured if you'd feel able to do the same. And may I call you Leonie?"

I said something appropriate – I hoped – in agreement but we were at the table by then and he was directing us where to sit. He sat at the head, with me and Lilyrose either side, and Perry and Brin next to us respectively. The conversation was pretty relaxed; mostly I just listened. Lord Neville did quite a lot of listening too. He reminded me of how Ma had looked the first time we'd all sat down for a meal – sort of happy and satisfied. Then I remembered that they were siblings and of course this was where Ma had grown up. That was pretty disconcerting, too.

"So, Lil'Lil," Perry said. "What's changed around here then?"

Brin snickered as Lilyrose glared at Perry, but she started to update Perry anyway.

"Why Lil'Lil?" I asked when she stopped for breath.

"It's short for Little Lily," Brin explained. He was being slightly less annoying than before. Maybe he was an acquired taste.

"She's much littler and younger than us," Perry added. "But she always had to join in with whatever we were doing, trying to keep up however much smaller she was."

I felt Lilyrose move to kick Perry under the table. And I felt the quick surge as he used telekinesis to stop her foot.

"Not fair!" she complained but Perry just looked at her innocently.

Lord Neville raised his eyebrows at her questioningly but she couldn't complain without revealing what she'd been trying to do.

Brin turned to me. "Now," he said, "what shall we call you?"

Back to being annoying then. I glared at him. "Leonie," I told him. "It's my name."

Perry and Lilyrose laughed. Brin just grinned. "I'll think of something suitable," he promised.

By the time the meal was over I was starting to feel quite tired, what with the journey and all the new people and places. I tried to hide it, but Lord Neville spotted me yawning. "Brother Benjamin and Lady Eleanor have both told me that on no account am I to let you get overtired," he said, smiling at me. "If I do, they said my rank would count for nothing in what they planned to do to me. And as I am scared of both of them – especially Eleanor – I'd be very grateful if you'd make sure you were well rested."

I wasn't sure why anyone was scared of either of them, but back home pretty much everyone jumped to obey when one of those two told them what to do, so I was perfectly happy to go and rest. Perry came with me, and Lilyrose ran after us. "I'll just introduce you to Declan and Dervla," she said.

They were to be our valet and maid. Declan was about my age, maybe slightly younger, all long and lanky and not quite grown into his body. This was his first assignment as valet and he kept stumbling over his words and blushing in embarrassment. I guessed it would be pretty nerve wracking being given the prodigal heir to look after on your first assignment. Dervla seemed a good partner for him; older than Perry, she was all calm and encouraging. I reckoned Declan would probably survive the experience.

Introductions made, they disappeared and Perry shepherded me off to bed. Once I was lying down, he kissed me gently. "I won't be far away," he said.

"It's okay," I said sleepily. "You don't have to stay close. I can feel you. There aren't any Shields."

"No, there aren't," he confirmed, smiling. "But all the same, I won't go far. I'll stay within your range, okay?"

I yawned and nodded, and that was that.

Chapter 29

Perry

Leonie safely asleep, Perry wandered back downstairs towards the veranda room, idly looking through any open doors, slowly reacquainting himself with the place and noting any changes. Just like early in his return to Deep River Farm, he felt a little lost, a little uncertain of his place, nervous about what was yet to come, and what would have to be dealt with.

When he reached the veranda room, Lord Neville was there, sitting comfortably in an armchair, papers on his knee and on the table beside him. He looked up, smiling, to welcome Perry. "Leonie resting?" he asked, and Perry nodded. "She's fast asleep. Are you working here these days rather than your office?"

Lord Neville gestured at the papers. "I'm trying to leave more of it to Brin and Lilyrose," he said. "But it still seems to creep up on me. Sit a while and keep me company."

Obediently, Perry sat opposite him, trying to relax into the armchair and hide the tension he felt.

"Is the place very different from what you remember?" Neville asked, curiously.

"A little, perhaps. A different way of life from the last few years, certainly." Perry hesitated and then decided he had nothing to lose. "I'm sorry that I ran away like that. I couldn't handle the expectations everyone had, nor how they conflicted with what I wanted to do. I wasn't thinking and I caused a lot of hurt and I'm sorry."

Neville shook his head. "We weren't fair on you. It was more about me and your ma than you and we should never have put you under that sort of pressure. I don't think you had a lot of choice. Gabriel's very proud of you, you know. Me, too."

"He is? You are?" Perry hadn't expected that.

"Hmph! Yes." Neville brushed the subject off with a wave of his hand and moved on. "Now, did Gabriel tell you that I said we'd work out a solution to suit us both?"

"He did. But I think I'm missing something here." Perry decided to get his confusion out in the open. "The way you greeted me, and Leonie, and the room we're in – it's not what I was expecting."

"I think it's fair to say that Gabriel has told me things which you don't know. But I'd rather wait until you and Leonie are both here. I'd like to discuss it all tomorrow morning."

Perry agreed. He didn't want to wait, but nor did he want to go into anything without Leonie, especially after what she'd said at the station when he and Brin had excluded her. "You've spoken to Lord Gabriel recently?" he asked instead.

"I have. And met with him a couple of weeks back, him and others. Your wife seems to have caused quite a stir. But that will keep. In the meantime, what is it that you would like to do? Where do you want to belong? What role would you like?"

"This isn't part of tomorrow's discussions?"

"In a way it is," Lord Neville conceded. "And yes, the things we have to discuss may affect what you can do. But right now, I'm more interested in what you want to do, ideally. I'd like to find a solution that suits us all. I'm assuming medicine – perhaps a senior role in the hospital here?"

"I think, most of all, I want to be somewhere because of my ability, not my birth." Perry's reply was sharper than he'd intended.

"You didn't hesitate to use your rank, your birth, your

connections at House Eastern."

"I used everything I possibly could to make sure Leonie's death counted for something. Then, it didn't matter what came after. Without her, I didn't care."

"St Peter's been the making of you, m'boy," Neville said. "Or Leonie has. Probably both. No wonder Gabriel didn't want to let you go. I'd name you as my heir now, but I promised Gabriel I wouldn't do that without your full consent. Hmph. Now, your preference?"

For a moment or two, Perry was silent, flabbergasted again by such praise from his Uncle and by the concession and promises that had been made. Slowly he found his voice and tried to respond positively. "Medicine, yes, and I do appreciate that offer. The hospital role, I mean. Only, either I would want to work within my specialism – and there's far more scope for that at St Peter. Or in making a difference to people's lives at an everyday level, the sort of thing I'm doing at Deep River. As to where, I don't know. House St Peter, and here, and Deep River all have their attractions. I think that depends more on Leonie. For now, she has several years of study to finish."

"What does she want to do?"

"Mostly, I think she'd like to work rescuing nestlings and runaways. The sort of thing that Taylor House does, I guess."

"That makes sense, from what I've heard. No House preference?"

Perry's response was slow as he thought about it. "I don't really know." He paused a moment. "Trader, perhaps?"

Neville smiled at that. "I'm sure they'd welcome her. Both of you." He put his papers to one side and got to his feet. "Brin and Lilyrose have gone over to the practice ground," he continued.

"You tempted?"

"It's been a long while…" Perry said.

"You don't forget. It'll come back. You look pretty fit."

"Defence only." Perry was wavering but he had to put that condition in.

"Even with Brin?" Now Neville was grinning at him, alluding back to the highly competitive relationship he and Brin had had in the past.

Perry grinned back. "Perhaps an exception for Brin. He's got Leonie pretty annoyed already."

"Has he? How?" Neville was definitely amused.

"He thought she was too small and delicate to have any experience of guard duty."

"Foolish boy," said Neville. "She's not much smaller than Lilyrose. He should know better. Want to sort him?"

"I thought I'd leave that to Leonie. She'll do it just fine."

"I'll send Declan to tell her where we are when she wakes and bring her over."

He arranged that, and then, companionably together, past resentments set aside, they headed towards the practice ground.

Leonie

The bed was warm and soft around me. I reached for Perry and found him. Not there in person, not in the next room, but not far away and he felt happy, enjoying himself, though I couldn't tell what he was doing. I slid out of bed and wandered into the next room where I found a snack set out for me. Hungry as ever, I ate that first and then decided to set out in the direction of Perry.

As soon as I opened the door, Declan was there, loitering. "Lord Perry and Lord Brin have gone over to the practice ground," he said, almost stutter free. It clearly wasn't me that made him nervous. "I've come to wait for you and show you where, if you like."

That was thoughtful of him and I would like, definitely. "Practice ground?" I asked. "Practice what?"

I could tell Declan was trying not to look at me as if I were slow. He almost managed. "Well, fighting," he said. "Swords, knives, weapons, hand to hand, whatever they choose."

"Perry? Fighting?"

I was astounded. That didn't sound like Perry, although I was more than happy for him to sort Brin out. Though come to think of it, he'd been wrestling with Matt that first Sunday we'd been at Deep River. Was this another side of him I didn't really know?

"Well, yes," Declan said. "I wasn't here when Lord Perry was here before but they tell me he's a real match for Lord Brin. It used to be quite something to watch them apparently. Most everyone's gone over to see."

I'd panicked when Perry and Matt had been fighting by the lake, terrified that Perry would be hurt. Now I could sense that Perry was perfectly happy but I still really needed to go and see too. "Come on," I urged. "Which way?"

The practice ground was in a courtyard to one side of the house. Almost the whole courtyard was an open arena, with seating banked around the sides. Declan told me that the buildings behind the seating were changing rooms and indoor training spaces. For now, my eye was caught by the activity to one side of the arena.

There was a small group of people, hovering around Perry and Brin. Brin looked relaxed, watching while Perry appeared to be trying a couple of swords for weight and balance. I didn't like to distract Perry but he must have realised I was there because he looked round, smiled at me and waved for me to come over and join them.

"Hey, beautiful," he said. His eyes and his voice were glowing with eager, almost mischievous anticipation. "Did you sleep well?"

"Yes, fine," I told him. "But, Perry, what's going on? Are you really fighting?"

"Just a little practice for old time's sake," he said grinning. "Brin and I used to be sparring partners all the time. We're well protected and they're just training weapons. No one's going to get hurt."

"Not even Brin? Just a little bit?" I whispered so no one else could hear.

"Would you like me to? I thought you'd rather sort Brin out yourself." He was grinning at me.

"Could I? Is it allowed?" Now I was the one who was eager for conflict.

"I'll set it up for you, after this, okay?" He told me where to sit for a good view. "And don't worry. Brin and I are evenly matched. I'm a little out of practice and he was always slightly better with a sword, but I'll make him work for it and I promise I won't get hurt."

It was Perry's tone and attitude that reassured me more than his words; I could feel his mind and he was happy and excited so I went to sit where I was told, beside Lilyrose and Lord Neville. Certainly no one else seemed worried so I guessed the likelihood of injury had to be pretty low. I felt someone switch a Shield over the area. That seemed fair, stopping Perry using his Gifts against Brin but it also meant I couldn't sense Perry and I never liked that. He felt it too, and, understanding how I'd feel, he turned and waved at me again, still grinning with pleasure.

Lilyrose bounced in her seat beside me. "I love watching them," she said. "They both annoy me like crazy, but to watch them fight, it used to be such a treat."

Lord Neville shook his head indulgently, but he wasn't taking his eyes off the practice ground, where Perry and Brin were now circling each other, warily. There was someone on the ground with them – some sort of referee I guess – who gave a signal and suddenly it was all underway. To distract myself from worrying I tried to analyse technique, strengths and weaknesses. I'd no real experience in sword fighting but it was pretty easy to tell that Perry was out of practice and that, for the first moments at least, Brin was going easy on him.

Then Perry got in a good parry and lunge. That boosted his confidence and I could see the muscle memories flooding back. Suddenly Brin had to really work at it. I studied Brin closely, looking for anything I could use against him later. He was right handed, which was even enough against Perry, who was also right handed, but he had a tendency to keep his guard just a little bit high which left him exposed lower down. And sometimes he left one side open, just for a moment. Perry spotted that too, and took advantage of it, getting a couple of good blows in. I thought Brin's main strength was that he was very fast.

Perry was noticeably slower but he was out of practice. He got faster as the bout progressed. I figured he was definitely stronger, probably fitter and also a more strategic fighter, planning his attack better. I didn't know how they were scoring but it was clear that Brin won. Perry was cheerful about it, happily congratulating Brin. They both stripped off their protective gear and Perry's shirt rode up and came off, showing the scars on his arm, shoulder and ribs. He'd got rather tanned working out in the fields which meant they stood out more than usual as fine lines across his skin.

"He never had those scars before," Lilyrose said. "How'd he get them without fighting? In a monastery of all places?"

"He had a fight with a window," I told her.

Lord Neville raised his eyebrows but didn't ask anything more. Perry pulled his shirt back on and we went down to join them.

"Care to take Leonie on now?" Perry asked Brin.

There was mischief in his eyes and a wicked lilt to his voice. Brin couldn't have noticed. His face suggested he was thinking about how easy it would be and how little he'd have to lose. "Okay then," he said. "What terms?"

"The maze," Perry said firmly. "You challenged her ability to guard. Leonie can guard the central flag. You have to take it."

I didn't know what the maze was, but I trusted Perry to set this up fairly. Brin nodded agreement. "What weapons? If I was attacking in the maze normally I'd have a sword, throwing knives and smoke bombs."

"I'd rather have a dagger over a sword," I said.

"Okay," Perry agreed. "A sword for Brin, a dagger for Leonie, and six throwing knives and smoke bombs each. And the Dampener Shield switched off."

"Then I want a personal Shield," said Brin. "And no contact

between you and Leonie during this."

Perry agreed to that. "Defender and Container Shields then. That's probably a good safety precaution anyway."

I was trying not to giggle at Brin's desire for a personal Shield. He thought it meant that I wouldn't be able to tell where he was – but what I actually saw if someone used such a Shield was a blank space, which gave away their location just as easily. And I hadn't yet met a personal Shield that I couldn't disable.

"One more rule," Lord Neville said. "A few bruises are fine, and the odd scratch but no real bloodshed, nothing broken and nothing that shows in formal dress. We've got a formal dinner tomorrow."

"And absolutely nothing I have to stitch," Perry added.

Brin gave him a look but I thought that sentence was mostly directed at me. I'd never used weapons in front of Perry but he knew what I was capable of, and the danger Brin could be in.

"Real weapons then?" I asked, trying to sound hopeful to wind Brin up.

Both Perry and Lord Neville jumped in instantly to deny it. "Practice weapons only," Lord Neville insisted.

I wasn't going to do much damage with those. The practice knives were nicely weighted but the blades were designed to retract once they hit. The smoke bombs were real enough except that the smoke was a harmless fog rather than something that would leave the victim coughing, spluttering and struggling for breath. The maze was much more fun. With the quiet whirr of well-maintained motors, the floor of the practice ground retracted to reveal a maze underneath. It must have been several metres deep and I spotted a ladder leading down into it. In the centre was a slightly raised mound with a flag. That was what I was supposed to be guarding. Around it was not so much a true maze as an area with walls and – fake – shrubs and trees and rocks, some of which could provide cover for an attacker and some which couldn't. From the central mound some of the surroundings were visible and some were obscured. Anyone sitting on the seats around the edge had a pretty good view of everything.

Perry came with me to the central mound. "Okay with all this?" he asked although he must have known I was.

"Fine," I told him with glee. "This is going to be fun."

"Remember the rules. Don't hurt him too bad," Perry told me.

I pouted at him in disappointment, but he just laughed, kissed me then headed back to the seats. It didn't matter to me which way I faced, so I sat down with my back to Perry, Lilyrose and Lord Neville so they wouldn't distract me. Then I stretched my mind across the arena looking for Brin.

The blank area was easy to spot so I turned slightly to keep my back to it and make him think his tactic had worked. He took advantage of that to lob a smoke bomb and move elsewhere quickly. I let that one land, then scooped it up with my mind and threw it back to where he had been. He scarpered sideways to get out of its way before it went off, and threw another one at me. This time I threw it in the opposite direction to the one in which he'd moved, just to confuse him. The third time he threw one – he should have known better – I threw it back to exactly where he was now and turned to face that direction. The resultant scuffling as he tried to get out of the way before it went off gave me a very good glimpse of him so I threw a knife to skim across his shoulder. Personal Shields were all very well but people tended to forget that they only extended a short distance from their body. That meant I had telekinetic control of the knife until it was nearly upon Brin. From that point I was a bit inaccurate because I could neither see him nor sense him in detail. I thought he'd dropped to the ground, trying to duck under the knife but I definitely hit him. If it had been a real knife, he'd have been bleeding.

He decided to go for knives too, sending one back at me – I was a pretty good visual target where I was with no cover. He was a very good marksman, I'd give him that. I batted the first knife to one side and let it fall to the ground. The second I ducked under. The third I caught and turned round, boomeranging it back at him. Now it was his turn to duck.

Such a shame he'd given up on the smoke bombs. I was having such fun with those. So I reached over and turned his Shield off – Lord Neville had said no breakages so I figured I'd better not damage it. Brin was reaching for a fourth knife; I nudged his hand and the knife fell. He jumped sideways to stop it hitting his foot and went for a smoke bomb instead. I pulled his three remaining smoke bombs free from his belt pocket and started them bouncing around him. He grabbed for one, clearly thinking he'd dropped them, so I set all three off. To his credit, he didn't panic. Instead he used it as a reason to move towards me, gambling that the smoke would cover him and he could reach cover much closer to me faster than I could react. He was right; I knew he was fast and this used that advantage. I did throw a knife at him but it was half hearted, more a threat than with any real intention or indeed likelihood of hitting him.

He clearly thought it had been a successful move towards me because then he decided his best option was to rush me. It was another good choice; he was faster, heavier and physically stronger than me and I hadn't given him any real indication of danger from the throwing knives.

I laid a line of fire in front of him, just a small one. No one had said anything about burns but I thought they were sure to be covered by the 'no visible damage' rule. He leapt it and dived towards me, so I gathered the power and pushed him back, aiming it hard at his left side. Perry had told me doing that was a form of telekinesis; I didn't really mind what it was called as long as it did the job. It did today. Brin slowed and wobbled off balance, so I took a leaf out of Lilyrose's book and knocked his feet from under him with another blast. He landed on his backside hard again, so I pushed him right over with a third blast as I raced towards him and landed on his chest. I was more than light enough for him to throw off and get up from there, but before he could move I had my dagger at his throat. Not that the practice weapon would have hurt him but with a real one I could have slit his throat before he moved. I wouldn't but he didn't know that. Nor did he know that those three blasts of energy had pretty much exhausted me. I couldn't have mustered a fourth.

"Surrender?" I asked him quietly.

"Surrender," he agreed so I got off and let him up.

He bent low over my hand. "My deepest apologies, Lady Leonie. I only wish I had you in my squad."

Perry, Lord Neville and Lilyrose appeared beside us. Perry slipped his arms round me and even without looking I could tell he was grinning all over his face. "Reckon Leonie could manage guard duty now?" he said to Brin.

"And some," Brin replied, fiddling with something at his belt. "Damn Shield must have malfunctioned. And I think it triggered the smoke bombs."

I tried to smother my laugh by turning to hide my face in Perry but it didn't really work. He touched my mind to find out why and then started laughing himself. "There's nothing wrong with your Shield," he told Brin. "Leonie turned it off."

Brin looked up at me absolutely flabbergasted. "You.

Turned. It. Off?"

"I would have blown it up," I said. "It's easier. But Uncle Neville said not to break anything."

That was too much for the others and I stood there looking from one to other of them while all four of them burst out laughing.

"You set off the smoke bombs, too?" Brin asked when he got his breath back.

I nodded. "And I made your knife drop and the smoke bombs bounce around you."

That started them all off again. Perry was the first to recover. "You know what else you did?" he asked me quietly.

I looked up at him, puzzled. I didn't think I'd done anything else particularly imaginative or unusual. "You set a line of fire. Did you not realise?"

I'd done it without thinking and it took a moment for what Perry had said to sink in. And then I started jumping up and down in delight. "I can firestart. I can firestart again!"

Perry wrapped his mind round mine and oozed calm, clearly concerned that I might set fire to us all in my excitement. That was a bit of a risk. My abilities were a little erratic whenever one of my Gifts returned. By now there were a whole lot more people around us; other spectators, congratulating me and teasing Brin who was complaining that he now had bruises on both buttocks – one from Lilyrose earlier and one from me just now. We headed back to the house in a group. Several people clustered round Lord Neville asking how they should take on someone like me.

"The chances of having to do so are so low as to be near

enough zero," he said. "The main lesson to learn from this is never to underestimate your opponent."

Perry agreed. "There wasn't anything Leonie did that you can't do a different way. Her main advantage was that she knew exactly where Brin was. Personal Shields are all very well – and Leonie is the only person I've ever come across who can disable them – but you can't rely on them. Some adepts see them as blank spaces so that tells them where you are just as well as if they can see you. And they can't stop physical attacks."

"But she could handle more weapons at once than we can," someone said.

"Not really," Perry told them. "I know what Leonie can manage, and she and Brin had the same number of smoke bombs and knives."

Brin winced at the knowledge he'd been set up, but Perry went on, "There are very few adepts who can handle more with their mind than you can manage with your hands. So one strategy is to practice being very fast and accurate with multiple knives or bombs." Perry was well into lecturing mode. "And Brin had a good plan when he rushed Leonie. Basically, what they were doing then was hand-to-hand combat. It was just that Leonie had the advantage of being able to do it from a distance. Getting up close – if you can – reduces that advantage."

I tuned out from Perry's lecture. Brin appeared beside me. "Next time," he said. "Next time, I'll know better. And be better prepared."

He was smiling at me, so I smiled back. I'd be well prepared next time, too. Lilyrose appeared on his other side. He looked back and forth between us. "No way," he said. "No way am I staying close to you two. I've got enough bruises for one day."

Lilyrose laughed as he left and she took my arm. "Well done," she said. "I always like to see someone get the better of Brin. Now, tomorrow we've got a formal dinner. Perry's easy to sort out and Brother Edward has sent something for you. But he said it would probably need adjusting to fit properly. So after dinner tonight, we'll go find Annie and get that sorted, okay?"

I nodded. Brother Edward had sent me something? That meant he – and therefore Lord Gabriel – knew about this formal dinner, whatever it was, and that supported Perry's theory that there was something going on we didn't know about. But Perry was still busy talking, so I thought I'd mention it to him privately later.

Lilyrose bubbled on, "Everyone who lives or works within the castle walls usually eats together in the main dining hall. Tomorrow, for the formal meal, there's a seating plan, and servers. Lots of people don't come to formal meals if they don't have to but this time pretty much everyone's coming."

I nodded to show I understood, but she barely paused for breath, "Tonight's just a normal meal. It's self-service so you can sit wherever you want."

***

I chose to stay close by Perry for the evening meal but we didn't have to sit with Lord Neville or anything like that, quite the opposite. There were a lot of people aiming to sit with us, wanting to catch up with Perry; I got introduced to them but I never quite got all the names straight. There were just too many. Mostly I listened and watched. But I did notice that someone – I suspected Lilyrose – had put a large cushion down where Brin was about to sit and he was clearly getting teased about his bruised backside.

Afterwards Lilyrose dragged me off to meet Annie, who seemed to have a similar role to Brother Edward. Declan took

Perry off somewhere on a similar mission. Once more, Edward had excelled himself with the outfit he'd sent for me and it fitted perfectly. I didn't know how he did it.

"Brother Edward sent another package for you, too," Lilyrose said, finding it and thrusting it into my hands. "He said he hoped you and Perry enjoy it."

Knowing Edward, that made me suspicious from the start. Lilyrose and Annie were hovering over me, both encouraging me to open it, eager to see what was inside. So, in trepidation, I undid the ribbon round the box, lifted the lid off and folded back the tissue paper I found there. I was right to feel cautious. I never did buy Edward the lace he'd asked me to get at House Eastern but he'd got hold of some anyway. And some silk, and made me the various items he'd promised me, the ones a monk wouldn't be expected even to know about.

Lilyrose and Annie were oohing and aahing as I lifted the items out. They were beautifully made and absolutely exquisite. It was just their nature that was making me blush.

"You say these were made by a monk? Really?" Annie asked in a disbelieving tone as she inspected them. "What sort of a monastery is that?"

"A very good one," I said defensively.

Annie rushed to assure me she hadn't meant anything by it, she was just surprised. And very admiring of Edward's skills she added.

"Edward always says it isn't what you know that matters, it's how you use it that's important," I told her. "But he also says he likes making stuff for me because it gives him variety from the day-to-day stuff."

Just then, there was a knock at the door, and Perry put his

head round as we scrambled to put everything back in the box out of sight. "Declan's done with me," he said cheerfully. "I'll see you back in our room when you're done here."

He disappeared again, and Lilyrose burst into giggles as she brought out a couple of items she'd been hiding behind her back and put them in the box. "I think Perry's certainly going to enjoy these," she said, and I blushed again.

Chapter 30

The Next Day

Leonie

As we ambled into the veranda room the next morning, Lilyrose raised her eyebrows at me with such a wicked look on her face that I knew exactly what she meant and blushed deep red. Perry had his back to her as he sat down, so he didn't spot it. I curled up next to him, my feet tucked underneath me and chose not to look at Lilyrose again. She snickered.

Lord Neville was standing up and pacing a little, just like Perry did when he didn't know how to start something or quite how to phrase what he wanted to say. Then he sat down on the edge of an armchair and leaned towards me rather than Perry. "I don't know what you know about recent history? And the way Houses interrelate?" he asked.

I shrugged. Not much. Perry had sometimes teased me about my lack of knowledge of the social, geographic and historical structure of our world.

"You know that House Chisholm and House Lindum are opposed, normally at war with each other?"

I nodded. I did know that. Probably everyone did. It was relevant to Traders in terms of planning routes and avoiding conflict. Other than that I didn't think it was particularly relevant to me, except that I'd recently discovered my red hair meant I had connections with House Chisholm. Not that I cared and clearly they didn't.

Lord Neville took a deep breath then carried on, "Around twenty years ago or so, the heir to House Lindum had a relationship with a son of House Chisholm. She became pregnant, someone from her House killed the person they assumed was the father and then she died giving birth."

Another unwanted parentless baby. At least this baby would have had a family and a House to care for it. There were so many who didn't belong anywhere. I had found my place to belong but I wanted so much to find and help the others who hadn't.

"Her sister took the child and disappeared. Four years later, that sister and a child were found dead."

That had been starting to sound scarily familiar until he'd said the child was dead. But I could feel Perry tensing up beside me, clearly having much the same thought, so I nudged him. "I'm not dead," I said quietly.

"Well, no, you're not," agreed Lord Neville. "There's no easy way to put this. I said a child, not the child. The dead child was a substitute. You are the original child in this story, the heir to House Lindum, fathered by a Chisholm."

No way. Too much. I sensed Perry's shock and horror, mirroring my own. Everything seemed far away, like looking down the wrong end of a telescope. Somehow I was standing up. I felt Perry's hand reach for me, his mind reach for mine and there was something else there, in his head.

"Perry," I asked urgently. "Did you know?"

If he had kept this from me, this of all things…but he couldn't lie to me, not now, not with our minds touching.

"Sort of," he said.

That was the last straw. I tore away from him knowing only that I needed to run. It didn't matter where, I just needed to move. Running was the only way I was going to be able to handle this, the only way to control my actions while I sorted this out in my head. If I stayed, I'd launch it all at Perry, my heart breaking at his betrayal. I had no idea how to get out of the building or where I was going, I just ran.

Perry

"I'll find you," Perry called after Leonie, but he didn't think she heard before she disappeared.

Lord Neville signalled to Lilyrose to follow her, to send bodyguards, but Perry swivelled back towards him. "Don't chase her. Don't follow her. I'm watching her," he snapped. "She's scared witless already. You'll make it worse." He took a deep breath to try to calm himself and then decided not to bother. "No wonder you greeted us the way you did. Heir to Lindum! And Gabriel made me hide it from her. Now she's terrified and alone. And she thinks I betrayed her."

"She was in danger. Gabriel tried to protect you both. But too many people out there know or suspect now. You both had to be told before you found out somewhere by accident. And she has choices to make." Lord Neville was fiddling with a large envelope, tapping it on his desk.

It distracted Perry slightly. "What's in that envelope?" he demanded.

"Photographs, family trees. Proof." Lord Neville shrugged.

"Give it to me." Perry took it from his hands. "I'm going after her," he said. "Don't try to follow us."

He had no chance of catching her, fuelled as her speed was by anger and the energy generated by her emotions. And the sense that she was being chased would scare her, so he settled for keeping pace at a distance, waiting for her to tire and stop, tracking her with his mind. He calmed too as they ran, the anger he had turned on Lord Neville cooling as he turned his thoughts to how to make this better for Leonie. She did stop, eventually, in a clearing overlooking the river. He slowed and approached cautiously.

She was standing with her back against a tree, like a hunted animal at bay, but he could sense her barely controlled fury, generated by his apparent betrayal.

"You knew?" she asked again as he approached, her voice tight and low.

He nodded, committed to telling her the truth, no matter the consequences.

"You didn't tell me!" she accused him, her anger now in her voice. "You didn't tell me! You. Didn't. Tell. Me!"

The power crackled around her, as she gathered it and launched it at him just as she had at Brin yesterday. He stood still, unshielded, welcoming the attack in recompense, punishment, for what he had done. Instinctively, he closed his eyes, then opened them sharply as the attack stopped, dissipating to nothing immediately in front of him.

Leonie had slid down the tree and was now crouched at its base, tears pouring down her face, as she continually whispered, "You didn't tell me."

He moved towards her, desperately wanting to gather her into his arms and soothe her, but well aware he was already pushing the boundaries of what she would tolerate from him at this point. He sank to the ground in front of her, as close as he dared, and she looked up at him. "Why?" she beseeched him. "Why did you keep it from me?"

He sighed. "It would be true to tell you that I was made to, that Gabriel blocked my memories so that I couldn't tell you, but..."

He was interrupted as she fell into his arms, sobbing against his chest, relief that he hadn't chosen to lie to her coming off her in waves. He wrapped himself around her, stroking her and rocking her, gathering up his own courage to complete his confession. He took a deep breath. "Leonie, Gabriel did block me from telling you, but he could only do that because I let him, and I agreed that I shouldn't tell you."

Calmer now, emotionally exhausted, she didn't pull away, but lifted her head and asked, "Why? And when?"

He didn't know where to begin and it just came out. "The day you agreed to marry me, you showed me your memories of your aunt. She looked familiar to me, but I didn't recognise her then, really I didn't or I'd have told you straight out. Then we were with Gabriel and he sent you off to Pedro to get a picnic. While he and I were talking I realised that your aunt was Augusta Lindum which meant that you were Helena's child, and I just blurted that out to Gabriel."

He paused as Leonie moved in his arms. "Helena," she said. "Helena. I never even knew her name." That rendered him speechless for a moment, but she nudged him. "Go on."

"I think Gabriel might have had his suspicions already, I don't know. We agreed it wasn't safe to acknowledge you as Helena's daughter, or even suggest that you might be her, and the fewer people who knew the better."

"I wouldn't have told anyone," Leonie protested.

He smiled at her. "I know that. I don't think that was Gabriel's concern, and it certainly wasn't mine."

She looked at him, puzzled, and he carried on. "There are people out there who want you dead, others who'd want to kidnap you, use you to further their own ends. Some of them will stop at nothing to get to you. If you'd thought that you were putting the people around you in danger, what would you have done?"

"I'd have left," she whispered, starting to understand.

He nodded. "Exactly. And I'd just spent the night searching for you, getting more and more frantic when I couldn't find you. And that was when there was no particular reason to think you were in danger. I only found you because you made a mistake, one you wouldn't make again. It was selfish of me, but I couldn't bear to risk that. So I let Gabriel block it so I couldn't tell you. I'm so sorry, can you forgive me?"

It was her turn to nod, twisting round and reaching up to kiss him, one hand in his hair, the other round his neck. He took it as a token of forgiveness but realised just how desperate she was for reassurance.

"I love you," he told her. "There's nothing in this world or the next that can change that. And I would have spent the rest of my life searching for you if necessary, but I'd much rather spend it with you."

She nestled back into him. "I was so mad at you. I wanted to hurt you but you didn't even shield and I couldn't do it."

"I felt like I deserved anything you might throw at me. You have a right to know who you are."

She was concerned. "Is it still dangerous to be me?"

"I don't know," he said. "I guess marrying me and what happened at House Eastern and coming here kind of made you more noticeable. Uncle Neville said too many people out there know now, so we had to be told before we found out by accident." He paused. "I shouted at him. He didn't deserve that. I'm sure we're safe here, on Tennant lands, but out there...I just don't know. I suspect Uncle Neville has more to tell us."

She accepted that but questioned him, "I don't really understand it all anyway?"

"How could you?" he agreed. "You'd need to know who you were and your family history and politics for at least a couple of generations, and you've had no chance to learn. I know I tease you that your knowledge of history and society and geography is appalling, but how could it be otherwise?"

She poked him gently in the ribs. "Not helpful, Perry. So tell me. You must know the background at least as well as anyone."

He reached for the envelope he'd taken from Lord Neville and eased the contents out, spreading them on the ground, looking for something to help him. He found a photo of an elderly gentleman. "This is the High Lord of House Lindum, your great grandfather, Lord Leon. His eldest child and heir was Alfred, your grandfather, and Alfred's eldest child and heir was Helena. As both Alfred and Helena are dead, that makes you, Helena's firstborn, direct heir to House Lindum. In that House it passes down through the firstborn, whether male or female, inside or outside marriage."

He paused to sort through the photos, selecting one to pass to her. "This is Helena when she was a little older than you. I hadn't realised how like her you look. Anyone who knew her well would recognise you." He breathed in suddenly as a memory came back to him, and Leonie looked up from the photograph.

He shook his head. "I showed your picture to Lord James. When I took the nestlings over to Taylor House, I showed Lord James your picture. There's no way he wouldn't have recognised you. He didn't say a word."

"How does he fit in?"

"He's Lord Leon's youngest son, Helena's uncle. But they were very close in age and pretty much brought up together."

Leonie went back to the photo, studying it carefully. "I never saw her before, she's beautiful."

"So are you."

She looked at him in some disbelief then changed the subject, "Lord Leon, like Leonie?"

He agreed, "Very much so. It's a family name and your mother was said to be very close to her grandfather." He passed her another picture. "This must have been taken about the same time. These three are your mother, her eldest brother, Anthony, and Augusta. Anthony was born between the two girls."

Leonie was unable to speak as she gazed at the photograph, one finger stroking the image of Augusta. He sat silently, letting her come to terms with her memories. Eventually she looked up. "So what happened?"

"What happened was Helena became pregnant. No one knows for sure who your father is. Chisholm has always acknowledged that it was one of his sons, but he's never been prepared to admit which. The youngest are twins and most people think your father was Jaim, one of those. Just after Helena's family discovered she was pregnant there was a fight – a border skirmish – in which Jaim was killed. If anyone from Lindum thought he was your father then killing him was probably the point of the battle. Helena was considered a traitor for what she'd done. The thought that her heir, the heir to the House of Lindum, had been fathered by a Chisholm was intolerable to many."

"Did they love each other?" She looked up at him, eyes wide, voice almost pleading with him to say yes.

"Did your aunt tell you they did?" he asked.

Leonie nodded.

"Then I'm sure they did," he confirmed. "Augusta would have known how Helena felt."

Leonie relaxed, apparently reassured, so he carried on, "The normal penalty for treason is death but I don't think Lord Leon would have condoned that. It doesn't tally with what I know of him. I think he would have arranged for Helena to live quietly somewhere with you. Disinherited certainly, and probably under a form of house arrest, but allowed to live."

"But then she died when I was born."

"Yes. That was tragic, but I don't think it was suspicious. Whatever their plans for you were, Augusta must have thought you were at risk, because she took you and disappeared. And that made her a traitor, too."

"But then she died."

"Yes. She was found dead along with the body of a young child that everyone assumed was you."

Leonie was still puzzled. "How do they know I'm me? I mean maybe that was the right child and I'm someone else altogether?"

That made him laugh. He rifled through the papers and photographs for something that had caught his eye earlier. "Well, you know you're you," he said. "You remember Augusta. Isn't that rather telling? But Benjamin has samples of your blood and from that he's done a genetic analysis and compared it with Helena's to show that you are her child." He showed her the report he'd found and explained what the various terms meant.

"Couldn't that also show who my father is then?" Leonie

questioned him.

"Well, it could," he confirmed. "But only if we had the detailed analysis of the possible candidates and Chisholm won't allow that. Instead, it simply shows that you are his grandchild."

"So Benjamin knows. How many other people knew this and kept it from me?" she asked bitterly.

He shook his head. "I don't know. My guess would be quite a few."

Leonie thought for a few moments. "If that's who I am why do people want me dead? You said they wanted me dead."

Chapter 31

Leonie

I needed to know all Perry could tell me. It was the only way I could cope; I needed facts because I didn't know how to deal with what I felt. I didn't even know what I felt. I'd been absolutely furious with Perry for keeping things from me but mostly I'd just been so terribly alone, abandoned again. I'd forgiven him, of course I had – how could I not? – and I understood why he'd done what he had but I still didn't know how to cope. And I had to deal with who I was now and what that meant.

I was heir to House Lindum. For my mother's brother, Lord Anthony, who must have spent most of his life believing he was the heir, that had to be personal. I'd displace him so I could see why he'd want to get rid of me. But it turned out my very existence could tear House Lindum apart.

"There'll be those who think you should be heir no matter who your father," Perry told me. "And those who think you must not inherit because of your father. And those who want to use your Chisholm heritage to take over that House."

House Chisholm wasn't any better; either I was a threat from House Lindum or a tool they could use against it.

"But I don't want to be heir to Lindum!" I protested to Perry.

"I'm not sure that's relevant to those who want you to be," he said carefully. "Or those who don't. And it's not just Lindum and Chisholm. You're Gabriel's daughter and my wife. That brings St Peter and Tennant to the table." He touched the mark on my wrist. "And the Traders. You bind together the four leading Houses and the main Nomadic clan. No wonder Gabriel thought you would change the world."

"Lord Gabriel thought I would change the world?"

"I told you, way back, about his visions? How he pushed us together? I know I did. After House Eastern, but before we came here."

He had, but I hadn't paid a lot of attention. We were together. That was what mattered to me. It didn't matter how it had come about. And I certainly hadn't cared about any of the consequences. In fact, I'd pretty much ignored Lord Gabriel's visions because they'd said I'd be dead and here I was, alive.

"Perry," I said. "You said you thought your Uncle had more to tell us? I don't think I can handle more."

"I can't think what more there could be either," he said slowly. "I think it will be things that have happened that we don't know. He's been with Gabriel recently. Maybe they've got a solution, an answer to all this."

And maybe they haven't.

There was only one way to find out. We had to go back. We gathered all the photographs and papers together to put back in the envelope. I saw my name on one and picked it up.

Perry looked over at it. "That's a copy of a birth record," he said. "It's yours. Look." He pointed at the writing as he read it. "On twenty ninth February, to Helena Jessami Lindum, heir in turn to House Lindum, a daughter, Leonie Helena Augusta Lindum, likewise heir in turn to House Lindum." He looked at me. "That's your name. Leonie Helena Augusta."

My name. I'd never even known my own name. I had to ask. "Did you know?"

He shook his head. "I never heard your name at all. You were always referred to as the child in polite circles."

"And impolite ones?"

I was being flippant, I knew I was. Perry winced. "There you would be known as the traitors' bastard," he said. His voice was tight, full of pain.

As we headed back to the house, I held Perry's hand for security. I knew he was trying to broadcast reassurance but he didn't try to touch my mind. I hoped he sensed I wasn't ready for that, not after what he had kept from me, however inadvertently.

Lilyrose was watching out for us from the veranda, and Brin and Lord Neville were right behind her. "Are you okay?" she called as we approached.

I didn't know how to answer. I was a long way from okay.

"Not hurt, anyway," Perry responded as we climbed the steps onto the veranda. He looked up at Lord Neville. "I'm sorry for shouting at you. I shouldn't have done that. It's not your fault."

Lord Neville brushed it off with a wave of his hand. "Don't worry about it. It's not your fault either." Then he turned to me. "Shall we leave this for a while?" he asked. "Come back to it when you feel a little stronger?"

I shook my head. "No, I need to know. I need to know now."

"Very well," Lord Neville said. "I can understand that." We sat back down in the veranda room. I curled against Perry on one of the sofas. Lord Neville leaned forward in his chair, elbows on knees as he looked at me. "I assume Perry has filled you in on the background," he said, and we both nodded. "What has only recently come to light is that Augusta did not die of natural causes."

Perry sat up sharply. "Twenty one," he said. "Of course.

Twenty one. She was assassinated, wasn't she?"

Perry might have understood this but I didn't so Lilyrose explained the nature of assassins to me.

They took money to kill Aunt Gusta? And now they're coming after me? Let them try it. They might have been paid, but I'll make them pay.

Then Perry had his arms around me, pulling me down beside him, trying to wrap calm around me. And Brin was grinning at me. "I, for one, am quite sure you'd make them pay," Brin said. "And I'll help you. I wouldn't want to be in their shoes. But it might be better directed at those who commissioned them."

I'd said that out loud? And I was standing up? I sank down into Perry, embarrassed.

"It's okay," he whispered to me. "I feel like that, too."

Brin, Lilyrose and Lord Neville all murmured agreement so I felt slightly better. All the same, I stayed close to Perry for the rest of the conversation, refusing to let go of his arm which was wrapped around me.

"Personal as it is," Lord Neville said, "the real issue is not the Assassins. There's someone, maybe several people, who want you dead. Right now, you are as protected as is possible while we seek to neutralise that."

He went on to talk about his recent meeting at House St Peter with the High Lords of Lindum and Chisholm. Perry sat up sharply again. "Lindum and Chisholm? Under the same roof? Eating together?" he asked in total disbelief. "World changer," he muttered to me as he sank back.

"Not only that," said Lord Neville, "they have also agreed to sign a mutual non-aggression pact."

Perry just shook his head, wordlessly. Obviously, I was missing the significance of this, but I didn't really understand enough to care. Lord Neville continued, "Actually, that pact's got a bit out of hand. Leonie, ultimately you'll have to choose your House allegiance. Lindum and Chisholm were both concerned that if you chose the other one, you could act or be used to act against them so we suggested a non-aggression pact. But of course you could also choose Tennant, or St Peter, so they wanted me and Gabriel to sign it, which isn't a problem." He sighed. "But somehow the news got out. And now there are any number of other Houses who see the advantage of signing such a pact, and are eager to offer you a place, in whatever role you want. And we think such a world-wide peace treaty is well worth the effort."

I could hardly deny that, even though this all seemed way over my head. Not so long ago the boundaries of my life had been about finding enough food and keeping warm and dry and safe. Now they seemed to encompass being responsible for the safety of the world. I didn't know how I could do that and nor did I know how to refuse to do it. I took a deep breath. "What do I have to do?" I asked.

"Mostly, you've already done your part," Lord Neville said. "What happened at House Eastern told the world you were still alive and that meant Lindum and Chisholm had to face up to things. Gabriel and I will deal with the rest although you'll need to be formally involved at some point. You will need to choose which House to belong to. You can stay at St Peter's of course. I would welcome you unreservedly as one of my heirs. Both Lindum and Chisholm are eager to meet you and would consider you heir."

"Is that what tonight's formal dinner is about?" Perry asked suddenly.

"What? That? Oh, no, no." Lord Neville looked utterly surprised. "That's about welcoming you two home. I should think you both need time to get used to things before meeting either Leon or William. And certainly before making any decisions."

I definitely did. When I'd got up this morning I'd thought I knew who I was. Now I was sure I didn't.

"If there are Assassins out there," Perry asked, "how do we protect Leonie?"

To my surprise – I thought Brin was the security expert – it was Lilyrose who answered. "Assassins really aren't an issue. They won't come onto Tennant lands, they won't act for more than two years and, in the meantime, they will protect Leonie from others. The issue is whoever commissioned them and we are trying to find out who that is. Lindum and Chisholm have made it known that they will act together against anyone who takes action against Leonie."

That led to another intake of breath in disbelief from Perry and another mutter of "world changer", both of which Lilyrose ignored. "Tennant will join them in doing so if necessary," she continued. "Additionally, there are a number of Houses indebted to Leonie as a result of what happened at House Eastern. Anyone who tries to harm her risks both a significant loss of support from those Houses, and the chance that those Houses will also take action against them. And all the Houses that want to join the pact will also support Lindum and Chisholm in this. That's one of the conditions."

"And practically?" Perry insisted. "What's being done to protect Leonie? Here and now."

"Whether you realised it or not, you have had bodyguards since you left House St Peter. That will continue. And after yesterday I'm feeling a lot more confident in your ability to protect yourselves."

"Is that what yesterday was about? At the practice grounds?" Now Perry sounded indignant.

Brin shook his head. "No, that was pure chance. And nobody expected Leonie there, least of all me. But it made Lilyrose feel better seeing what you can both do."

So I'd been right about bodyguards all along then. And they had to be pretty good for me not to have spotted them. I wasn't particularly worried about my own safety but there was one thing that I was now so concerned about that I broke my silence to ask it. "House Eastern," I asked. "That didn't happen because they were after me, did it?"

Perry looked horrified. He obviously hadn't got there yet in his thoughts.

"No," said Lord Neville, quickly and firmly. "That has been thoroughly investigated and we are quite certain it had nothing to do with you."

I shrank back against Perry again in relief. Now what was concerning me was how I was supposed to make a choice between Houses. It seemed to me that I could be heir to Lindum, Chisholm, possibly even Tennant, just for the asking. Or stay at St Peter, or choose any one of a number of others. How was I supposed to make such a choice? How was anyone? How could I take one of these roles from someone who thought it was theirs? Someone like Brin, or Lilyrose? I couldn't work out how I would ever know what the right choice was.

Perry must have sensed how I was feeling because he held me close and spoke to the others. "I think Leonie's had more than enough for now," he said. "We need a bit of space to think about all this, to take it in. I'm sure we'll end up with lots of questions, but for now, we just need a break."

Lord Neville nodded agreement and spoke to me, "There's a Trader caravan nearby," he said. "In about an hour or so, maybe a little more, I'm heading to their site to join the Merchant for a meal. You'd both be very welcome to join me if you would like to."

I thought I would very much like to. I understood the way things worked in a Trader campsite and if I couldn't go running back to the security of House St Peter – and obviously I couldn't – that would make me feel more grounded, more able to deal with things. Perry said it was up to me, so we agreed to go with Lord Neville.

"Good," he said. "I'll send Dervla or Declan to find you in plenty of time."

Chapter 32

Leonie

Perry took us back to our room. He seemed more wound up, more tense than I was. I curled up tight on a corner of the sofa but he needed to pace, running his hands through his hair, muttering to himself. It was his way of dealing with things so I just let him be until he'd calmed down and unwound a little. I needed to focus all my concentration on holding the shreds of me together before I disintegrated.

He came and sat in front of me, holding his arms out to me. "I'm sorry, my love," he said. "This must all be rather too much for you. I'm so sorry. I don't know how to make it better."

I gave up trying to hold myself together and trusted his arms to do it. "Perry," I sobbed into him, "I don't know who I am. Or who I should be."

"You're you," he said instantly. "Always and forever you. All this history and ancestry and stuff, they don't change the person you are inside, the person that I love. You're still you, no matter what."

Am I? I'm not sure.

"Look," he carried on, "when you discovered I was an heir to House Tennant, I know you were mad at me, but it didn't change how you loved me, did it? I was still the same person that you knew? You're still the same person, too."

That was true. Whatever he had or hadn't told me, he was still the same annoying, caring, impulsive, thoughtful, know-it-all, loving Perry.

"But, Perry," I sobbed, "it makes me one of the bad people."

He understood that; throughout my childhood I'd come to the conclusion that it was those of high rank who did bad things to those of lower rank.

"No, it doesn't," he said firmly, stroking my hair. "People are people, whatever their background. Some do bad things but most are good. You just came across a lot of bad ones. Think about all the good ones you've met since. And your family will be good, too."

That bit hadn't really sunk in. I had a birth family, blood relatives. And that brought up another issue. "My family?" I said bitterly. "Either they didn't look for me or they wanted me dead. Either way, they didn't want me."

"We don't know they didn't look for you," he said soothingly. "All we know is that they didn't find you." He went on holding me, rocking me, trying to comfort me, before he continued, "I'm beginning to wonder if the entire purpose of Taylor House wasn't just to find you," he said.

That distracted me enough that I looked up at him in surprise.

"Lord James set it up," he explained gently. "Not that long after you disappeared. And he was very close to Helena. I wonder if somehow he knew the other child wasn't you."

Thinking that might be true made me feel an awful lot better. We sat quietly, curled together, not really talking, just being peaceful. I was pretty sure Perry was praying quietly; I could always tell because he felt a particular way, sort of connected and focussed at the same time. I couldn't find any words to use, so I sat listening to the quiet and feeling the shreds of me start to weave back together. Eventually, I stretched and stood up. "Guess we'd better get ready to visit the Traders," I said.

Perry smiled at me. I could tell he was relieved I appeared to be starting to come to terms with everything.

***

Three of us walked over to the Trader encampment – me, Perry and Lord Neville – although I assumed there were covert bodyguards somewhere. It wasn't far, within the castle walls and down near the river, about a five minute walk. If I'd run in the other direction earlier I'd probably have ended up there. Perry was twitchy, continually looking around us, obviously worried about danger.

I nudged him. "You're not on guard duty. Either it's safe or there's someone already doing that job. We have to trust Lilyrose."

He nodded and smiled, a little embarrassed, acknowledging that I was right and that I'd caught him out. "I just worry about you and keeping you safe," he said softly. "I couldn't bear to lose you."

The Trader guards knew we were coming and would have seen us from some distance so we walked unchallenged into the camp. Headwoman Karina and Merchant Evan were waiting for us by the main campfire. Lord Neville greeted them formally as equals – I liked that – and introduced both me and Perry. They responded with equally formal greetings and then Karina turned to me and greeted me in Trader language, as a Trader.

Such greetings had a set formal structure, each offering the other a place or share in their caravan, which was very politely declined. As I responded, I realised I could do so with honour because I did have a share in another caravan and that gave me a feeling of rootedness which helped combat my earlier feelings.

Only, Karina addressed me as *Liaprima*, Princess.

No way. I'm not a princess. And I can't handle any more

revelations today.

Princess was a term reserved for someone who was the *lia* – child – of both a Headwoman and her Merchant and also for the person who had already been chosen as the next Headwoman or Merchant of a caravan. The first was unusual simply because Merchants and Headwomen were rarely in that sort of relationship. And I certainly didn't fit in either category.

I thanked her for the honour but told her she was mistaken. I was not a Princess.

"Yes, *Liaprima*," she said firmly. "*Lia* to Katya and *lia* to Ethan."

Lord Neville touched my shoulder gently. Perry didn't really understand Trader so I would have to explain this to him later, but Lord Neville clearly did. "Accept it," he said quietly. "I have heard Merchant Ethan claim you as his daughter and seen evidence that Headwoman Katya did."

I looked at him in amazement but I took his advice. Merchant Evan brought out a small box and presented it to me. "For you, Princess. From your caravan and ours, and from all caravans."

I decided Lord Neville's advice applied to this too so I took the box and opened it. Inside was a Trader bracelet, the pattern showing the eight spoked wheel of the Traders unadorned by any caravan insignia. But four of the spokes were set with jewels and there was another jewel at the hub.

Evan touched each jewel gently as he spoke. "Ruby for your mother and House Lindum, diamond for your father and House Chisholm, sapphire for your salvation and House St Peter, emerald for your husband and House Tennant." He smiled as he touched the central one. "And, at the hub, for after all it is a Trader bracelet, turquoise for the Traders because you are always one of our own, Princess."

He lifted it out and, as he placed it round my arm a bit more of me wove back into place. Perry might not have understood the words, but he understood the sentiment and smiled at me, as pleased as I was.

We ate by the campfire as all Traders do, everyone together whatever their rank or role. It isn't just a campfire, although it's a fire in the centre of the camp. It's the cooking fire, a place to heat water for laundry or washing, and a place where anyone who needs fire for a task works. And not everyone eats at the same time, not at midday, because tasks don't necessarily fit like that. So, things were happening all around us as we ate.

It made Perry a little jumpy again. He kept glancing around, unsure that we were safe, but I was certain that I was in no danger whatsoever in the middle of a Trader camp. Our conversation was in the common language out of respect for Lord Neville and Perry – Traders needed to be fluent in that as well as their own language. Then Karina started talking to me in Trader and then some of the other women came to join in. Mostly we were discussing things any Trader women would – medicines, routes, sources of various herbs, recent or complex cases, tips and advice – but we also talked about the Gathering. It was almost due to start and the caravan was on its way there, this being their last stop on the route.

"To lighten the waggons for a quick journey," Karina said dryly to much laughter as we all knew that really meant unmissable opportunity for a highly profitable trade. "And to see you, Princess," she added. "It is an honour to be the ones to bring your bracelet."

I smiled and thanked her again then we went back to talking about the Gathering. It felt so good to be talking Trader and I wished I was going to the Gathering. I'd been to one, but it had not been long after I'd joined the caravan and I'd still been very nervous of people. I'd spent most of it watching from a distance, either under or on top of Katya's waggon. This time, I would have joined in to the full. It was where nearly all Trader caravans met together, once every five years, to celebrate and discuss and plan and party. Naturally, there was a lot of courtship that went on and few caravans would leave with exactly the same members as when they'd arrived. There would be plenty of weddings during a Gathering, and a considerable number of babies nine months later, and not just to the newlyweds.

The conversation got a bit…intimate…after that. A lot of teasing, plenty of laughter and quite a bit of blushing. And I was fully included, like I belonged, like I was in my own caravan and had never been away. I felt content, relaxed, although I decided I'd better not share much of this conversation with Perry later. The women did look him up and down and give him their seal of approval.

Probably a good thing he doesn't speak Trader.

Perry

"Are you passing through House Sabden before you return this way?" Uncle Neville asked Merchant Evan. "Our bowmakers are perfectly good, but Sabden have the best and I'd like a new longbow as a gift for Lilyrose."

Perry leaned forward and paid a little more attention. "A bow would make an excellent gift for Leonie, too. I'd be very interested if you could find something for her."

"Can she shoot?" Uncle Neville asked.

Perry shrugged. "If not, I can teach her."

Merchant Evan looked shocked. "She's a Trader. Any adult Trader can shoot well enough to feed and protect those she's responsible for. Of course she can shoot."

"She's probably better than me, then," Perry said. "Perhaps she could teach me. Either way should be fun."

Merchant Evan laughed. "Don't you worry, I've got excellent contacts at Sabden. I'll get you something top quality for Leonie. And for the Lady Lilyrose, too. And what about yourself, Lord Perry?"

"Turns out my favourite bow is still in the armoury," Perry said. "I spotted it there yesterday."

"Kept it safe and well looked after, in case you needed it again," Lord Neville told him.

"We'll be back this way in about six weeks," Evan said. "I'll bring the bows then."

Perry nodded his thanks to both of them and lapsed back into his thoughts. Part of his mind was concerned about safety and uncomfortable with unknown people wandering around, however well he knew that a Trader camp was safe. A very small part was a little resentful; it was all very well yesterday Uncle Neville offering him the chance of a role to suit him – there was no way he would be able to fulfil a medical career with Leonie as High Lord of some House. He was trying hard to squash that part. By far the largest part of him was concentrating on Leonie and her reaction to today's news and how to deal with it.

Right now, she was laughing and happy, taking a full part in the conversation with some of the other Traders, looking like she belonged in a way he hadn't seen before. He wasn't sure what they were saying – was he feeling a little excluded? – but some of the looks he was getting from the Trader women were making him feel rather uncomfortable. If Leonie chose to live among Traders, could he be comfortable in this society? He was very much afraid that, if she did, he'd always feel something of an outsider and that made him feel resentful again, and then guilty because that was probably how Leonie felt all the time.

He tried to dissipate those feelings, aware that he was being selfish and self-centred. Instead, he chose to think about the day's revelations and how to handle them. He had called a break to the earlier discussions as much because he'd needed it as because Leonie had. A hot rush of anger and frustration had risen through his chest at the familiar conflict between what he wanted and what was going to be required of him by others and he'd had to get out of there. Then – and he wasn't proud of this – he had needed to get his own reaction and feelings under control before he could offer Leonie any support at all.

It had been patently obvious that she was falling apart, not knowing who she was, utterly lost. And he had promised that he would always find her. That promise, as much as anything, had been what had enabled him to pull himself together and somehow, he had found her. He didn't deserve her trust after what he'd done, but she still had total faith in him.

And prayer seemed to have soothed her and it had helped him. Despite the residual resentments he was feeling now, he'd realised that whatever the future held, they would still face it together, that Leonie would not put him under the same pressures and conflicts that had all but destroyed him in the past.

Even the very thought of losing her made him feel panicked, his stomach churning, and right now every movement seemed a possible threat.

But truly, this visit was worth it just for the sheer joy on Leonie's face when the Merchant had given her the bracelet. Perry hadn't understood many of the words but it was easy to tell what the jewels represented. Then, ever so gradually, she'd started talking to the others in Trader and drifted further away from him, looking like she belonged in a way he knew he didn't.

She moved back next to him, nestling in where he felt she belonged, sighing with contentment.

"What were you talking about?" he asked.

She looked at him almost shyly. "You might be the only man who'd understand," she said.

Although she didn't tell him anything else that one sentence was enough and somehow it didn't matter any longer. He slid an arm round her. "I love you," he said quietly. "I can never tell you that too much."

She smiled at him with unmistakable pleasure. "I love you too," she whispered.

He resolved then and there that, whatever else they had to deal with, his focus would be to make it as easy for her as he could. Leonie stayed close against him as they returned to the main house, clearly tired by the events of the day so far, and he guided her up to their rooms so she could sleep.

"Stay close," she pleaded, her insecurities returning.

"No way am I leaving you alone today," he told her, lying down beside her and pulling her into his arms. "Sleep now. You'll be safe here. I won't leave you."

She blinked sleepily and then, to his delight, twisted her mind into his before almost immediately falling asleep. He had intended to spend the time praying and meditating but with a sleeping Leonie in his arms and mind, it wasn't long before he too slept.

He woke to find her kissing him, her desire flooding through his mind. With the desire came amused realisation. "This is what you women were talking about, isn't it?"

She grinned back at him, wickedly. "Don't worry," she said. "You got their seal of approval. Just."

He flipped her over so he was on top. "It's only your approval that matters to me."

With that simple statement came an incredible sense of freedom. The conflict and pressures that had led to his past problems had been about trying to seek the approval of different parties with conflicting views and expectations of him. These no longer mattered. All he should seek was to do God's will; it might not be easy – almost certainly very difficult – but it wouldn't be destructive.

With his mind now at peace, he turned his attention to the matter in hand. He twisted his mind deeper into Leonie's, and ran his hand down her bare leg, revelling in the sensations and reaction he elicited.

Chapter 33

Leonie

In the past, Perry has said that I used sex to make us both feel better. Today it did make me feel better, more of me weaving back into place. But that wasn't why I'd wanted to make love. I'd been trying to find a way to show Perry how important he was to me, that he mattered more than any House or history.

He lounged in a chair, watching me finding my clothes and getting dressed. "We've got plenty of time before the dinner," he said, "and nowhere we need to be. Would you like it if I showed you round the House and grounds? Not a formal tour, but all the places we used to get up to mischief or hide out?"

I grinned at him and nodded. "I'd love that," I told him.

We started with the attics which were pretty much the same as attics anywhere, full of forgotten items. I'd always found attics pretty good for pilfering supplies – if I could get into them I could be long gone before anyone noticed. The attics at House St Peter were way too organised to be safe for pilfering.

"We used to hide out up here," Perry said. "But today we've come up for the view."

From the attics we could get out onto the roof and there was a sort of pathway round. Perry was right, the view was amazing. The layout of the whole area enclosed by the castle walls was visible. On one side it led down to the river, on another the view stretched right out over the town. Perry started pointing out places and telling stories to go with them. I listened, but I was also watching him, his face and body animated, his voice happy; this was clearly a place he loved.

"Am I boring you?" he asked, apparently noticing that I was watching him and not the view.

I shook my head. "No," I said. "I was just thinking. It sounds like you really love your lands."

He smiled. "I guess I do. But it's people that matter, not places. And however much I love here, in the end I'll only be happy if I'm doing what God has planned for me, wherever that is."

That was typical of the Perry I knew and loved. We wandered back down through the attics past a pile of old toys that caused a shadow to cross his face. "They were Danny's," he explained. "Lilyrose's older brother and my cousin. He was about the same age as me and Brin but he died when he was fifteen. He was never very strong. And his mother died a year or so later which was pretty tough on Lilyrose." He sighed. "I think Danny's death just strengthened my desire to be a doctor, even if by then I knew it wasn't what anyone else wanted for me. I can't help feeling that children shouldn't die, not so young, not before they've had a chance at life."

I was with him on that. It struck me that death and illness were no respecter of rank or position. Great House or no House, we all suffered when we lost those close to us. I'd always thought of those in Great Houses as being above all that pain, that it just didn't happen to them. Now I realised that it did and they hurt too; neither money nor position could stop death or illness. Suddenly, for me, High Lords and their families became people, too.

For once, Perry didn't realise what I was thinking. "Come on," he said, far more cheerfully. "I'll show you the rogues' gallery of past High Lords."

This turned out to be a long wide corridor with portraits of previous High Lords going back generations. The last portrait was a family one, a couple with four children – three girls and a boy – ranging in age from perhaps twelve down to a fat little baby.

"Recognise anyone?" Perry asked me with a grin.

I shook my head. The mother had quite a look of Lilyrose and there was a general family resemblance but that was all. Perry pointed to the boy. "That's Uncle Neville," he said. "And this" – pointing to the baby – "is Ma."

He waited for my disbelieving reaction before he named the other two. The older girl was Elise who died many years ago, the younger, Naomi, mother to Brin. We ambled on, turning a corner and then Perry stopped dead at the sight of the wall in front of him.

"Wow," he said. "This was never here before."

The wall was covered with family photographs, starting with one which was obviously Uncle Neville's wedding.

"That's Rose-Marie, Lilyrose's mother," Perry said, pointing at the bride.

We wandered along, looking at all the pictures – a young couple with their first baby, obviously Danny, children growing up, including Brin and Perry and some of their siblings, a baby Lilyrose – all the evidence of a growing and extended family. I concentrated on the ones of Perry, watching him grow from a child to a young man. There were some lovely ones of him and Danny and Brin, and then him and Brin and a very young Lilyrose, all happy and laughing together. Then one of Perry riding a beautiful chestnut horse, absolutely oblivious to the camera, totally one with his mount.

"That's Ginger," Perry told me. "I wonder if he's still around. He'd be pretty old now, for a horse."

As time progressed along the wall, the pictures became more centred on Brin and Lilyrose. But to our amazement, they were interspersed with pictures of Perry, taken over his time at at

House St Peter, showing him as a monk and as a doctor, again clearly unaware of the camera. He shook his head in disbelief while I studied them carefully. Perry as a monk was just so much more peaceful than the pictures only a few years earlier.

I pointed that out to him. "Look at the difference," I told him. "Never doubt that you made the right choice, it's just obvious in the difference between you before and you after."

"I don't doubt, not really," he said, running his hands through his hair. "Only when I think about the effect it had on others."

That was what worried me about making a life choice. It was one thing to make a choice for yourself, quite another to choose the consequences for other people. And there would be so many people affected by the choice I had to make. Not just those people I knew, but tens, hundreds of thousands, millions of others that I didn't. How could I ever take responsibility for them?

I looked up at the final photograph on the wall and my mouth dropped open. "How on earth did that come to be here?" I asked. It was a picture from our wedding, just outside the Old Chapel, Perry smiling all over his face and me looking up at him, laughing and happy.

Perry shook his head. "I don't know. I don't know how he got any of these. Personally, I suspect Lady Eleanor."

"He must be so proud of you," I said. "Uncle Neville, I mean. To do all this."

"He said he was," Perry replied slowly. "Yesterday, he said he was. I always thought I was a disappointment. Because I wasn't Danny, and I didn't want all this, and I wanted to be a doctor and then I ran away."

He turned towards me, and I ran my hands into his hair

and pulled his head down onto my shoulder, wrapping my arms around him while he dealt with all these thoughts. "Idiot," I said softly. "Of course he's proud of you. You stood up for what you believed to be right. How could he not be proud of you?"

After a while, he lifted his head up and smiled shakily at me. "Come on," he said. "Let's go and see if Ginger's still around."

We went via the kitchens where we managed to acquire hot pastries, fresh from the oven, something Perry had obviously done many, many times. The cook – Molly – pretended to chase us out, brandishing a spatula at us, and we went, giggling.

The stable yard was quiet in the late afternoon sun, apart from an old man sitting, slowly and methodically polishing harness. He looked up at our arrival and his weathered face crinkled into a wide smile. "Ahh, Perry-lad," he said. "You've come home then."

"That I have, Ronnie," Perry replied. "Are you well?"

"Well enough, boy, well enough." The old man – Ronnie – looked at me. "Welcome, Princess."

I didn't know what to reply but I didn't have to as he turned back to Perry. "Ginger's out in the back field. There's carrots in the sack."

Then he went back to his polishing, and we were clearly dismissed. Perry dragged me over to grab some carrots and then led me through the stable yard and down a path to a series of fields. At the end, we reached a gate and Perry leaned on it and whistled. A horse some way across the field lifted his head and swivelled its ears towards us. Perry whistled again and the horse headed slowly towards us so we climbed over the gate to wait for him.

He was the horse from the photograph, stiff and slow with

age, greying around the muzzle but he recognised Perry and nudged him for the carrots, huffing and whickering around him. I stayed back a little while they had their reunion. And then it was time for us to head back to the house to get ready for the evening meal.

"There's one more thing I want to show you on the way," Perry said. "And I'm really sorry, I forgot about this, I know you're going to be mad with me, but I just forgot all about it."

I looked at him, astounded. Forgetting to tell me things I should know was typical Perry. He often just didn't realise that I didn't know them and he was always sorry afterwards. But I didn't know what this could be, not after the rest of today, nor why I would be mad at him, although he didn't seem too worried. He took us back into the wing of the house on the other side from the veranda room and then stopped and looked at me guiltily. Now I understood.

"Perry!" I said reproachfully. "You didn't tell me this was here."

"I know," he said. "I'm sorry. Forgive me?"

In front of us was a swimming pool, empty of users and so inviting. I took my time but then I grinned at him. "Of course. Can we swim now?" I asked eagerly.

He shook his head. "I'm sorry again, I really don't think there's time. But tomorrow, I promise."

I let him off with that, and we hurried to get ready. The dress Edward had sent was beautiful – silk rippling with gold and silver, close fitting and then flaring out into a fuller skirt. I wore my new Trader bracelet high on my upper arm, and Jenny's bracelet at my wrist.

Perry ran his fingers delicately across the new bracelet.

"People will start to understand the symbolism of this," he said carefully, as he trailed his fingers up to my face and across my cheek.

I nodded. "I know. But I've got to get used to it, too, haven't I? And it's Trader. It makes me feel like I belong."

He left it at that.

***

The dining hall was packed; not only had most of those living within the Castle wanted to be there but Lord Neville had also invited anyone from Karina's caravan who'd wanted to come, which included both Karina and Evan. I found myself chatting away happily in a mixture of Trader and the common language, sometimes in the same sentence. After we'd eaten, people started moving the tables and stacking the chairs to one side. Lilyrose turned to me and Perry, her eyes alight. "We're going to have dancing. I love it when we have dancing. I could dance all night."

"Perry," I said excitedly, almost jumping up and down. "Can we dance?"

"It's been a long time," he told me. "Do you know how? I'm not sure I remember."

Merchant Evan overheard that. "Any Trader girl can dance, and well," he said. "Princess, if my Lord Prospero is unwilling, would you allow me to be your partner?"

That aroused Perry's jealous and possessive streak. I figured Merchant Evan knew that it would from the look on his face.

"With all due respect," Perry said firmly. "If my wife is going to dance then the first dance will be with me."

He took my hand and led me out onto the dance floor. As

he settled his arms around me he whispered in my ear, "If I make a total fool of myself, this is all your fault, you understand?" But his voice was full of laughter and happiness so I just grinned back.

He didn't make a fool of himself, not at all. I could have danced all night. I danced with Evan, and Perry, and Brin, and Perry, and Declan and Perry and even Lord Neville. It seemed like Perry could only manage to let me dance with someone else for one dance at a time before I danced with him again. But I was fine with that; dancing with Perry was by far the best. I did see him dancing with Lilyrose, and with Dervla and with Molly, so he wasn't exactly unoccupied.

Eventually, Lord Neville brought the festivities to an end. "I know it's still relatively early," he said to me, "but I've told you, I'm scared of Lady Eleanor and I don't want you getting too tired."

To be fair, I did answer him with a yawn—I couldn't help it, however much I was enjoying myself. He laughed and sent me and Perry packing.

Chapter 34

Perry

As soon as they reached their rooms, Leonie headed straight through to the balcony that opened off their bedroom. Perry followed her; he was sure she knew he was there, but she didn't turn around or greet him. He went to stand behind her, meaning to put his arms round her to check on her and comfort her. He hesitated, afraid he wouldn't be welcomed, that her silence meant he was still unforgiven for his earlier betrayal.

"Are you still mad at me?" he asked softly. "About not telling you who you are?"

She shook her head, so he ventured closer, pulling her gently to him, feeling the softness of her skin against his, cool in the evening breeze.

"It's not that," she whispered. "I know you were trying to protect me. It's just, just..." She turned round in his arms to look up into his eyes, and the torment in her soul was reflected in her voice. "Perry, I have to choose. How do I choose? Who am I? And who am I going to be?"

She turned back and gestured across the courtyard. "I could choose this. Do you want it? You could be High Lord here."

He shook his head. That was the last thing he wanted. "This is your choice. You can't make it just on the basis of what I might or might not want."

"What other basis do I have? How do I know the right thing to do? It was a simple choice at House Eastern and still I caused consequences for so many people who had no choice. It led to all this. And this choice isn't even simple. How can I know what I'm doing? What it will mean? Who will be affected and how? How did you ever make the choices you made?"

He pulled her back into his arms, her head against his chest, stroking her hair with one hand. He ached with the need to take this torment away from her and even more with the knowledge that he couldn't. "You don't have to choose yet. You've got plenty of time. Months certainly, years if you need them. You can't pledge to a House until you're twenty one. And I'll be right with you. We'll work it out together."

She sighed, her breath whispering across his skin, but gradually he felt her relax a little.

"As to how?" he said quietly, resting his cheek on the top of her head. "We'll investigate all the options, visit the Houses we don't know, meet the people. But most of all, we'll pray for God to lead us."

"I don't know how to pray about it," she confessed. "I don't know what to say, what words to use."

He smiled slightly. "I should think everyone who has ever prayed has said that at some point. When you were injured, unconscious and I didn't know if you would ever wake up... Then, even with years of prayer and worship behind me, I didn't know how to pray. I couldn't form the words."

She looked up at him in astonishment. "What did you do?"

He shook his head at the memory of those days and answered obliquely, "Prayer's a conversation between you and God. Sometimes it's okay just to sit silently, knowing that God will understand what's worrying you."

That wasn't enough for her; he hadn't really expected that it would be.

"Isn't that a bit of a cop out?" she asked. "I mean, it's like saying I don't have to pray because God knows what I'd say anyway."

He smiled at her response which he considered typical of her, challenging, questioning, never taking the easy way out. "Well, yes and no," he said. "I didn't mean all the time, just those occasions when words totally fail you. Like, I told you about when I hit rock bottom and Andrew was there for me? Sometimes I talked and he listened, and sometimes all I could manage was silence and he sat there, with me, understanding. I meant sort of like that."

Leonie

I was lost in the night and in my worries, but even then Perry had found me and rescued me. He held out prayer as a lifeline and told me God would understand, like Andrew had when I'd needed him.

Perry went on talking about different ways to pray, things he'd found helpful. "There's formal, written prayers," he said. "Ones that have been written by someone else. Some of them have been used for centuries, millennia even, but that doesn't make them any less meaningful. Sometimes when you don't know what words to use, they're a start. I find saying them helps me get to a place where I can use my own words."

I thought about that and I must have looked puzzled because he found another way to explain it.

"When you greeted the Traders," he said, "you used formal phrases that must have been used thousands of times by thousands of people. But they still have meaning; they were still a way of starting your conversation, still conveyed the message you wanted to give. And then you went on to a conversation in your own words."

Now I followed what he meant.

He carried on, well into his stride, "You can use your own words in prayer. Just like you do with me or anyone else you're talking with. There doesn't have to be anything different about them. Many of the Psalms are the writer pouring their heart out to God, trying to express exactly what they felt. You don't have to be polite or on your best behaviour or anything like that. You can share your anger, or confusion, or happiness, whatever you're feeling. The Psalm writers did."

He paused and looked at me, his eyes a little amused. "It's okay to shout at God, get mad, if that's how you feel. I have, many times. If you hide your feelings from God, you're not being yourself with him. And he doesn't want that."

That was a liberating thought. But there was still something puzzling me. "You called prayer a conversation," I said to him. "But a conversation is two way, like you and me talking. How can it be like that with God?"

Now he was definitely amused. "That's the other question everybody who's ever prayed has asked," he said. "Firstly, you have to take the time and patience to listen."

I gave him a look.

"Yeah, okay," he acknowledged. "I'm not the most patient person and God has had to yell at me several times to get me to hear. But I usually get there in the end."

Well, probably. Andrew and I were pretty much agreed that Perry was often slow to realise important stuff.

Perry carried on, "It's very rare to actually hear a voice, though it does happen. More often, there'll be something you read, perhaps in your Bible, or something that someone says, or a thought that comes into your head. And it might not be immediate. You have to be open to it and learn to recognise it. I guess it's not easy."

That was for sure, definitely not easy. I shivered slightly from the breeze out on the balcony.

"Come on," Perry said. "Off to bed. I don't want you getting cold."

***

Despite being curled up warm and safe in bed beside Perry, my thoughts were still buzzing around the choice I needed to make. I was sure Perry could tell that because he was broadcasting calm and reassurance, trying to encourage me to sleep.

"I still don't know what I have to do, how to choose, who to be," I told him.

"There's time," he said soothingly. "There's a Bible verse that helps me when I'm uncertain. Want to hear it?"

I nodded.

"It's from the book of Jeremiah. It goes, '"For I know the plans I have for you," declares the Lord, "plans to prosper you and not to harm you, plans to give you hope and a future."' Does that help?"

It did. I might not know what to choose but God had plans for me and he knew.

I do know who I am. I'm me and I'm loved.

I could trust in God for the rest. Who I should be could wait until tomorrow.

***

The Them loomed round me, arms outstretched, reaching for something. One of Them leant over me to grab at Perry, sleeping peacefully beside me. No way, that was not happening. I was not going to let them touch Perry. I felt for the power, took hold...and it fizzled out.

No, I'm still me. Even without the power I'm still me. And I can deal with a bunch of the Them.

I rolled off the bed, using my body to knock their feet from under them as I landed on the floor. They dissipated as I touched them, reforming behind me. Light shone from one side of the room so I headed towards it, the Them following. The light led to a rocky ledge, revealing a ravine beyond. I'd need my Gifts to get me across that. The Them coalesced in front of me, into one large Them with a Shield that was stopping me accessing the power.

Easy.

I'd switched off Brin's Shield; I could destroy this one. I twisted it until it blew up, grabbed the power and leapt through the fading Them.

Perry

The explosion ripped across Perry's mind, a deluge of sensation bringing him instantly awake. He twisted towards Leonie, finding her side of the bed empty. Cold fear gripped his heart, the night accentuating his worries. He couldn't breathe.

Where is she? Has she left me? Is it a nightmare?

He lunged out of bed, reaching for her with his mind. He lost his balance as a sheet of mental colour prevented him spotting anyone at all and he had to grab the foot of the bed to stop himself from falling.

Where the blazes is she? What's happened? Is she hurt?

Catching sight of the billowing balcony curtains out of the

corner of his eye, he rushed towards them. The balcony was empty but the courtyard below was full of odd dark shadows, some stationary, some moving. Could that one be Leonie? Nothing was clear in the dark of the night and he still couldn't sense anyone in the aftermath of the explosion. Wherever Leonie was, she needed him. If she was down there, the quickest way down was to jump – and he'd exited this building by a first floor window more times than he cared to remember. It was only as he leapt that it struck him – if he couldn't sense anyone, could he still use his telekinetic ability to land safely?

The story concludes in

Cloth of Grace

Choices and Consequences Book 4

Release date: February 2020

When the fate of the world rests on your shoulders, how do you choose between what you ought to do and the only thing you really want?

Leonie finally knows who she is. But now she needs to decide who she is going to be. Her choice will affect not just her family, not just those she knows but tens, hundreds of thousands, millions of people that she doesn't. And every path that's open to her will put Perry under the pressures that caused his breakdown before. How can she do what she must and still protect Perry?

Perry desperately wants to make things easier for Leonie. Somehow he has to find the strength to face the things that all but destroyed him in the past. But every way he turns some aspect of his past lies waiting to pounce – even during his happiest moments. And he can never forget that Leonie's life is in danger from someone, somewhere. That danger may be much closer to home than anyone suspects.

Gabriel has managed to negotiate peace, at least in theory. Now he must put that into practice and reunite Leonie with the family she never knew she had. Then disaster strikes right in the middle of his own sanctuary. Can he still protect those he loves, or has he been harbouring a villain the whole time?

Get it now at **https://www.books2read.com/clothofgrace**

Can't wait? Sign up for my occasional newsletter to be the first to hear the latest news and to get early extracts. Just visit my website at **www.racheljbonner.co.uk** or go directly to the sign up page at **https://www.subscribepage.com/webpage**.

Please consider leaving a review! Reader reviews are crucial to a book's success by helping other readers discover them. Please consider taking a moment to review Weave of Love at **https://www.amazon.co.uk/dp/B07VLMV52C**. Your review doesn't have to be long or detailed – one sentence about how the book made you feel would be great.

Want to make contact? I'd love to hear from you. Please visit my Facebook page at **www.facebook.com/rachelbonnerauthor** or connect with me on Twitter at **www.twitter.com/racheljbonner1** – or both!

Not read **Strand of Faith yet?**

It's available at all major ebook retailers and can be ordered at all good bookshops.
Or get it at **https://www.books2read.com/strandoffaith**

Strand of Faith

Choices and Consequences Book 1

A girl. A monk. An unthinkable sacrifice.
When the choice is between love and life, how can anyone decide?

In a post-apocalyptic future, a girl and a monk, both with extraordinary mental powers, have compelling reasons not to fall in love. But their choices will have consequences for the rest of the world.

After the troubles of his youth, Brother Prospero has found comfort and fulfilment in the monastery. Then he discovers something that forces him to reconsider his whole vocation. How can it possibly be right to leave a life of worship and service for human desire? And if he does leave, will the pressures from his past destroy him?

Orphaned and mistreated, Leonie has found sanctuary and safety at the Abbey. When she comes into contact with Prospero everything spirals out of her control. Everyone she's ever loved has died. She can't do that to him. But how can she walk away from the first place she's truly belonged?

Abbot Gabriel is faced with an impossible choice. He can do nothing and watch the world descend into war. Or he can manipulate events and ensure peace – at the cost of two lives he is responsible for. Is he strong enough to sacrifice those he loves?

And what about **Thread of Hope?**

It's available at all major ebook retailers and can be ordered at all good bookshops.
Or get it at **https://www.books2read.com/threadofhope**.

Thread of Hope

Choices and Consequences Book 2

What if your secrets are so dangerous they could destroy the one you love?
Is honesty always the best policy?

Leonie may have run away but Prospero *will* find her. He loves her and he wants a future with her by his side whatever the consequences. Only when he does find her, he ought to tell her who he really is, outside the monastery. That'll make her run again. Dare he risk it? But if he doesn't tell her, someone else may...

Marriage to Prospero is what Leonie wants most and the one thing she knows she can't have. If he found out what she was really like, what she'd been, what she'd done, he'd despise her and she couldn't bear that. Better to leave now than live a lie – but it's harder than she expected. If only...

Gabriel is starting to discover the secrets inherent in Leonie, secrets that not even she knows, secrets that will tear the world apart. And the secrets he is keeping are tearing him apart. How can sacrificing those he loves possibly achieve peace when everything he discovers risks the death of millions?

Acknowledgements

As always, this book has been a team effort and my deepest thanks go to all those who have been a part of its creation.

I may have thought of the story, but it is my editor Sarah Smeaton who has made it what it is. Sarah nudges me to polish it here, adjust it there, take out this bit, expand that bit... Without Sarah it would not be half as good as it is. Should you ever need an editor, I recommend her unreservedly.

The cover has been designed once again by Oliver Pengilley, working under very difficult circumstances. Thank you, Ollie, for all you have achieved, and for responding so fast every time I discover a last minute problem. If you'd like to see more of Ollie's work, visit his website **https://www.oliverpengilley.co.uk/** and his Etsy shop **https://www.etsy.com/uk/shop/oliverpengilley** .

Rachel, of Rachel's Random Resources at **https://www.rachelsrandomresources.com/** organised the blog tour for Weave of Love achieving amazing results, despite the interruption of the summer holidays. I wouldn't have known where to start on publicity and social media without Rachel's help.

My husband, my sons, Adam and the other one, my Mum and my friend, Kathy have been there for me all the way through. Thank you so much for your support, your encouragement, your questions, and for reading what I've written – again and again. Without you, these books wouldn't be here at all.

And thank you to my Bible Study group for your encouragement (although possibly not for the threats when I end a book with yet another cliff hanger...). You've no idea how much your support means to me.

Last, but by no means least, my thanks to you, the reader. I hope you have enjoyed reading this as much as I have enjoyed writing it, and that you will continue with me to read the rest of the series.

Deo Gratis

Rachel J Bonner

October 2019

Lightning Source UK Ltd.
Milton Keynes UK
UKHW010841161019
351703UK00001B/27/P